Family Blood

A NOVEL

by
Mary Hazzard

For Fiora

Mary Hazzard

December, 1999

Ariadne Press
Rockville, Maryland

Library of Congress Cataloging-in-Publication Data
Hazzard, Mary, 1928–
    Family blood : a novel / by Mary Hazzard.
    p. cm.
    ISBN 0-91-805610-1
    I. Title.
    PS3558.A96 F35 1999
    813'.54--dc21

                                                    98-40992
                                                    CIP

Jacket Design: Leslie Murray Rollins
Typesetting: Barbara Shaw

This publication is supported by a grant from the
Maryland State Arts Council, an agency funded by the State of
Maryland and the National Endowment for the Arts.

Ariadne Press
4817 Tallahassee Ave.
Rockville, Maryland
20853

For
Edith, Laura, Betsy, and Bill,
who will recognize these times but not these events

Also by Mary Hazzard:

Close His Eyes (as Olivia Dwight)
Sheltered Lives
Idle and Disorderly Persons

PROLOGUE

Sometimes when Clara Davenant's most painful recollection comes back, she remembers—or almost thinks she remembers—a stream of blood running along the hall floor in her family's house and dripping down the stairs toward her all the way to the landing—from one step to another, while she screams and tries not to step in it with her bare feet. But that must be wrong; there wasn't any blood, or none that she could see. And she doesn't think she screamed.

1941

The plays of children are nonsense,
but very educative nonsense.

—Ralph Waldo Emerson, *Experience*

I

Five children in one car—or in one house or one family—are too many, Grace Davenant was thinking as her husband drove the long black Buick, diapers flapping from both rear windows, toward the Lower Peninsula.

It was early September of 1941, and it was the end of the Davenants' yearly escape from ragweed. With the homeward trip barely begun, Robert's jaw was already set, and he was concentrating grimly on the road. Some people do manage large families, though, Grace told herself; look at the Roosevelts, for instance. If she said this to Robert, however, the name would only set him off. She wished he could see that shouting at the children didn't help. She let her thoughts stray to Amelia Earhart—the aviatrix, welfare worker, and non-mother who had crossed the Atlantic in a plane called *Friendship* just before Clara Jane, the first Davenant child, was born. AE (as Amelia called herself in her memoirs) had disappeared four years ago, but Grace clung to the hope that she was still alive.

One of Grace's other fantasies was of having a set of Edwardian servants to go with her Depression family. When she went to the hospital for Cricket's birth, her sister Eleanor had given her the first volume of the Random House edition of Proust to read during her two-week stay. That, of course, would be Eleanor's idea of entertainment. Grace herself wasn't a Proust person; the very look of the author's mournful mustache made her impatient. Also, the book was translated from a language she had studied—so that, apart from the difficulty of deciphering nuances through a linguistic screen, she felt guilt at not reading it in the original. What she hadn't expected to feel, besides a grudging interest, was envy.

The person she envied was the narrator's mother. Not only was there just one child, but his mother wasn't his main caretaker; he didn't even eat dinner (not, of course, cooked by her) with the rest of the family. All that fuss about kissing him good night was nothing to the trials Grace went through every day. And there was the whole leisured atmosphere—the consultations on what little Marcel should eat and read, and which plays he should attend. Grace had all she could do to keep her children clothed and fed and reasonably clean. She didn't know how to discipline them, or to educate them beyond what they picked up at school or from independent reading. It was a pity; she looked at their eager faces and noted their absorbent minds, which, as Robert complained, they were filling with junk from movies and radio programs. But there were too many children, and they had come too quickly.

Marcel's family worried about his health? They should try having five of them. Whenever Grace came upon a shivering child crouched over the hot-air register in the front hall, she knew that flu or strep throat was about to sweep through the family, obliging her to call pompous expensive Dr. Wernimont. That Marcel's upbringing might not have been ideal—that it had led him to devote the rest of his life to the writing of an enormous book—was unimportant; writers had to find their material somewhere.

In graduate school, Grace had been proud of her advanced—though still theoretical— ideas on birth control. Just before her marriage, conquering a deep reluctance, she had visited the Sanger clinic in New York and obtained a diaphragm, which she thought she could trust. The result, however, was Clara Jane, unlooked for but conscientiously welcomed. Harold, in spite of further precautions, arrived two years later. Next came Freddie, and by the time Mellie was on the way, Grace was in despair. She and Robert had tried douches, withdrawal, mental effort, jumping off the kitchen table—and even condoms a few times, though Robert complained that they were cumbersome. "All I have to do is *breathe* at you," he shouted when, after a deceptive three-year respite, she broke the news about Cricket. "Why in Hell do you have to be so fertile?"

She had heard him swear only once before, when he was changing a tire and the car fell off the jack. Some men, she mentioned, wouldn't consider fertility a defect. At this he hurled her douche bag across the bedroom with its orange tube trailing and leaking on the rug.

Cricket (formally Herbert Theodore, for two great-uncles) was almost two now, and Grace and Robert were apprehensive. The children took it for granted that the babies would keep right on coming, though Harold did point out from time to time that the Buick wasn't designed to carry more than three passengers in front and four in back. The car had once belonged to a funeral home. The children called it the hearse, and in it they were sometimes mourners, sometimes movie stars with a chauffeur. It had cut-glass flower holders, a collapsible dividing arm in back, and two jump-seats, which the older children had talked the younger ones into preferring. The coarse gray upholstery took the light like pussy willows. "Mama can hold the new baby," Clara Jane said to Harold now as they rolled past green Midwestern fields.

"What makes you think there will be a baby?" Grace asked in alarm.

"Well, there always is," Clara Jane said reasonably. She would help to take care of it, of course, and mostly she wouldn't mind. During the past month, though, she had often rowed to the middle of a pond in a sun-warmed rubber boat, allegedly to fish but mainly to be alone with the sound of lapping water and to read—*Emily of New Moon, While Rome Burns, Benchley Beside Himself*, any book she could find in the rented cottage. She liked to lean over the edge and watch threads of sunlight dancing through bright sifting specks, with brief clusters of bluegills or sunfish or minnows. She would narrow her eyes at the dual image—trees and sky on the surface, fuzzy rocks and waving weeds below: Seeing fish swimming through the branches of trees, she felt as if something had squeezed her heart.

On the day-long drive home, Clara Jane was thinking that though she hadn't quite lived thirteen years yet, she had already forgotten more of her life than she remembered. She would almost certainly forget this very moment, and being crowded into the car while her brothers and her sister sorted the candy they had bought for the trip. Through the triangular side window she saw an ash-gray bird with a slanting tail, bouncing from one branch of an elm tree to another; she saw utility poles, and trees passing other trees, and clouds in the shapes of animals—none of which she would remember. She might even forget what she was thinking now. But she wouldn't. She stared through the glass, fixing the flat Michigan landscape in her mind: For the rest of my life, I will remember those telephone poles and that exact sky.

"Six licorice whips, four Tootsie Pops, forty-nine jelly beans," Mellie crooned.

"Spearmint leaves," Freddie said. "Necco Wafers."

Their father frowned at the rear-view mirror. "Candy again? You'll ruin your teeth."

"It's all right, Daddy. We're just gloating," Mellie said, and Clara Jane feared that she saw her mother making a mental note.

For Grace Davenant didn't always regret the size of her family. Sometimes she actually took advantage of it. A Ph.D. in anthropology wasn't much use to the mother of a young family, she reasoned; so, just until they were grown, she kept her hand in by writing a biweekly column about the children's doings for the local newspaper. "Our Harold," she had written last May, "has suddenly lost interest in his marble collection and turns cartwheels on the front lawn every afternoon. This is because, it seems, a little *girl* is visiting next door. Until now, the only girls Harold has known have been his sisters, whose pigtails he regularly pulls..." And so on. Grace tended to think of her children as having been drawn by Ernest Shepard or Norman Rockwell.

The actual Harold, as it happened, wouldn't answer to any name but Hal, disdained marbles, and had no idea how to turn cartwheels, which anyway were sissy. And, he told his mother, there were plenty of girls at school. She tried to explain about artistic license, but of course she couldn't expect him to understand.

She reached now for the notebook she always carried. "Our gang," she wrote, "is packed into the car, amid much disputation over who owns the most jelly beans. I suspect it will be Harold in the end, as he is a prudent little character, much like his grandfather the banker. Our generous Mellie, on the other hand, is scattering sweetmeats with no heed for tomorrow." These notes were interrupted by the sound of retching, and Grace turned to see Mellie, with a pale green face, vomiting into a paper bag. Freddie, leaning away and holding his nose, jogged the checkerboard on which Hal was arranging jawbreakers in rows.

"Dummy," Hal shouted, jabbing with his elbow. "Stupid idiot!"

"Clara Jane!" Robert Davenant ordered as Freddie began to howl. "Do something!" This trip—with the wrangling children and the smell of vomit from poor Mellie—was the usual nightmare, though Robert had to admit it had been worth the trouble. Apart from other physical problems, he suffered from agonizing hay fever. Because the Conservation Department allowed him to work in the Upper Peninsula each year during August, he and his allergic family had been able to breathe for the last month.

Grace started to sing "Row, Row, Row Your Boat" in a thin soprano, and Cricket, in the car-seat next to her, bounced in rhythm and sang "Wo, wo, wo," exactly on pitch. "Listen," Grace cried. "Listen to him." Maybe he would be the genius who would compensate for the delay in her career. He certainly looked like a genius, with his radiant hazel eyes and the little frill of copper hair at the back of his head.

Grace, Robert reflected, might very well describe this journey afterwards as jolly family fun. However, it wasn't right to criticize her, when she had to cope with the children now and cook dinner afterwards. "Before we get home tonight," he said to make up for his thoughts, "why don't we stop for hamburgers?"

"With milkshakes?" Clara Jane cried, in rapture. The Davenants didn't eat out.

"Milkshakes too," her father said recklessly, and she decided to order strawberry. It was still morning now, and they were driving through a small town. Clara Jane saw birds flying low across wet green lawns, cats creeping around the edges of shrubbery. Leaning her cheek against the cool glass, with her elbow on the scratchy gray upholstery, she reminded herself of the image she was going to preserve.

And it worked. For the rest of her life, Clara Davenant could recall that parade of telephone poles against the sky. She sometimes wondered whether it was a mistake to have chosen such an ordinary scene, but no, something more unusual could have stuck in her memory spontaneously. Clara doesn't believe she did this more than once—took a deliberate snapshot in her mind—but whenever she wants to place herself in time or recapture a sense of her family before their worst trouble came, she can think back to those telephone poles and that journey.

"Do you want me to drive now, dear?" Grace offered after their picnic lunch by Lake Michigan in Traverse City, but Robert declined. People were often surprised that Robert Davenant, with his handicap, was so active. Not that it had been a truly devastating case of infantile paralysis, but his right leg was weak, and occasionally he wore a brace. Between field trips and conferences, he worked at the Fisheries Institute with his foot propped on the bottom drawer of his desk. He never complained, and his colleagues admired his integrity even when it made them uncomfortable. He wouldn't, they said, take home so much as a paper clip from the office.

This summer, the Davenants had had an entire island to themselves. The children swam in the icy water of Lake Superior or dug in the sand, and when it rained they painted pictures or wrote stories or played the wind-up phonograph. Their favorite record was "I Wish I Could Shimmy like My Sister Kate," but they also imitated Caruso's "Di quella pira," complete with surface noise. With a whole island to play on, the children quarreled less than at home, though Clara Jane sometimes retreated to the rubber boat and ignored calls from the shore. Grace said this was a normal sign of adolescence, a thought which made Robert shudder. If only he could keep his children exactly as they were, safe from change and outsiders and the coming war.

Because nobody knew how he cherished them—their smooth skin and treble voices, their growing vocabularies. Although Robert might not have wished for the children in the first place, he cared more for them than for anything else.

It was because he cared that he had to correct them. Lunch by the lake today had been an ordeal, with too much mayonnaise in the sandwiches, and the children whining and failing to help; people who described unpleasant experiences as 'no picnic,' Robert reflected, didn't know what they were talking about. Afterwards Grace had taken the children off to the swings—all but Clara Jane, who sat at the table running her finger along the words that were burnt officially into one corner. "Murray D. Van Waggoner," she murmured. "State Highway Commissioner." Clara Jane had always read everything in sight. When she was five, Robert had seen her read a cookie, spelling out "National Biscuit Company" before putting it into her mouth.

Today he remarked on her fingers, which were long, with oval nails. "Such lovely hands," he said, and she smiled. But then he noticed the unnatural shine of her fingernails. His child? "Is that polish? No daughter of mine—" he said, and saw her flinch. Hurt by her reaction, he rose and limped toward the shore while she continued to sit on the bench, looking down. It was true that Robert spanked his children, but not for things like this. Back in the long black car, coping with Saginaw traffic, he told himself it could have been worse; the polish might have been pink or even red. But he still hated the thought of his perfect child disfiguring her perfect hands.

Since Robert was away so often—hunting or fishing or doing field work—he tried to put the rare times with his family to good use. "'Ozymandias, king of kings,'" he said now in his reciting voice, "'Look on my works, ye Mighty, and despair.'" If he didn't know what to say to his children, he could at least expose them to poetry. Next week the family would move to a larger house. They could expand, with a room for each child, a study upstairs, and two parlors below. Robert walked through the new house in his mind, admiring the stained glass in the dining room and the Dutch tiles around the fireplaces and all twelve of the tall rooms.

Clara Jane was beginning to worry. They had reached the outskirts of Ann Arbor and were approaching the last hamburger stand, but her father had given no sign of stopping. Mellie's anxious eyes and Hal's frown showed that they were thinking the same thing. "Dad," Freddie finally said in a small voice.

"Possess yourselves in patience," their father said. "We're almost home."

"But Daddy," Mellie wailed. "You said we could have hamburgers."

Clara Jane hoped the tears that sprang to her eyes were redundant, but then her father, driving right past the stand with its red-striped awning, said, "It's too late. Why didn't you speak up sooner?"

As if even bold Freddie would have dared. The warm tears spilled down Clara Jane's cheeks. Before the car pulled into their driveway, she had reduced her last piece of Kleenex to a ball of white shreds.

"What's the matter?" her father said as she came into the lighted kitchen, turning her face away and lugging the carton of mayonnaise, ketchup, and other supplies. "What's the matter now?"

"Nothing." Did he really not know?

"Don't be so selfish." Selfishness was the worst thing anybody in the family could be accused of, except for stupidity. "Help your mother for a change. Peel some of those potatoes."

"No!" She let the box crash to the floor and ran toward the stairs, hoping he was too tired to follow.

II

Before Clara Jane Davenant was two years old, her parents began to tell her stories. Grace, believing that children were nourished by legends, did research in Perrault, Hans Christian Andersen, and the brothers Grimm and then, at bedtime or naptime, repeated the tales to however many children she had. Robert read to the children too, but his verses from Kipling and Robert Louis Stevenson didn't have the personal resonance of the fairy tales. Clara Jane, only too well, could imagine a bad fairy at her own birth, decreeing that she would lose her temper whenever it was most inconvenient; and she could feel a sliver of ice in her heart, placed there by the wicked hobgoblin in Andersen's story of the Snow Queen. There were good things in the stories too, like the release of the children at the end of "Hansel and Gretel," but how had those children met the witch in the first place? They had been abandoned by their parents, that was how. Clara Jane wasn't just entertained by the story-telling; she was terrified.

It seems to her in later years that she was afraid from the moment of her birth—afraid of her parents as much as of anything else. She liked visiting fish hatcheries with her father, passing between troughs of minnows and huge lurking sturgeon. And she liked hiking with him, learning to follow trails and hold back branches so they wouldn't snap in the face of the person behind. He pointed out animals' burrows and showed her how to find the tender young leaves of wintergreen. On the island in Lake Superior that summer they mapped the pond together, tying lengths of toilet paper to trees on the bank and sighting toward them from two positions. In the woods, her father didn't frown. His voice was gentle. But as soon as they left the wilderness, he changed.

With Grace it was different, but no easier. Clara remembers wanting to hug her mother and simply to be hugged back, with no need for a reason, but she doesn't know whether that ever happened. Grace was always imagining some scene, in which Clara Jane was the oldest child or the timid one or the one with the bad temper. It was the same with the other children. "Oh, maybe *you're* the genius," Grace exclaimed to Freddie when he'd written a jingle for her birthday. None of the children were sure she loved them. Perhaps all of them, not just Clara, harbor slivers of ice.

The house the Davenants bought in the fall of 1941 had a lawn with a maple tree, and beyond that was a street full of traffic. Just after they moved in, Clara Jane was sitting in the swing on the front porch. Hal, who was obsessed with Sherlock Holmes, sat next to her, wearing their father's checked hunting cap. "His eyes had the brightness of fever, there was a hectic flush upon either cheek," he read with expression, from "The Adventure of the Dying Detective."

For the third time in fifteen minutes, a boy's bicycle whizzed by on the sidewalk, ridden by a tough-looking girl with skinny blond braids. She reached out without a glance, and two objects flew through the air and clattered onto the porch. "What's that?" Hal's head came out of the book.

Clara Jane stopped the swing with her foot. "Blackjacks." Pink, black, and white anise-flavored taffy. She gave one to Hal and unwrapped the other. "That girl threw them."

"A capital shot, my dear fellow," Hal said, chewing.

The next morning, the girl with the braids wheeled her red bicycle up their front walk and tossed it into the barberry bushes. Her name was Nadine Applegate, and she lived next door, she announced, straddling the sidewalk with stout legs. Nadine wore riding pants and a leather jacket with fringe, and her raw pink forehead looked as rough as a vegetable grater. "Why do you leave your mouth open?" she asked Hal.

"Singular. Most singular indeed," he said, and closed his mouth, looking hurt.

"He has hay fever," Clara Jane explained. She didn't think Nadine was very polite. A shrill three-note whistle came from the other side of the communal driveway, and Nadine leaped to attention. "I've gotta amscray," she said, and rode off.

When Robert met the Applegates, he wished he hadn't taken the realtor's word about the lovely family next door. The mother seemed inoffensive, but she was away all day at her University secretarial job while the children ran wild and the father stayed home and drank. Mrs. Parmelee, the faded widow on the other side, was more the sort of neighbor Robert had hoped for. Mr. Applegate's drinking was obvious; he started every morning in pale silence but got redder and louder as the day went on. Grace, who tried to see the best in everybody, defended him. "He's quite jolly," she declared. "A real character."

"Oh, Grace, please!" Robert sometimes wondered how he could bear to live with a woman who exasperated him so much. He never intended to speak sharply to her, but sometimes he couldn't help it. He was aware too, though, that he could never have found another woman with her goodness. It was because Grace was so guileless herself that she failed to recognize other people's complexities. "She's a typical old maid," she would say about his sister Mildred, not seeing devoted, conscientious Mildred at all. Their plumber was a typical warm Italian, and Mr. Twist the grocer was gruff but kindly—as if, complete with his name, he had stepped out of Dickens. This combination of ignorance and the assumption of knowledge inspired some of Robert's cruelest remarks. How could Grace, trained supposedly in the study of humankind, see it in stereotypes?

"What do you mean, stereotypes?" Grace asked once, looking thoroughly crushed.

15

Robert went on, in spite of himself. "I mean there's more to Mr. Twist than a white apron and a rude way of talking."

"Of course there is. Did I say there wasn't? I'm sure he's quite different at home." Her voice shook.

He didn't believe her. He didn't believe she knew Mr. Twist had a home. And the next day, as if the conversation had never taken place, she made one of her references to the grocer's rough humor. How had Robert, a failed but once aspiring poet, come to marry a woman with no aesthetic sense?

She was actually proud of her deficiency. "I have no style," she used to boast, referring to a criticism made by a professor in graduate school. "He wanted me to put in some *style*." She laughed, as if the missing quality were an affectation, a matter of forced similes and la-de-dah language.

However, as it turned out, the Davenants didn't have to see much of Wayne Applegate, who was busy listening to Gerald L.K. Smith and Father Coughlin on WJR or lying under his precious Studebaker in his garage. And Wayne Junior—a juvenile delinquent, Nadine boasted—was at a military academy in St. Louis. "Thank goodness for that," said Grace, who did admit that a few people had defects. But Nadine, she added, tomboy or not, could be a playmate for Clara Jane. And Norma, the youngest Applegate, was just Mellie's age.

The broad oak stairway in the new house had a square landing with a leaded window and a built-in bench. A second set of stairs, narrow and steep, rose from the kitchen to the hall outside the master bedroom. Each child had a room, with the three boys on the second floor and the two girls on the third. Grace and Robert were to share the study that opened out of their bedroom, and one of the first things Grace did was to hang their two doctoral diplomas, one above each desk, to remind them that Robert wasn't the only one with a Ph.D.

There wasn't much else to remind them. At the time of their wedding, when they were still in graduate school, Grace and Robert had thought that they would simply get their degrees and start out on their scientific careers. The wedding itself would make no difference except that they could share an apartment and not have to look around for people to marry.

But then Professor Alois Freundlich, Grace's thesis supervisor, heard the news. "How could you?" he demanded of her in his intimidating accent, British on top of Viennese. "How could you do such a thing?"

Grace hadn't realized that marriage was against the rules; she pointed out that a number of her fellow students were married.

The professor pointed out that these students were men.

Grace was disillusioned. Professor Freundlich had welcomed her into his graduate program. He had claimed to be a feminist. But now, on discovering that she had been unfaithful to the program, he dropped her from it. "Men may marry," he explained. "In fact, it is better if they do. Marriage helps to direct their energies. But women ..." And he made a disgusted noise behind his little beard.

"Yes?" Grace had never felt so much indignation.

"Women," he said with an indulgent shrug that enraged her even more. "The trouble with women is that they put their husbands first." As, of course, they ought to do, he hastened to say, but not if they wished to be anthropologists. How could he send a married woman to live with a primitive people for months or even years? And besides that, there was the danger of pregnancy. Professor Freundlich was disappointed in Grace.

She was disappointed in him too. So much for feminism. The worst part of it was that he was right; she did value Robert's work above her own. At the moment, for instance, he was preparing for his language exams, and Grace was coaching him. It made sense, she told herself, since he would surely find a job more easily than she, and the sooner he got his degree, the better. Apart from anything else, she simply felt more comfortable looking up to Robert. She couldn't have married a man to whom she felt superior.

But she had truly hoped for a degree of her own. Grace and Robert were going to be scientists, working side by side; it had been their dream. She wasn't sure how an ichthyologist and an anthropologist could collaborate, but they might at least work in the same territory. In the West, for instance; he could manage streams while she studied Indian tribes. But Professor Freundlich dropped her, and that was that. It was a pity, he said, but she must clear out her desk in the office next to his. His wife would send her an embroidered linen tablecloth and matching napkins.

And so, possibly, she became pregnant through a mixture of frustration and carelessness, as well as a helpless obedience to Professor Freundlich. When she discovered a few months afterwards that the diaphragm hadn't worked, she was barely surprised. "You see," she imagined her professor saying with a small Continental smile above his Oxford gown as he swept past her baby carriage on the campus. "You see I was right." And he would instruct his wife to send her an embroidered bib.

She regretted her pregnancy but then thought, Why not? She was helping Robert and working part-time in the dean's office, but between them they should be able to care for a baby. And then, without warning, Professor Freundlich died. He had had a brain tumor, it turned out. His successor saw Grace on the campus—before there was a need for a carriage—and invited her to enroll in the program again. It didn't matter if she was married or even if she had a child. She could be his assistant.

Again, she thought Why not? The baby, due in two months, shouldn't make a huge difference. She could carry it on her back in a basket from L.L. Bean and go on with her studies. However, when Clara Jane had become an actual colicky, insomniac baby, Grace found that being a mother took up more time and energy than she had expected. Sometimes it seemed that continuing with her graduate studies was only an elaborate way of fooling herself. But she did continue. When she took her orals, Clara Jane was in a portable crib outside the examining room.

Grace did get the degree, but the degree was all she had. She hadn't dreamed how cranky Robert could get if a room was untidy or a meal was late. Before Clara Jane was a month old, Grace felt she had more in common with the most uneducated woman in the maternity ward than with anyone professional.

It was when Clara Jane was six that the newspaper columns began. Robert, by then, was publishing articles on fishing, and Grace was glad to type them, but she thought she might also do some work of her own. She was celebrated for her letters about her growing family—people were always urging her to do something with them. Why not? So one August when the Davenants were at Copper Harbor, Grace sent copies of her letters—about mischievous children fishing with bent pins and tracking sand into the cabin—to the local paper. The letters were printed, under the title "Notes on a Modern Family," and she had ten dollars more for groceries every other week.

Robert, for some reason, disapproved of the newspaper columns. By the time the family moved to the new house, in fact, he seemed to scorn a great many things about her. "Grace," he would say after a perfectly innocent observation of hers, "how can you say that?" And he would limp out of the room. This scorn of his, this tone of voice and withering eye, made her dry up to nothing. It was a tone she recognized from her childhood, when her father reacted to some statement of her mother's—an irreverent remark, for instance, about a politician he admired. When Grace was a girl, she had taken her father's side, and she had vowed never to become as silly as other women. It wasn't that she'd wished to be a man—but an angel, perhaps, or a youth without gender. Ariel. Peter Pan. She would be simply spirit, without a troublesome body. And look at her now.

In the meantime she had her newspaper column with its local fame, as well as her diploma on the study wall; she had her brilliant lively children and a large house and a husband who supported them all as well as he could. What more could anyone want?

III

THE MEANING OF ARMISTICE DAY IN 1941
by Jane Davenant, Grade 8B

Armistice Day has more meaning now than it did a few years ago. Right now most of the world is at war, and we are almost in the war ourselves. We should be glad that we don't have a dictator at the head of our nation, and that our country isn't fighting yet. Armistice Day is celebrated in honor of the soldiers who lost their lives in the First World War ....

Clara Jane, sitting in the window seat halfway up the stairs, finished writing her Social Studies essay, though it was hard to get up much enthusiasm for the topic. Most of her compositions were attempts at humor, but you couldn't very well be humorous about Armistice Day.

The very thought of war made her shiver, and yet in a way she didn't believe in it—especially in the one that everybody said America was about to get into. People—her teachers and parents and the news commentators on the radio—talked as if it were just going to happen and there was nothing anybody could do. If they were so sure, why didn't they stop the fighting before it began? She asked her parents this, but they only smiled sadly in the way that meant she was too young to understand. It was like the fights that took place in the family, she supposed; the children knew quite well when they were about to hurt each other's feelings, and yet they went right ahead and said whatever it was, even if they didn't mean it. But she would have expected kings and presidents to have more sense.

The window seat was Clara's Jane's favorite place in the house. Soon after they moved in, Grace had made heavy damask curtains and fitted them to the edge of the alcove rather than to the window itself. With the curtains closed, Clara Jane could sit undetected on the cushioned bench and read. On rainy days she watched the drops running down the glass and saw the lights of the Applegates' house on the other side of the driveway. Some of the books she read in that first year were *Scaramouche, Enquiries into Human Faculty* (from her mother's bookshelf, and full of case histories), *Life with Father*, and *Leave it to Jeeves*.

It was a wonderful house, the whole family thought. The attic contained decayed silk dresses and albums of brown photographs, as well as a majestic hand-painted chamber pot, which Grace moved to the bay window of the dining room and filled with paper-white narcissus. She had the downstairs walls repapered too, although the paperhanger—chosen out of sympathy for his poor eyesight—hung several of the pieces upside down. The effect wasn't so bad in the rooms that were patterned in stripes or climbing ivy, but the pastoral landscape in the front hall was a disaster; even Grace admitted that it was unsettling to open the front door to a scene of inverted horses and country roads. Clara Jane wrote a description of the wallpaper for English class and got an A-, and Grace moved the coat rack to cover the worst part, but Robert, who thought of the house as a new beginning, was saddened.

A curtained archway led from the large hall into the living room, where sliding doors opened into a back parlor. "We can give plays, with real curtains," Clara Jane exclaimed, "and the audience can sit in the hall." They had put on shows before, but without enough room for spectators. There were twelve-foot ceilings in the new house, and fireplaces in both rooms. If Grace's battered upright piano and the couch and chairs with scratched maple arms looked shabby in such grand surroundings, that was just too bad. The kitchen didn't have enough cupboards, and there was a rusty pump beside the sink, but that didn't matter either. Any drawbacks, the children pointed out, were made up for by the back stairs. "We can sneak down for crackers," Freddie exulted.

Mellie and Clara Jane, on the third floor, were a little unhappy because Clara Jane couldn't reach her room without walking through Mellie's. "Get out of here!" Mellie would screech, and Clara Jane would tramp through all over again, to establish her rights. When Grace suggested a rule about knocking, the arguments died down. As she said to Robert, Mellie (whose real name was Mildred Eleanor) was so pretty, with her blue eyes and straight black bangs, that it was hard to fight with her.

"Both of them are beautiful," Robert said.

"Well…" Grace was at her desk, typing an exaggerated account of her daughters' quarrels for her newspaper column. With any luck, Clara Jane would grow into her serious face. She had a wide calm brow and hazel eyes and thick gold-brown hair which she insisted on braiding. If only she would hold her head a little higher. And if she would make some friends besides Nadine. "Get out in the fresh air," Grace was always urging. "Play with your chums." Chums were what Grace had had in her own youth. Robert had been one of them, and he had hit her with a snowball once. She had wished she could preserve that snowball forever.

Clara Jane's age might be the real problem. "Our eldest," Grace wrote, "is poised on the brink of the nest, ready to test the water." Because she had no feeling for metaphors, she could mix them without noticing.

"A letter for you, dear," Grace called from the kitchen as Robert limped into the house one afternoon in late November. The envelope on the brass tray in the hall was from his sister. Mildred was a devoted correspondent, sending details of Eastern Star banquets and Grange meetings in their home town in upstate New York. She was engaged to Willard Cooper, the local funeral director, a hearty, graceless man whom Robert was unable to like. However, Mildred was forty-two and probably wouldn't find anyone else. Robert stretched out on the couch to read the letter. His leg was giving him trouble.

Not nearly so much trouble as he was about to have, he saw.

22

Mildred's engagement was broken. There had been times when he'd been unsure of the engagement, and Grace openly doubted it. It had gone on for five years if indeed it did exist, but Leonard was not attentive, and Mildred didn't wear a ring. Now it was definitely off. Mildred was wondering if, since Robert had such a nice big house now, the family would like her to visit. She could help with the children and the housework.

Robert pulled himself together and followed an odor of scorching to the kitchen, where Grace was mangling sheets while a pot of foul-smelling cabbage stew bubbled on the stove. Freddie and Clara Jane were making fudge all over the table, and Cricket, doing his loudest siren imitation, was running a toy fire engine over Grace's feet. It was clear that she did need help; Mrs. Kepler, whose wages were paid by Grace's father, came only two mornings a week to do the laundry and part of the cleaning. It might not be the moment to bring up Mildred, though.

"Happy news," Grace announced the next evening at the dinner table as she dished out baked beans and hot dogs and applesauce. "Auntie Mildred is coming to visit." She knew Robert was glad. Mildred had brought him up after their mother's first stroke.

"Auntie Mildred?" Mellie squealed happily—apparently forgetting the last visit, when she had wet the dining-room floor twice and Auntie Mildred had accused her of being jealous of the new baby. "Oh, goody."

"You're mixing her up with Aunt Eleanor, dummy," Clara Jane said. Grace's sister, whose paintings of churches and vegetables decorated the Davenants' wall, was popular with the children. She wasn't strict, and she brought them things like all-day suckers and materials for making marionettes. "Don't you remember?" Clara Jane said. "Auntie Mildred is the one who makes us chew our milk."

Mildred did have a theory, Grace remembered, that milk—as a food—should be chewed, and the children had found this ridiculous. Still, she might be off on another tack by now

"Dummy," Freddie said, and kicked Mellie under the table.

"You know we don't use that word." Grace was worried. Mildred would need a room to herself, and the only plan Robert approved was to give her Clara Jane's room and put the two girls in together. The double-decker bed, now separated into twin beds, would have to be reassembled. "We're all going to be especially nice to Auntie Mildred," Grace told the children.

"I thought she was supposed to get married," Clara Jane said. "To the undertaker."

"The undertaker!" Freddie spluttered through a mouthful of beans.

"Not anymore. But you mustn't say anything to her about it." Grace looked at Robert for help, but he was frowning at his plate. "Auntie Mildred is very sad," she said. She would explain the sleeping arrangements later.

IV

Sunday, December 7. Mildred Davenant had been with the family for over a week, and kept to her room except for meals, when
she poked at the food with her fork. She knocked before going
through the girls' room and didn't comment on the mess, though
she cast pointed glances toward the dolls' village that occupied half
of the floor. Today Grace and Robert had actually persuaded her to
go with them to the Institute Christmas party and left Clara Jane in
charge.

Clara Jane, sprawled over the funnies while fleas from Mischief
the cat bounced on the paper, saw Jiggs sneaking into his house
carrying his shoes and felt her usual discomfort. Nadine Applegate
loved "Bringing Up Father," but Clara Jane couldn't stand to see
Maggie chase Jiggs with the rolling pin; it reminded her of 'hen-
pecked,' one of her least favorite words. She did have to agree with
Nadine that Boots and Her Buddies were cute, though, with their
little snub noses set directly above their jaws as if they were Labra-
dor retrievers. She could never hope to look like that.

Besides her looks, Clara Jane despised her name. It was bad
enough having the wrong kind of nose, without being called
Clarabelle Cow whenever anybody at school wanted to tease her.
She had asked her teachers to call her Jane, and even her father
often did, perhaps because the original Jane was his saintly mother.

The radio, gothic with a mottled orange dial, was playing
Beethoven with static. Their father forbade popular music, which
he referred to as jazz, but Clara Jane thought that if she could hear
more of it—and more radio programs in general—her status at school
might improve. As it was, her ignorance of song lyrics or the charac-

ters in "Little Orphan Annie" or "I Love a Mystery" was almost total. She had heard a few illicit programs at Nadine's house this fall, and she had memorized "Three Little Fishies" and even read some comic books, but she was afraid she would never catch up.

"Why can't we find a different station?" Freddie whined.

"You know perfectly well," Clara Jane said, but then she changed her mind. "All right, if you don't beg me any more till five o'clock, maybe we can turn on 'The Shadow.'" This was forbidden too, but she felt reckless. They were all fascinated by the playboy Lamont Cranston, who became invisible to do good deeds. His evil laugh bespoke hidden depths.

Hal laughed evilly, stalking invisibly around the room, trampling the newspaper. "The weed of crime bears bitter fruit."

"Don't you have any homework?" Clara Jane demanded in her father's voice. She had finished her math problems, but she still had to design her ideal wardrobe for her Home Ec Charm Book. She took out her colored pencils. She would draw a picture of herself in the gray wool skirt and green Sloppy Joe sweater she wished she would get for Christmas. What she dreamed of, besides the sweater, was a pair of loafers and some thick cream-colored socks. "Not unless you stop pronating your ankles," her mother said whenever she mentioned the loafers, and Clara Jane knew she was doomed to wear Girl Scout shoes with Thomas heels for the rest of her life. She gave the girl in her self-portrait lank brown hair and a dejected face.

The music on the radio stopped in the middle of a violin obbligato, and a man's voice spoke in deep, excited tones.

"The Japanese have invaded Pearl Harbor," Clara Jane wrote that night in her line-a-day diary—the first entry she had made all year. "We are At War."

V

The war made people feel useful who hadn't felt that way before. Mildred Davenant regained her appetite and dominated the dinner table with chatter about the war effort. The sewing machine hummed as she ran up dark curtains for all the windows. She taught the girls to knit woolen squares for afghans, and she and Grace folded bandages for the Red Cross every week in the junior high cafeteria. Blackouts were practiced, and there were air-raid drills at school. Candy, except for Horlick's malted-milk tablets and something called Tastyeast, nearly disappeared from the stores. Grace tried recipes for inedible sugarless cakes. Everyone collected bacon fat, rubber, and metal. Gas and tires were rationed. "Is this trip necessary?" posters inquired.

Robert, with his bad leg and large family, was excluded from this war as he had been from the last. However, the new restrictions appealed to his sense of economy. The son of a Methodist minister, he had been brought up to suspect extravagance. His studies of both poetry and science had reinforced this training. Though he had long ago thrown off formal religion, Robert retained a respect for larger purposes and for what mathematicians call elegance. Art and science, he believed, both take the materials at hand and form them into shapes that have been inherent in them from the beginning. In nature there is no waste. Dead leaves and dead plants fertilize the ground. Trees spring from the droppings of birds. He could put a drop of pond water under a lens and see a universe.

So Robert applauded the war effort. War itself horrified him, and he distrusted all governments and politicians, in particular Franklin D. Roosevelt, who had created the bureaucracy. Franklin's cousin Theodore, founder of the conservation movement, was his man. Or

Lincoln, who used words well and put up with a foolish wife and suffered from moods as dark as Robert's own. The war, he hoped, would purify the country.

One night in December, Grace was awakened by noises from downstairs. Burglars didn't seem likely, in spite of the pistol Robert kept in the drawer of the bedside table, separate from the ammunition; the pistol, to her, was only a symbol of Robert's concern for his family. But definite sounds were coming from the kitchen. The children must be after crackers again; it was too bad the back stairs were so convenient. They were convenient for her too, though. She slipped out of bed, put on her blue chenille robe, and made her way down the steep, narrow stairs. A light streamed under the door at the bottom. It would be Freddie, as usual—charming, naughty Freddie.

Grace opened the door to the kitchen. "Now, you know you're not allowed..." she began, but then she saw her sister-in-law Mildred, in a lace-trimmed negligee and bunny slippers, standing on tiptoe on the kitchen stool in front of the cupboards. Mildred wasn't getting crackers. She had taken all the cereal boxes and soup cans out of the cupboards and was scrubbing the shelves with Old Dutch Cleanser and a dampened sponge.

Mildred gave a start, then looked furious, then smiled. Her first angry expression could have been a reaction to the light that hit her eyes as she turned and focused on Grace. Mildred was not quite five feet tall, a small woman in pincurls and a hairnet, but her position on the stool gave her authority. "I was just ..." she said.

Robert had mentioned more than once that Mildred didn't think Grace kept the house clean enough, and by Mildred's standards, Mildred was right; the house was not perfectly antiseptic. But if Grace ever came to value a spotless linoleum floor over a page of tidy prose, she might as well not go on living. However, she reminded herself of Mildred's troubles with the funeral director. "Couldn't you sleep?" she asked. "Maybe some hot milk..."

Mildred muttered something in which Grace could distinguish only the word "filth." Then she said, through tight lips, "Nobody's going to mind this. Nobody's feelings are going to be hurt." And she turned around and attacked the cupboards again.

Grace let herself see that her feelings were meant to be hurt. "Good night, then, Mildred," she said. "Don't work too long."

Mildred Davenant's visit to her brother's family was the least of their troubles in a world overturned by war. It was only more immediate than bombs or invasions or European despots, which figured in family conversation as well as in the children's nightmares. They were all frightened; the whole country was frightened. It didn't matter that Europe and Japan were far away or that there was no such thing yet as a jet plane or an atomic bomb. Nobody could see the future, and nobody knew who would win.

Clara Jane and Mellie both acquired a fear of Asians, reinforced by torture stories from Auntie Mildred and Nadine Applegate. Nazis were just as bad, Hal maintained, but Clara Jane wasn't sure; Japanese people read backwards and didn't even use the alphabet. Mellie feared the Chinese too, even after the older children explained that they were good. "I don't care," she said. "They *look* bad."

Clara Jane was especially frightened by dictators in newsreels, with their quacking voices and stern gray faces. It was the inexorability, the steamroller quality, of movies that scared her most: Even when a story was made up—even when it was innocuous—there was no possibility of its changing. As a rule, the children saw only films that featured Shirley Temple, Deanna Durbin, Sonja Henie, or Jeanette MacDonald and Nelson Eddy. By some oversight, however, last year Mrs. Kepler had been allowed to take Hal and Clara Jane to *The Letter*, with Bette Davis as the straying wife of a rubber planter, and both children had developed strep throat the next day, with temperatures of a hundred and two. No matter how often Clara Jane turned her pillow to the cool side, the image of Bette Davis's big selfish eyes wouldn't go out of her head. She saw the moon sliding through clouds and the actress standing on the steps of a verandah firing a gun over and over, and later working at a huge piece of lace until she was finally, deservedly, strangled. Bette Davis had nothing to do with the strep throat, Grace said, and Clara Jane knew this, but she still connected the mysterious East with danger and pain. She had been ashamed of her fear, but now the deceitful emperor Hirohito was proving her right.

Who could tell when the war would cross the water? Americans, it was hoped, would withstand it as well as the British and French and the noble Russians. "The American people in their righteous might," as President Roosevelt had said when he declared war. Daylight Saving Time became War Time and lasted all year in most places—to the irritation of Robert, whose state-run office was an hour ahead of the city. People who lived through World War II would refer to it ever afterwards as The War, and other people from the same era would know which war they meant.

When a month had gone by and Mildred hadn't mentioned leaving, Grace ventured to ask when she was expected back in the house she shared with a married brother in upstate New York.

"Oh, I couldn't go back there," Mildred said. "I couldn't face it." Her voice trembled.

Grace reported the conversation to Robert when he got back that night from duck hunting. He had shot four mallards and was in a good mood, though his leg was aching and he had put on his brace. "I'm not sure she expects to leave at all," Grace said, half joking. "She may be here for the duration." That was another wartime phrase, and it meant until the end of the war, which was expected soon.

"Just one more sacrifice to make for our country," Robert said, also joking. "But why don't you turn the household over to her and shut yourself up in the study? I'm serious. You could go back to your research."

"Research?" Grace echoed. Did he think it was like embroidery, something she could pick up whenever she had a spare minute? "Do you imagine I've even had time to keep up with my field in the last twelve years?" Besides, she said to herself but not to Robert, Mildred wasn't all that much help: She undertook small jobs without fitting them into a larger plan, as when she had mopped the kitchen floor today and forbidden Grace to cook dinner before it dried. "And," Grace did say, "the children are afraid of Mildred."

"Nonsense," Robert said, not recalling his own childhood trepidation. "She loves the children."

A week later, Mildred announced that she had enrolled at the University for graduate work in Education. Her courses would begin in February. Neither of them dared to object, though Robert did apologize to Grace. "We'll have to make the best of it," he said.

Grace resigned herself. Mildred would provide material for her column, anyway. Under another name, she had already figured in two episodes as the brusque but plucky maiden aunt. Grace had received letters from readers who were reminded of characters in their own families.

One afternoon that winter, Clara Jane sat on a crate in Nadine Applegate's chilly clubhouse above the garage next door, leafing through a pile of comic books. She had seen such things before, but she was surprised by some of the pictures in these, with gangsters aiming guns at each other and women being tied up and tortured. Her favorite comics, to Nadine's scorn, were the ones about Li'l Abner or Nancy and Sluggo. It was hard to turn the pages with mittens on, but if the girls stayed out of Nadine's house, they could avoid her father, who lurked in his chair by the radio and made remarks.

The comic that Clara Jane was looking at now had an ad in the back, for a necktie that would light up and say, "Kiss Me in the Dark, Baby." She laughed out loud. "Look at this."

"What about it?" Nadine said, looking defensive.

Clara Jane was still laughing. "The person who wrote this ad seems to think it's romantic."

"So what?"

"If you were with a boy and his tie suddenly..." But Clara Jane already knew that their sense of humor wasn't the same. Nadine didn't even agree with her about Charles Atlas's muscles.

"Why don't we play Cassino?" Nadine breathed on her cold fingers and tapped a ragged blue deck of Bicycle cards against a crate.

Mittens were for sissies. She shuffled the cards expertly, but Clara Jane, who didn't care for cards, pretended not to notice. So Nadine went back to an earlier conversation about her brother, Wayne Junior, who used to share a room with her. She was glad her parents had sent him away to school. "You know how it is," she said, casting her eyes to the fiberboard ceiling of the clubhouse. "You can get really tired of fucking." She sighed and thrust her hands into the pockets of her riding pants.

Clara Jane hadn't heard that word before, but she understood its importance—if not its precise meaning—right away. Any word introduced to her by Nadine, whose vocabulary was smaller than hers, had to be taboo. "Oh, sure," she said, feeling uneasy.

It wasn't the first time she'd felt that way. Nadine acted as if they were best friends, and yet Clara Jane wasn't sure they even liked each other. More than their sense of humor was different; a lot of things about the whole Applegate family worried her: They used slang and yelled at each other, even the grownups; the children were allowed to eat Vienna sausages whenever they wanted, straight from the can; Nadine chewed on the ends of her pigtails and made spelling errors, and she followed the Phys Ed teacher around town on her bicycle. Clara Jane was always thinking of the criticisms her parents would make if they knew these things.

Nadine was critical of the Davenants, too. "Your family has too many kids," she liked to point out, rolling her eyes. "Which proves you-know-what." This meant, Clara Jane understood, that her parents had done shameful sexual things. Nadine's parents must also have done them, of course, but not so many times.

Besides, Nadine said, all the Davenants were stuck-up and skinny, and it was obvious that they were poor. Although these comments wounded Clara Jane, she was impressed by Nadine's assurance. Other things impressed her too: The Applegates used Lifebuoy soap, which Clara Jane hadn't seen until then outside of a store. Her mother would never buy soap like that, with its medicinal smell and octagonal shape and its dirty-orange color; there was something anti-intellectual about it, as if it weren't meant for people with graduate degrees. The word Nadine had said gave Clara Jane the same feeling. Just because the Davenants didn't use it, that didn't mean it didn't exist; there might be millions of people in the world who bought Lifebuoy soap and said "fucking."

It wasn't in the dictionary, she found out when she got home. Maybe she had the spelling wrong. But she was sure it was connected with sex. A few years before, her mother had caught the younger children playing doctor in the garage with Eloise Gaddis from the next block. They had persuaded Eloise to pull down her underpants and stand on a ladder facing the wall while Freddie, wearing a discarded lab coat of their father's, scribbled in a notebook and made diagnostic comments. Clara Jane was supposed to watch the others that day, but she had gotten caught up in a story about a tractor salesman in the *Saturday Evening Post*. Eloise's mother was horrified, and so was Grace in spite of her advanced views. She got Robert to spank them all, and Clara Jane was horribly ashamed.

A ghost of that shame came back that day in the Applegates' clubhouse. Clara Jane knew by then that sex games were more prevalent than she had thought, though she still believed that they were confined to children. She was afraid to ask Nadine for details, in case she heard more than she really wanted to. During the next few weeks, whenever Nadine invited her over, Clara Jane said she was busy.

She had feared at the time of the Eloise episode that her mother might expose the family disgrace in her newspaper column, but except for an oblique reference to youthful high spirits and natural curiosity, there was no mention of what had happened in the garage. No matter how much Grace might scold in person, she never wrote as if she minded anything her children did.

It was hard for Grace even to know what she ought to mind. She wanted to guide her children toward happy and productive lives, but most of her general principles were hard to apply to particular situations. She knew it was wrong to scream at them, for instance, and yet once, when Freddie had accidentally knocked a newly frosted cake from the kitchen counter into a pan of dishwater, Grace heard herself shouting, "Freddie, you fool!" before she was aware of having opened her mouth. She reproached herself intermittently—for that incident and others—and wondered how much she was damaging her children's egos.

She worried especially about her daughters. Should she encourage them to pursue careers, as her parents had encouraged her? Or would this only lead someday to their screaming at children of their own? When she had started out on her studies, she had considered herself a pioneer. Her father, a small-town banker with a respect for learning, had approved of her ambition. She suspected now that he and her mother had thought of her scientific education as insurance for a plain, serious-minded girl who might not attract a husband. But then she had surprised everybody—including herself—by marrying Robert.

Not that Grace had ever thought herself unmarriageable, exactly, but she wasn't confident of her appearance. She had distinctive features and faint eyebrows obscured by glasses. Her body was slender and wide-hipped, with heavy, swinging breasts—not the sort of figure to be flattered by the fashions of the Twenties. She was grateful when waists came back and showed how slim she had been all along. Were her parents disappointed when motherhood put a stop to her profession? Probably, in some ways. Her mother's letters now were full of the artistic doings of her unmarried sister, Eleanor.

Still, Grace supported her children's projects, like the doll village they had built from orange crates a few years before and moved, intact, into the new house. Smithville was an elaborate community, where murders, robberies, and weddings regularly took place. One of the more talented dolls had painted murals on most of the walls. Another was a spy, still another a dentist. There were love triangles in Smithville—but no adultery, which the children hadn't heard of. When Robert brought up the moral ambiguity of the doll village, Grace reassured him: The dolls might be immoral, but the children didn't take their adventures any more seriously than the ordeals of Helen Trent, Mrs. Kepler's favorite soap-opera heroine.

This, in a way, was true. There were very few evils, besides the war and their own everyday problems, that the Davenant children took seriously.

VI

In October of 1941 Grace took her annual Christmas picture, of the children and Mischief by the empty fireplace hung with empty stockings, under the mounted head of the mule deer that Robert had shot several years before. She would send copies to relatives, acquaintances, and readers who had written to her about her column.

On Christmas Eve the same stockings were hung again. Robert read *A Christmas Carol* aloud, skipping most of the Past and Yet to Come sections and getting a catch in his voice, as usual, when he came to the Cratchits. Later Freddie crept down the back stairs in the dark and betrayed himself by tripping over the cord of the electric clock at 4:46, but escaped punishment because of the season. Each of the children received a toy, a book, and a new pair of pajamas. Feeling the big soft pajama package, Clara Jane allowed herself to hope briefly for a sweater, but of course it wasn't. Her book, Hendrik Willem van Loon's *The Arts*, looked good, at least, and she was glad about her new cribbage board. She had bought little plaster images of Disney dwarfs—Grumpy for Hal, Dopey for Freddie (with whom she was annoyed at the time), Sneezy for Mellie, and Happy for Cricket. Her parents both got Doc, because of their Ph.D.s. Auntie Mildred presented the whole family with flashlights loaded with Eveready batteries, for air raids. "We ought to have gas masks too," she fretted as she sat in the alcove with her lap full of lace-edged handkerchiefs and little blue bottles of Evening in Paris cologne from Kresge's. "I suppose the President will set up some kind of agency."

"No doubt," Robert said bitterly. Just like the WPA and the CCC camps, he was implying—anything to waste the taxpayers' money.

"I'm sure he will, dear," said Grace. Mrs. Roosevelt, in spite of those unfortunate teeth, seemed practical. She would see to it.

Clara Jane imagined the family in gas masks, with big insect eyes and elephant trunks, crouched under the round oak dining table while Japanese planes dropped flaming bombs. Mellie would be whimpering the whole time, and Freddie and Hal would be pinching each other, and it would be up to her to control them. If Alf Landon or Wendell Willkie had been in charge, there wouldn't even be a war.

Robert, deaf to all Grace's hints about an imitation pearl necklace, had given her a chenille robe exactly like the one from last year, but rose-colored instead of blue. She tried not to be disappointed. This was quite a usual Christmas, she thought, except that Mildred was there. By anybody's standards, Mildred was a difficult person. For one thing, she finished other people's sentences for them. "We've all been under a lot of—" Grace had begun at the dinner table last night, after Robert's abrupt departure when Cricket knocked over his milk for the second time. "Of strain," Mildred had murmured as she rushed to the kitchen for a sponge.

A few weeks after Christmas, sitting uninspired before a blank sheet of typing paper, Grace considered the problem of her sister-in-law. In high school Mildred, a grade ahead of Grace and Robert, had tried to prevent them from walking home together. Even then, tiny as she was, she had a commanding presence. She looked nearly the same now, with springy dark hair pulled into tight braids around her head, and dark eyes glittering behind thick lenses. Her teeth projected like Eleanor Roosevelt's, but unlike the First Lady, Mildred didn't compensate by smiling. And now she had settled into her brother's family as if it were her right. Perhaps she thought it was; she had lived for twelve years with her brother Wesley in New York, and now it was Robert's turn.

On the very day of her arrival, Mildred had begun an alliance with Mrs. Kepler. Grace would enter the kitchen on one of Mrs. Kepler's cleaning days to find the two of them huddled at the chipped enameled table over coffee cups, chatting away. She was fond of her cleaning woman, in spite of an initial distaste for the bright, metallic vermilion of her lips. It couldn't be lipstick, Grace had thought on the day Mrs. Kepler applied for the job; from the side, it had a strange greenish cast. And then Clara Jane reported seeing Mrs. Kepler at the bathroom cabinet, painting her mouth with Mercurochrome. Poor thing, Grace thought, and hoped it wasn't toxic. Since then she had come to think of Mrs. Kepler as an ally. She passed on discarded clothes and sympathized about her drunken husband. But there had been nothing like the conspiracy that was developing now, with silences and exchanged glances when Grace came into the kitchen. Mildred was confiding her grievances, Grace suspected.

Robert, too, was different now. Grace knew better than to venture even a slightly critical remark about Mildred, but he responded to remarks she didn't make. "She's earned anything I can do for her," he snapped when Grace dared to wonder aloud whether the family in New York missed Mildred. "Without her, I would have died." It might be true. Mildred had nursed him through infantile paralysis when he was eighteen and had helped him learn to walk again. Grace reminded herself of this every day.

Robert was also more impatient with the children than before. They failed to understand the value of work, he said. They whined and quarreled and used slang expressions. One day Hal asked why they weren't allowed to listen to Fred Allen's radio program. "All the other kids—" he began before Robert broke in to explain that kids were goats and that Fred Allen was broadcast too late on a school night. It was Robert's favorite program, as it happened, except for the Metropolitan Opera, but it was often spoiled for him by the sound of stealthy feet on the upstairs landing. Maybe the children's behavior hadn't degenerated, but Robert noticed it more.

Grace ran her hand along the typewriter keys and looked down at the paper, on which she hadn't even typed the heading for her column. She was having trouble maintaining her daily routine. Soon after the start of her life with Robert, she had discovered that he couldn't bear to see her idle, and at first she thought this meant that she had to work every minute she was awake. She actually did so for a while, before concluding that a certain amount of deception was permissible, or even necessary, in marriage. Since the birth of Clara Jane, therefore, Grace had timed her own naps or reading times to coincide with hours when Robert was away. He could come home from the office to find her cleaning windows or baking biscuits, and the implication was that she had spent the whole day that way. With Mildred around, subterfuge was more difficult.

Robert didn't even like to see Grace at her desk, unless she was typing for him. Letters were all right, of course, but more often than not she was working on the newspaper column he disliked so much. She didn't mention him in the column; his reaction to a playful reference in the first of her "Notes on a Modern Family" had taught her better.

Grace had adored Robert since they were in sixth grade, when he had hit her with that snowball. She wasn't injured, but she was smitten; it was a sign of attention. She tagged along after him in high school—class secretary to his president, salutatorian to his valedictorian. His illness separated them, and they went to different colleges, but Grace's devotion continued. When she found out where he had applied to graduate school, she happened to apply there too. By that time he was in love with a girl named Judith Rabinowitz, but both sets of parents opposed the marriage. For nearly three years, as his chances with Judith diminished, he confided his sorrows to Grace. She and Robert gradually became closer, until he agreed to marry her.

No, that wasn't right. She blushed now when she heard the words in her mind. *She*, of course, had agreed to marry *him*. He loved her by that time; he said so. But neither of them ever had to puzzle over whose love was stronger.

"He has invited me to marry him," she had written to her parents, before changing it to "We have decided to be married in the spring."

When the family moved last fall, Grace and Clara Jane had come across a trunk filled with clothes from Grace's trousseau. There were gum-boots from L.L. Bean, tweed knickerbockers, and striped man-tailored shirts. No negligees or lace nightgowns; Grace and Robert had spent their honeymoon on a field trip at Cranberry Lake in the Adirondacks with eleven male biologists. Grace had been expected to cook.

"Oh, Mama," Clara Jane cried. "Weren't you disappointed?"

"Of course I wasn't," Grace said to her daughter. "It was lovely being out in the wilderness." This wasn't true, she saw now. There were two of her former wishes that she usually kept in separate imaginary boxes: She had wanted to do work of her own and be respected for it; and, since childhood, she had wanted to marry Robert. If she had put the two desires together, would she have expected to achieve both? Yes. Certainly. Only the children had prevented her. But no, it wasn't true; her surrender had taken place before children were ever thought of. She had spent more of that camping trip in tears than she cared to remember. She had been too squeamish to bait a hook, and her leaking air mattress lowered her to the stony ground before the middle of every night. And Robert, even then, had been impatient.

She didn't know now where she had picked up the notion that wedding trips ought to be spent in Florence, but since the age of fifteen she had pictured herself standing on a foreign bridge, in ankle-length skirts and an overpowering hat, next to a man whose arm was placed tenderly about her waist as they gazed down at the water. Grace hadn't supposed that her real honeymoon would be like this, but she hadn't been prepared, either, to wear clumsy rubber boots and heat baked beans over a campfire and scrub greasy tin plates with cold water and sand. She was all too used to those things now. At the time, though, 'disappointed' was putting it mildly. And yet when Clara Jane used the word, Grace denied it.

It wasn't camping or sleeping in a tent that had discouraged her. Before her engagement, when she hoped to be an anthropologist, she was prepared for those very things, along with inedible food and dysentery and Pidgin English. The field trip had failed her because it was part of Robert's work and not her own.

Without him and the children, where would she be? New Guinea? Arizona? She had dreamed of studying in London with Malinowski; exhilarating days in the British Museum and discussions of Melanesian marriage customs over strong tea with the milk poured in first. Now, she would never cross an ocean in her life. Grace wondered how many lies she told and thought each day. But it might be as well not to know: Would it do any good to say to Clara Jane, "You're right. I hated my honeymoon. I felt swindled and subjugated"? She would only disillusion her daughter, who might have a honeymoon of her own someday. A happier one than hers, Grace hoped.

Sitting at her desk with no notion of what to write in her column or what to do about Mildred, Grace felt like pounding her fists against the typewriter keys. If only her sister-in-law would find something to concentrate on besides the family and her studies. If only she could make a few friends, for instance.

VII

One morning soon afterwards, when everybody but Auntie Mildred was seated at the breakfast table, Grace Davenant suggested to Robert that they give a dinner party. "Who can we invite for Mildred?" Grace asked. "There must be lots of single men in the Institute."

"What?" Robert asked crossly. The prospect of people entering his house—not necessarily strangers, but people who didn't belong there—disturbed him. Grace had a way of allowing mere acquaintances to practically move in. One woman, Mrs. Waterhouse, appeared every so often and collapsed in the living room, billowing over the edges of the couch. Grace had met her at the Co-op and made the mistake of inviting her for tea. He couldn't imagine what they found to talk about. Or, rather, he could: Grace would tell Mrs. Waterhouse about her trials with Professor Freundlich in graduate school and about how she had breast-fed all her children in spite of the doctors, while Mrs. Waterhouse would make responsive noises and eat arrowroot biscuits and not have to say a word. Whenever he came home to find Mrs. Waterhouse spread full-length in his living room with her crimson hat on, he felt invaded. And yet Grace objected to Mildred's being there, his own sister.

He wouldn't have minded friendships with fellow scholars. What he hated was to see his wife spending so much time with people he could only think of as her inferiors. The children didn't like it either. Grace always put a stranger ahead of them. All this might seem unconnected with her suggestion about the dinner party, but Robert knew better; she was proposing to bring outsiders into the family.

"Mildred ought to meet some of our friends," she said with an oblivious smile. "Now, think: What eligible men do we know?"

"You're going to invite somebody *for* her?" Clara Jane asked, "Oh, Mother, how awful."

"Yeah," said Hal. "She'll hate that."

"Yes, not yeah," Grace corrected. "No, not necessarily somebody for her, but it's the custom at dinner parties. An equal number of men and women."

"Grace," Robert said. "We've barely moved in. We can talk about this later."

"But I want to put my guest list together. Don't you have any ideas?" She went blithely on as if she hadn't heard the warning note in his voice.

"No!" He pulled himself to his feet and flung his napkin into his unfinished bowl of Wheatena. Coffee slopped from his cup. "I said later!" Nobody at the table moved or breathed. He stumped out of the room to the hall, got his coat from the closet, and left, slamming the door.

On the way to his office, limping through damp snow that stuck to his boots, Robert wished he hadn't lost his temper. It was probably true that Mildred needed to meet more people. If he could help her, he should. He owed her too much.

Mildred hadn't been sympathetic when he had polio; she had been outraged. How dared he get so sick? She had glared at him through her glasses and commanded him to recover. She couldn't believe in his paralysis. "Nonsense," she said. "Nonsense!" She had never been a noticeably loving sister, and if she pitied him then, she didn't show it. Lying there, unable to move anything but his eyes and the fingers of his right hand, he felt not only helpless but humiliated. Later he almost thought he had recovered just because he was so used to doing what Mildred said.

Grace had come to visit him in the following spring; he recalled her anguished face, nearly hidden behind a large bunch of lilacs. He didn't remember their conversation. By that time, he could sit up and was able to move everything but his right leg; Mildred put him through a series of exercises three times a day, and she had bought him a red rubber ball to squeeze twenty-five times every hour in each hand. He might have been holding this when Grace came in with the lilacs. He might have felt tempted to toss the ball at her and make her drop the flowers, though he was pretty sure he hadn't done it. But he couldn't remember. He had never noticed Grace enough to memorize their meetings.

Mildred had come in soon and shooed her away, he did recall. She had thought it was pretty funny of Grace to bring lilacs when there were so many in their own front yard. "Coals to Newcastle," she said. "Isn't that just like poor little Grace?"

That evening in their study, Robert apologized to Grace. "I didn't mean we can't ever invite anybody to dinner. All I meant..." But that was what he had meant: He didn't want strangers inside his front door.

"Of course," she said timidly. He hated the cowed look on her face, hated knowing he had caused it. Why hadn't she married somebody who would treat her better? "I thought it would be nice for Mildred," she said. "She doesn't know anybody here."

Men, she obviously had in mind; Mildred didn't know any men. "I'm not sure she's in the mood to meet anybody new," he said.

"But that's just it. She's so caught up in her own troubles." She brightened, seeing that he was open to the idea after all. "We could invite the Clines and the DeGroffs, and... Now, who's a nice single man?"

It wasn't unreasonable. Robert tried to think. "There's Malcolm Wolfe, I suppose. At the Science Library. He's a little odd, though."

Grace laughed. "Robert, it's only a dinner party. What's wrong with Mr. Wolfe?"

"Nothing, really. He's quiet. Plays the guitar. His wife died a few years ago." Malcolm Wolfe was no more peculiar than he was himself, Robert reflected, but that wasn't saying much. Malcolm would have to do.

The children had never heard such a funny name. Freddie developed a habit of singing "Who's Afraid of the Big Bad Wolf?" either loudly for the benefit of Mellie and Cricket or under his breath at the dinner table.

The Clines were familiar already. Mr. Cline was a large, extraverted zoologist who smoked cigars, and Mrs. Cline was a biologist who worked in the same lab and tried to prevent him from molesting female graduate students. The children didn't know about the students, of course, and Grace scoffed every time Robert, in privacy, referred to the subject. Mr. Cline was very eminent in his field, she always said. Which might be true, Robert had pointed out, but had nothing to do with his personal behavior. Mr. Cline the eminent scientist was one more of Grace's stereotypes, and she never even registered the way he looked her up and down at Institute parties.

The DeGroffs were another matter. Mr. DeGroff had reached a pinnacle in the departmental hierarchy through personal connections, charm—and, Robert darkly hinted, through membership in the Democratic party. Mrs. DeGroff, on the other hand, was a fine woman, very attractive and perfectly content to stay home and look after her husband and child. Grace could see why Robert admired Hazel DeGroff, but she herself couldn't feel comfortable with Hazel. The children couldn't either. She was too much like the snobbish society women in movies, they said; the very flesh of her feet, bulging over the edges of her high-heeled shoes, frightened them. Mrs. DeGroff needed only to glance at the Davenant children to let them know that there were too many of them. She didn't think much of their frayed overalls and shrunken cardigans either. For a small fee, she passed down her daughter's dresses, and Clara Jane and Mellie were sometimes mortified by meeting Peggy DeGroff when they were wearing her former clothes.

Grace didn't want the children to know that she shared their feelings. Hazel might not actually mean to make her feel pale and dowdy and too fruitful. With just one adopted child of her own, she might simply be envious.

A week before the party, Grace started to plan the menu. It was too bad that pheasants and brook trout were out of season. Robert had shot his annual deer, but somehow on the Davenants' table, venison tended to be stringy and dry, sitting in puddles of congealed grease. Maybe roast beef, in spite of the expense. With mushroom gravy?

For dessert, ice cream and some of those thin expensive chocolate wafers would have to do. Grace was too impatient a cook to succeed at baking. Her sponge cakes were tough and chewy, with splinters of aluminum from the pan glinting along the surface; her spice cakes were studded with lumps of undissolved soda; she couldn't even make blanc mange without burning it.

At the breakfast table once more, she announced that the dinner party would take place on the following Friday. The girls were to wear their navy-blue sailor dresses from the Macy's catalogue and the boys the blazers their grandparents had sent, and of course they must all be polite to the guests. The Clines, the DeGroffs, and Mr. Wolfe had accepted.

"Mr. *Who?*" Mellie cried, in ecstasy.

"Mr. Wolfe, dumbbell." Freddie began to hum his tune.

"Now," said Grace "that's enough." But maybe she could get a column out of the occasion. She noted Freddie's 'elfin grin.'

On the afternoon of the party, Clara Jane sat in the bathtub scraping soap scum from around the faucets, hardly aware of Auntie Mildred's complaining voice outside the door. She had just finished pouring vinegar onto her wet hair, when she had been distracted by the scum, which was gray and disgusting. The children were allowed to wash their hair just once a week, and only in the sink, to avoid ear infections. Lately, however, Clara Jane had dared to wash hers secretly, plunging under the bathwater and coming out afterwards with her filled ears echoing. Well, she had done her best on the faucets. She leaned back into the water, letting her hair swirl out around her head like Andersen's mermaid. When it was rinsed enough to squeak, she pulled out the plug and left the room, to walk, with a towel over her shoulders, past indignant Auntie Mildred.

A few years later, the Davenants' guests would think back to that evening and search their memories. Had anything unusual happened? Everybody in town knew the family, because of Grace's column. When the children bought groceries with their mother at the Co-op or walked down the aisle of a movie theater in graduated heights, people nudged each other. Within a small circle, the Davenants were famous. And yet hardly anybody really knew them. They were self-contained, playing their private games and doing their little household tasks, as the readers of "Notes on a Modern Family" all knew.

The Clines were acquainted with the family from the annual Institute picnic, where their own children had tried to get them to play softball. They were surprised to see the young Davenants at the dinner table, but they didn't object. Mrs. DeGroff, on the other hand, disapproved utterly. Little Cricket was certainly a charming baby, with his blazing hair and eager smile, but he didn't belong next to her, sitting there in his bib and making roads through his mashed potatoes. Besides, she was to say later, look what happened afterwards.

The evening got off to an unpromising start, with the three youngest children forming a ring around poor Mr. Wolfe at the front door and chanting the Walt Disney song that Freddie had been singing all week. Clara Jane ran to the kitchen to report them, and Grace was obliged to leave Mildred to finish the gravy while she rushed out to the hall in her apron. Mr. Wolfe was not happy, she could see. His oblong horselike face was flushed, and he was trying to laugh with the children, but he couldn't really think his own name was all that funny. He was carrying a white florist's box and his guitar, which Robert had asked him to bring.

Then, after the other guests had arrived and everyone was assembled at the table, Freddie gaped at the Haviland china as if he hadn't seen it every Thanksgiving and Christmas of his life. "Hey, Hal," he said. "Look. Everything matches." Mellie continued the theme by examining the mushrooms in her gravy and asking, "Do we eat the little buttons or leave them on our plates?" As Mildred had warned all along, it might be a mistake to include the children in the party. But Grace had thought it would be educational, and besides, she had wanted to show them off.

Mildred, for her part, contributed almost nothing to the conversation. She was wearing her new princess-style dress with the huge red roses, and two silver pins in the shape of seagulls swooped across her bosom. Grace thought she looked quite nice, considering. But she seemed to have been struck dumb. During the cream of celery soup, she turned her back on Mr. Wolfe and absorbed herself in Mr. Cline's description of a new fish hatchery in the Upper Peninsula, while his wife stared suspiciously across the table. Could Mildred have forgotten which of the two men was single? To fill in the general silence, Grace launched into a description of her graduate-school experiences with Professor Freundlich.

"He actually dropped you from the program, just because you were married?" Mr. Wolfe's long face was creased with concern.

"Well, yes," Grace said with a little laugh. It was just an amusing story. She hadn't expected anyone to take it seriously. "He was afraid I might have children."

"Yes," Robert said, looking grim. Other conversation at the table had died.

Oh, dear, Grace thought. "And of course, he was perfectly right." She gestured gaily around the table.

"Oh?" The expression on Mrs. DeGroff's heavy, handsome face was worse than grim, and Grace felt compunction; she hadn't meant to boast about her family.

"But," Mr. Wolfe said, still focusing on Grace, his fork suspended, "but you shouldn't have had to choose—"

"Between a family and a career," Mildred put in, as if the words were too predictable to be worth saying.

Grace was impressed to see him turn to Mildred without annoyance, as if she had helped him out. "Yes," he said. "Exactly, Miss Davenant. It shouldn't be necessary."

"Is that so," Mildred said ungratefully, and turned back to Mr. Cline.

"But it wasn't," Grace said. They were missing the point. "I have both. I got the Ph.D. after all." After another conversational hiatus, she brought up Hal's fixation on Sherlock Holmes, then Mildred's ambition to be a teacher, but neither Hal nor Mildred picked up their cues.

For a while, in fact, it seemed that nothing would bring Mildred to say another word to Mr. Wolfe, but then she turned to him and began to speak rapidly, though the only words that came out clearly were "to help Grace with the children," spoken in a martyrish tone. Well, at least she and Mr. Wolfe were conversing.

Before the ice cream and cookies there was another silence, which Grace broke with a lively description of the doll village upstairs, and her attempts to run the vacuum cleaner around it while the inhabitants protested, calling her "Grandma" and making her feel not only elderly but freakish, as the grandmother of several stuffed bears and a spotted pig. The children, during this account, scowled at their plates, and it was clear that Robert thought she was talking too much, but what could she do if nobody else would speak?

Mr. Wolfe asked Cricket then where his red hair had come from. "From the side of the house," Cricket solemnly said, and Grace explained that he meant it was from her side of the family, from her wicked Uncle John. What was wicked about him she had never found out, but his hair had been exactly that color. Robert, she said, used strands of Cricket's hair when he tied flies for trout fishing.

"That's right," Robert said. "He's a useful boy." And Grace got up, beckoning to Clara Jane, to clear the table for dessert.

Later in her life, all Clara Davenant can recall of that evening is a scene in the kitchen. The children, having asked politely to be excused like the characters in a Frances Hodgson Burnett book she had just read, were finishing up the left-over Neapolitan ice cream before it could melt. The coffee pot bubbled on the stove, filling the room with their favorite fragrance. "That smells so good," Hal said. "Why don't we try it?"

"Do you dare?" Mellie asked.

"Sure." Hal poured some into one of the delicate blue-and-white cups. Clara Jane took a sip and choked. "It needs salt." They added salt and passed it around, but it was still a disappointment. Sugar didn't work either, and they emptied the cup into the sink. Grace, coming in later, found less in the pot than she'd expected.

At the end of the evening, as Mr. Wolfe played his guitar and sang "I Saw Three Ships Come Sailing In," Grace decided that he wasn't so horse-faced after all. He was a little like Gary Cooper, in fact, just as earnest and shy. "Mildred made quite a hit with your Mr. Wolfe," she said generously afterwards to Robert.

VIII

On Monday morning after the party, Robert drove to East Lansing for the day, and the whole family felt a lessening of pressure. Whenever he left town, it was as if the big white house—with all its porches and rooms and bay windows—sighed in relief and settled into its foundation. Today, Grace was planning to visit the Science Library at the University. Since Mildred's classes hadn't started yet, Cricket could stay at home, with the baby gate hooked across the entrance to his room.

Grace picked her way through January slush under the yellow-gray sky, feeling oddly unencumbered. Robert was right; she ought to take more advantage of Mildred.

Her errand called for all her courage, though. It was a long time since she had acted in the world except as somebody's wife or somebody's mother, and she hoped she hadn't misinterpreted Mr. Wolfe's invitation. She also wished she had something more cheerful to tell him. He had spoken to her after dinner on Friday night, deploring her lack of opportunity to work in her field. "With your training?" he had said. "But that's criminal." The Science Library provided carrels for visiting scholars all the time. Her doctorate was enough to ensure her a place to work, with all the resources of the library. If she would come to his office, he would make arrangements.

The idea sounded miraculous to her at first. The study she shared with Robert was set off from the bedroom only by curtains, and it held his snow-shoes and waders and landing nets, as well as the rifles which made her nervous in spite of his keeping the ammunition carefully separated. All these things were neatly placed in a corner, but they did take up space. Even Robert's desk was crowded with fly-tying paraphernalia. A vise was attached to one corner, next to the bottles of glue and varnish and the envelopes containing pheasant feathers, fur, silk thread, and a lock of Cricket's coppery hair. Robert made beautiful flies during the winter and used them in the spring to catch beautiful trout.

But Grace had no area of her own, not for her real work. She used her desk only to pay bills and write letters and compose her column. She didn't think of herself as having given up on the work; in fact she felt almost as if her marriage and family belonged to an alternate life that ran parallel to the genuine one in which she was a scholar and scientist with her whole career ahead of her. Someday she would return to her profession, but until then she must simply sustain it in her mind. Not that this was easy. Her diploma, hanging there on the wall, was almost a reproach. She could describe her sufferings in graduate school all she wanted, without anyone's taking them seriously. Her children seemed to think that everybody's parents had Ph.D.s.

Over the weekend, Grace's initial joy at Mr. Wolfe's offer was diluted by such thoughts. Robert didn't help. "You mustn't count on Malcolm's being able to do much for you," he said on Friday night in the bedroom. "He was being polite to his hostess—like bringing the roses. I told you, he's a nice man."

"Yes, of course," she said, but she resolved to go to the library anyway, soon enough so that Malcolm wouldn't forget who she was. Not to go would be rude.

Malcolm Wolfe's view of Grace wasn't very different from her family's. He saw her mainly, that is, as a mother. Entering the Davenants' house on Friday evening, loaded down with his guitar case and half a dozen apricot-colored tea roses, he had been attacked by chanting children and wished only to escape. But then Mrs. Davenant, aproned and flushed, with her hair falling into her face, had come to his rescue. The thing was, she looked like an angel, and she obviously didn't know it. Goodness shone from her face. All through the evening, at the table with vigilant Mrs. Cline, slippery Mr. DeGroff, and despondent Mildred Davenant, Grace worked to rescue everybody. Malcolm had never seen anyone labor so hard or so transparently to make other people comfortable.

Not that her efforts could help very much. Robert was not a social being, and Mrs. DeGroff could dampen any gathering. But still, Malcolm was charmed. And once he had recovered from his reception at the front door, he was actually pleased by the children's presence. After that first rowdy greeting they were subdued, but their bright hair and shy energy added life to the gathering. They didn't interrupt the conversation but caught each other's eyes and exchanged signals. He himself had hoped for a large family and had been crushed when the birth of his daughter Annabel, twelve years before, was followed by his wife's fatal illness. Connie had tuberculosis, it had turned out. Annabel lived now with Connie's sister in Chicago and saw her father only on vacations.

Grace Davenant's children, Malcolm thought that night at the extended oaken table, were her string of pearls.

However, no matter how pretty a picture Grace and her family might make, it was clear that she needed a place to work. So he mentioned the library and the chance of her getting a carrel. He liked the thought of her being there. Wherever she was, he felt sure, emotions would spill over and make the world more interesting. The library was a little too tidy; to see her there would be refreshing.

On Monday, when Grace floundered into his office with her galoshes unsnapped and her muskrat coat trailing, his impression was confirmed.

"I've been thinking," she said earnestly, "and I have to be honest with you."

How she could be anything else he couldn't imagine, but he showed her to the large leather chair across from his desk. Her legs above the galoshes were slender and well-shaped, he noted—and chastised himself for noting.

It might be a good sign, though. Malcolm hadn't paid much attention to women for a while. Perhaps his present feelings meant that there could be a break in the atmosphere he lived in, as drab as the Michigan sky. Malcolm Wolfe was forty-three years old. His aim right now was endurance. If he could just get through the rest of his life honorably and cherish his daughter and do his job, he would consider what was left of his existence a success. The quarterly journal he edited for the library was gaining in reputation, and he tended it in much the same way as he cared for Annabel. For recreation he played chess, sang bass in the Episcopal choir, and read Victorian novels; Trollope offered almost total immersion, he had discovered during the last, torturous year of Connie's life. He had read most of the Palliser series to her, and now he was working his way through the rest of the books. But nothing he did was done with passion.

"The problem is," Grace explained to him, "even if I had a place to work, I'm not sure what I could do." She blushed, as if confessing some disgrace. "I don't have a project, you see."

He thought he did see. "Of course," he ventured, "the war has made it hard for anthropologists."

"Exactly." She hadn't put this idea into words, but now she seized on it. "Even if I could travel, I couldn't. I mean…"

"Yes." But he was disappointed.

It wasn't only the war, Grace knew, or even the children. Malcolm's offer had forced her, during the weekend, to think more concretely than usual about her life, and now she had the terrible suspicion that she had been deceiving herself for at least a decade: There was no parallel career after all. "I just don't know," she said, almost in tears at the sight of his long, anxious face. "Although I appreciate the thought." She started to rise.

"Please." He reached out to stop her. "Please don't go."

"I'm so sorry." She subsided. Of course it would be exciting to do research, but research on what? Defense workers, perhaps? The Ford plant at Willow Run was bringing new people into the area, and their way of life might be worth investigating… But not by her. "Not with the war, and my family," she said, and a wave of gold-brown hair fell against her gold-framed glasses.

"I can see that." And yet Malcolm couldn't let Grace go away feeling so miserable. There must be something he could do. "We've been looking for editorial help on the *Quarterly*," he said tentatively. "I realize you're trained for much more than that, and we couldn't offer a proper salary…" It was true; he did need somebody to deal with printers and see that articles were written in decent English instead of shapeless scientific gibberish.

"A job?" Her joy returned, full force. One of her deepest sources of shame was the smallness of her contribution to the family income. Robert considered this feeling unreasonable, but his saying so—and saying it so crossly—only added to her guilt. Even twenty dollars a week would be a help.

"It would only be part time," Malcolm Wolfe said.

Grace walked down the library steps feeling a new energy. As she crossed the campus, a large snowflake swerved diagonally past her eyes, followed by others until snow was falling steadily around her and the flakes were blown into piles along the sides of the pavement. She had never witnessed the birth of a snowstorm before. As the cold delicate edges of snowflakes melted against her face, faster and faster, she felt an extraordinary sense of triumph. Her children weren't evidence of cowardice or failure after all; they were additional achievements. A woman's life needn't be a matter of one choice cutting out another. Why shouldn't she give her attention to the family when she was with them, and when she was not, bring the same energy to other matters? This surely was what Robert did, and it was why he stayed away from home so much; the presence of his children would have distracted him from his trout.

She had believed that women were different, that they *couldn't* forget their children from the moment they were born. It was something biological, she had supposed. Even when Grace sat in the study, she was aware of tensions on the third floor, quarrels in the kitchen. She felt a change in the air when Mildred went out or came back. She was a spider in a web, feeling the slightest pull at the end of each shining strand.

No, not a spider—that was sinister, and too powerful. For Grace had no power. She was a boat rocked by storms; that was more like it. She had created these small tyrants and watched helplessly as they grew larger and went their own way into their own misfortunes. Like Robert, she longed to keep them from harm and knew she couldn't. And so she wrote about an ideal, invulnerable family instead. A part of her was aware that the anecdotes she sold to the newspaper had little to do with reality. Yet the stories tended to replace her actual memories. When she thought back on an incident in their joint lives, what remained was only what she had made of it.

Grace was thinking these things as she walked down East University through swirling snowflakes. It wasn't the first time she had had such thoughts, but the context had changed. Now she could see beyond them, to a world that had a place for her. She could be independent after all. In fact, she had better be.

Instead of walking on past Mr. Twist's expensive shop, Grace went in and bought half a pound of his expensive tea. It would have been cheaper at the Co-op, but who cared? When she reached home, she was only slightly irritated to find Mildred on the step-stool in the kitchen, clutching a curtain rod with one hand and straining to reach the ceiling with a scrub brush. "I saw your pal Malcolm Wolfe," Grace called. "He sent his regards." Well, he almost had; he had mentioned Mildred, and Grace had told him about the falsehearted funeral director and then wished she hadn't. But he had been sympathetic. As Robert had said, he was a kind man.

What Malcolm Wolfe was thinking as the snow fell past his office window was that Grace Davenant was an interesting woman and that her children were the most appealing thing about her—except for her name, left over from a time when baby girls were named for flowers and virtues. One of the things that had attracted him to his wife was her name, Constance.

"Who stole the pencil from the budget book?" Robert's voice roared that afternoon, from downstairs. Grace, seated at her desk, stopped rolling a sheet of paper into her typewriter and sat motionless, with a beating heart. She didn't think she had taken the pencil, but it was possible. This morning after coming back from the Science Library, she had dutifully recorded the forty-nine cents she had spent for tea. Then she had cut a slice of the fallen Karo Syrup cake that the children refused to eat and had escaped to the study with a tray. It was a luxury to sit in her rocking-chair with a steaming blue-and-white cup from the good set of china and think about the job Mr. Wolfe had offered her. Her thoughts had twined happily with the rising steam.

And now here was Robert, back from East Lansing earlier than she had expected and shouting about the pencil. Still shouting, after almost a minute. Grace would have to hurry downstairs and unearth one of the spare pencils she kept in the silverware drawer. She would certainly have to postpone telling Robert about her job.

In the dining room Robert, with his most tormented look, was displaying the open budget book to Mildred, who stood in the kitchen doorway wearing her flowered apron as if she had slaved over the stove all day. She had just come in, Grace knew perfectly well, and had slipped into the apron as soon as she took off her coat.

"Is it too much to ask?" Robert was saying piteously. "One pencil. Do I have to attach it to a chain?"

His leg was hurting, Grace guessed. But he was right; it wasn't much to ask. "I'm sorry, dear," she said as she rummaged behind the serving spoons for a pencil. She hoped nobody would be spanked for this. On her way down the stairs she had noticed one of Clara Jane's feet, in its scuffed brown oxford, sticking out from under the curtain on the landing.

"It's the principle," Robert said almost apologetically as he took the pencil.

Clara Jane, on the window seat, heard the commotion and knew she was responsible. Today in homeroom she had had the sudden thought that there might be a formula for the sum of all the numbers leading up to any particular number. But no sooner had she begun some trial calculations than it was time for Social Studies, and she'd had to postpone the problem. On her way home from school, walking through snowflakes as big as quarters, she had thought about numbers again, and she was still thinking, her shoulder against the chilly glass as she watched flakes fall like ashes out of the gray-white sky. She was writing down numbers and adding them up. The sum of the numbers till six was twenty-one, till seven was twenty-eight. If six is to twenty-one as seven is to twenty-eight, what is X? Clara Jane thought X was supposed to come into it, but her class hadn't begun algebra yet. X ought to stand, in each case, for the number the sum of whose antecedents she wanted to find. So X, in this case, was six. Or seven. Only it wasn't.

Hearing her father's voice downstairs, filled with bitterness and rage, Clara Jane sat still, with the guilty pencil poised over her paper. The snow would probably keep him from going out and cutting a switch from the forsythia. Then she heard him unevenly climbing the stairs, just a few feet away on the other side of the curtain. Her father almost always used these stairs rather than the steep back ones, with their narrow treads. He must be carrying his briefcase, weighted with reports on fish populations and stream conditions. He would go into the study and fill the room with smoke from his pipe.

With Robert occupying the study, Grace had to stay downstairs. Mildred, in her apron, was dithering around the kitchen, removing things from the refrigerator and making unworkable plans for dinner. Grace had already made plans. She had, in fact, set a casserole of soybeans to soak. She had just been thinking that she ought to drain them and add some kind of sauce when she had heard the shouting.

Mildred didn't care for soybeans, as she had already made plain. The children didn't either, but Grace was going to make the beans more appetizing this time, by adding chunks of Spam. There was a cabbage to grate for salad.

"We don't have anything for dinner," Mildred complained, taking out two shriveled baked potatoes and a bowl of old beets. "Were you planning to go to the Co-op?"

"There are these soybeans..." Grace began. It wasn't as if Mildred were paying any rent.

$^x/_2$ x X + $^x/_2$. Clara Jane felt a rush of joy, as if she had discovered a satisfying chord on the piano. The comparison came readily because Nadine Applegate had recently been practicing "The Lost

Chord" to sing to her rich grandmother, and she and Clara Jane had searched the keyboard in vain for the magic combination of notes. But now Clara Jane had found the equivalent. She had never experienced exactly this kind of exhilaration. Maybe she could be a mathematician, she thought, if she wasn't a portrait painter or an opera star. Math had never been hard, but she hadn't seen it as anything but a set of rules to be memorized and obeyed. This afternoon she had made the numbers obey her.

She would have to be careful not to get sidetracked, though. Most children seemed to want interesting professions, but when Clara Jane looked at adults, she saw no signs that they'd ever hoped to be different from the way they turned out. Even her own mother, with all her talk of tropical islands and the British Museum, had ended up with a pretty ordinary life. And what about Mrs. Kepler, for instance, or Mr. Applegate—who must once have been children, with dreams of becoming explorers or circus riders? Clara Jane was determined that this forgetfulness, or failure of nerve, or whatever it was that killed ambition, wouldn't happen to her.

She would have liked to tell her father her discovery about the numbers, if only she'd put the pencil back in time. She always meant to put it back, and she could see how annoying it must be, but today she had rushed in from school adding up figures in her head and needed to write them down before they got away. She hoped her father would forget before dinner time.

IX

A Saturday morning in February. Clara Jane always hated to see her mother sitting naked on the edge of her bed, waiting for her daughters to hand her her underwear. What upset Clara Jane wasn't so much the task itself, as the educational atmosphere that surrounded it. Grace's voice on these occasions took on the self-conscious quality that meant she was trying to set an example. The example in this case was that of the woman Clara Jane was fated to become, with a body so floppy and uncontrollable that she would have to bind it in the pink harness of a brassiere and a boned girdle which showed in lumps and ridges through the slip on top of it and the dress on top of that. Why couldn't her mother wear a Spencer foundation garment like the ones in *Good Housekeeping* ads, which would make her as streamlined as a seal? Mrs. DeGroff must surely wear a Spencer; even if she swelled to the size of the Hindenburg, there would be no inelegant bulges.

On Saturday mornings if Robert was away, the children liked to huddle in their mother's warm, rumpled bed while Cricket said things to make them laugh. Grace laughed too, and she wasn't anxious or critical. (Though it was, the older ones suspected, a time when she caught the children off guard and gathered material for her newspaper column.) But eventually they had to get up, and if Clara Jane didn't slip away in time, she—and sometimes Mellie too—had to go through the dressing routine.

So many clothes. Clara Jane told herself that even if she couldn't get out of turning into a grownup woman, she would never wear all those garments. A grayish-pink rayon undershirt with deep armholes, for instance. What was it for? She couldn't understand the slip either. So many shoulder straps, which divided her mother's flesh as if she were a package tied with string. After the underwear came the pinkish-brown lisle stockings and the perforated black shoes with Cuban heels and tasseled ties, and finally the cotton housedress— with the crescent-shaped shields pinned under the arms—patterned in plaid or outsize flowers.

The tone of her mother's voice during this routine was the same as when she called out from the bathroom to ask Clara Jane to bring her a Kotex from the cache behind her piles of underpants in the second bureau drawer from the top. It was Ozymandias: "You, too, shall come to this," it said.

But since last August on the island, her mother had stopped doing that.

Poor Grace. She hadn't known what to say to Clara Jane. Her own mother, in this situation, had pretended to ignore it while letting her know nevertheless that it was a matter for shame. They had no rituals, that was the trouble. In the Andaman Islands there were standard procedures for the first tooth or the first menstruation; these things were celebrated. As it was, Grace simply, matter-of-factly, asked Clara Jane to help wash the sheets.

The whole thing couldn't have come at a worse time, as it happened, when they were camping and had to do the laundry by hand. It wasn't Clara Jane's fault, of course, but Grace did feel provoked. "Why couldn't you have waited a month?" she asked as they bent over a tin tub of chilly pink water and scrubbed away together. She spoke in as jolly a tone as she could muster.

Poor Clara Jane. She had hoped, by the exertion of will power, to prevent this calamity from ever taking place. What it proved was that she had less control than she had thought—over her body and the rest of her life. What else might happen? Her customary dread was increased.

On this Saturday morning, Mellie escaped from the bedroom and Clara Jane was just about to follow, when her mother called her name.

Grace was already unbuttoning the top of her flannel pajamas, and Clara Jane could see her dangling breasts, with their long brown nipples. In a minute, her mother would expose her puckered white appendectomy scar. Without clothes, she looked bleached and vulnerable, like an animal without its fur. "What do you want?" Clara Jane said from the doorway, though she was afraid she knew. This time it wasn't just help with dressing. Miss Pettibone, her Social Studies teacher, had sent home a note the day before, and her mother had been too busy mashing potatoes to deal with it then.

"Would you just hand me my bra?" Grace asked, too casually.

"All right." Clara Jane picked it up gingerly from the cretonne-covered chair at the foot of the bed. Nobody but doctors ever sat on the chair; it was mainly there to hold clothes. She dropped the brassiere on the quilt and went to stand at the window, where she could see Mrs. Parmelee's house through a veil of gently falling snow.

"Why does Miss Pettibone call you Jane?" Irritation showed in Grace's voice.

"Because it's my name." Clara Jane couldn't bring herself to explain about Clarabelle Cow. The note wasn't too bad, though. It only complained that she didn't say enough in class.

"Well, really!" Grace said.

"It is!" Clara Jane stayed by the window, breathing in the bitter smell of dust from the curtain.

"Nonsense. But if she doesn't even know your name, she certainly can't know much else about you. You speak up often enough at home." Grace laughed. "Would you hand me my underpants, please?"

The underpants were pink, with wide, cuffed legs that reached halfway to the knees. Clara Jane handed them over and concentrated on Mrs. Parmelee's house, where the bottom edges of the gray shingles were beginning to be outlined by snow. At least now the main part of her mother's body would be covered.

"If you're quiet in school," Grace said, "I'm sure it's only a stage you're going through. Help me with this, will you?" She was reaching back to hook her brassiere.

Clara Jane struggled with the hooks, trying not to touch her mother's back, but she felt better. There wasn't going to be a fuss about the note or about her name. "I can't stand Miss Pettibone," she said. "You know what I told you about her knit dresses and how she smells." Miss Pettibone had been after her since last fall, when the class had given reports on the most recent Presidential election. The students who spoke before Clara Jane explained their electoral choices in terms of policies, and yet she noticed that none of their opinions were different from those of their parents. So when it was her turn, she simply said she had supported Wendell Willkie because her father did. Miss Pettibone expressed shock at her cynicism, and Clara Jane learned a little more about the risks of speaking in class.

"Here," Clara Jane said, picking up the rest of her mother's clothes from the chair and flinging them onto the bed. "Can I go get dressed now?"

"Yes, of course." Though Grace looked disappointed.

Clara Jane ran upstairs to her room.

Grace Davenant, gathering up her clothes, wished she knew how to talk with her children. She wasn't sure what Social Studies was or were, and Sarita Pettibone reminded her strongly of a teacher who had frozen her into silence in high school. However, if she let Clara Jane know such things, the child would cooperate less than ever. Also, Clara Jane's only specific complaints against Miss Pettibone concerned the two form-fitting knit dresses—one aqua and the other flesh-colored—that the teacher wore alternately, and her suffocating perfume; you could always tell when Miss Pettibone had been in a room, Clara Jane reported. These were hardly grievances that Grace could take to the principal.

Upstairs, putting on her overalls and cardigan, Clara Jane could hardly bear to think about yesterday. What she hadn't told her mother was that Miss Pettibone had kept her after school and asked whether something was wrong at home. Clara Jane denied it, of course, but she couldn't forget the question.

Her everyday fears had been bad enough before, but now she knew that they showed on her face. What she dreaded was almost everything. She was frightened of growing up, and of telephones and teachers and doctors and gangsters and Edward G. Robinson (whom she had seen in a Preview of Coming Attractions) and her grandparents, and of being caught without tissues when her nose was running; she was afraid of humiliation, and she was humiliated by her fear. It wasn't physical harm she was afraid of—though she wasn't brave about pain—but something worse, which she couldn't even name. The war certainly didn't help. Clara Jane didn't see how collecting tin cans and stepping on them was going to protect the Davenants from bombs. For it was the family she thought of, always the family. People outside hardly existed except as threats.

"Of course not," Clara Jane said to Miss Pettibone, but she felt her voice become untrustworthy, and she was almost tempted to throw herself on her teacher's broad aqua bosom. When she was younger, she had believed that her family was as harmonious as that of the Five Little Peppers or the Bastable Children or anybody in Louisa May Alcott. She had almost been taken in by her mother's sprightly newspaper column. As she grew older, though, it had seemed more false all the time, and now she knew that she herself was just as dishonest. The compositions she wrote for English class were all about the children's Bingo games or singing together around the piano—not lies but not the entire truth; she never mentioned the bruises they got from their father and from each other. Her brothers and her sister weren't as nice as she pretended, and she wasn't either.

She had always believed that she loved her parents: Now she wondered if it was only because she was expected to; it was like being a Republican. Whether they themselves loved any of the children except Cricket and maybe Mellie was open to question: They were always criticizing, and they hardly ever showed affection, though of course they must love each other.

She wished she had a true friend—someone kind like Pierre in *War and Peace*, which she was reading that winter. Aunt Eleanor the artist probably loved the children, but she lived in Ohio. Clara Jane's fifth-grade teacher, Miss Scarlett, had praised her book reports and said once that her hair was pretty. And then there was her father's friend Mr. Wolfe with the mournful eyes, who had told her about his daughter Annabel and not asked how she liked school; she thought about Mr. Wolfe quite often.

Miss Pettibone didn't like Clara Jane, though; she was only sorry for her. Clara Jane told none of this to Grace but mentioned the knit dresses instead.

Grace went into the study and seated herself at the typewriter. "Adolescence looms for our eldest," she wrote, "and my heart goes out to her. And yet she is plucky and bright. These next years, I tell her, are a time to grow and to taste the wonders that life has to offer. But how can she believe me? Adulthood seems a far-off goal to one who is a mere thirteen."

X

Clara Jane woke up to her father's six-thirty call one morning and looked down from the double-decker bed, and saw nothing but chaos. Mellie's clothes—the ones she'd worn yesterday as well as all the ones she'd thought she might wear—were strewn across the floor. The doll village, from a height, was a mere senseless heap of boxes. Auntie Mildred wasn't up yet, but soon she would clump through the room in her high-heeled mules and make one of her comments. Clara Jane tugged the covers carefully to the head of her bed and slipped out from under and climbed down the ladder. The village wasn't any more presentable at eye level. "Who's that supposed to be?" she asked her sister, pointing to a red-and-white Teddy bear propped drunkenly against a toy fireplace.

Mellie was still curled under the slippery maroon comforter her grandparents had sent for Christmas. It was filled with something she was allergic to, but nobody realized it yet. Mellie sneezed and peeked out. "I've got another cold again." In her blue Dr. Dentons, with her pink nose, she looked like an ad for something. She sneezed again and huddled under the comforter.

Clara Jane hoped they wouldn't all catch Mellie's cold, and make grouchy Dr. Wernimont come and examine whoever had the highest temperature. "Why don't we bomb the village?" she said with a sudden inspiration.

"What?" Mellie sat up, her blue eyes wide open.

"Let's have an air raid. After school." Clara Jane threw off her pajamas and began to put on her clothes.

At four o'clock that afternoon, she sat cross-legged on the top bunk, directing operations. Hal, downstairs in Cricket's room, piled blocks into grocery bags for the two younger boys to transport, while Mellie, in the pith helmet once worn by Great-uncle Henry the missionary, set up Red Cross headquarters in one of the orange crates. The toy mail truck had a red cross pasted on top, and dolls and stuffed animals waited to be victims.

"Bombs away!" Clara Jane cried, as Hal and Freddie circled the village with balsa-wood airplanes, dropping lethal blocks on civilians. The devastation was horrible. Cricket, shrieking, gathered up fallen ammunition and fired it back at the planes. Clara Jane hadn't decided whether the bombers were Japanese or German or possibly American. It didn't matter. "Bombs away!" she shouted again, and waved her arms like Leopold Stokowski, as Cricket screamed and the siren on Mellie's ambulance wailed. And then the door to the next room opened, and Auntie Mildred, her little eyes staring behind her rimless glasses and her mouth open, stood on the threshold.

Mellie peeked up charmingly from under the black strands of her bangs. "We were having an air-raid drill." But this time the charm didn't work.

They hadn't known Auntie Mildred was home, Clara Jane pleaded later, while her father was getting his walking stick out of the corner of the study. They hadn't known about her headache.

But somebody had to be spanked. It had nothing to do with Mildred, Robert thought; it was the frivolity that was wrong, the playing at war. It might be natural, as Grace declared, but it was wrong. He grasped Clara Jane's arm and raised the stick and struck her thigh through the thin cotton of her dress. She gave a yelp, and he hit her again in the same place, harder. "I hope you've learned something." He limped to the corner and leaned the stick back against the wall.

Clara Jane, leaving the room with a wet face, tried to think what excuse she would make if her gym teacher noticed the bruises this time; she couldn't keep on saying that she had fallen while she was roller-skating. Actually, it hadn't been necessary for her father to spank her; she was already ashamed, of having enjoyed the air raid too much. What made her feel worst wasn't the spanking or Auntie Mildred's interruption, but the thought of the devastated village. One of the falling blocks had broken off the toes of the Shirley Temple doll's right foot, so that the brown composition material showed next to the painted pink flesh. Mellie had cried when she saw it.

"Life and death are serious things," her father said. "You have to learn that."

After that day, Clara Jane left the dolls to the others and retreated to the landing with *War and Peace*. Hal had found the book in the glassed-in shelf by the fireplace and noted that it was as thick as *The Complete Sherlock Holmes*, but it turned out to have too many Russian names and no detectives. He bet Clara Jane a dime that she couldn't read it all the way through, and so she took it with her one night to the Moreaus' house, where she was minding their bilingual children for fifteen cents an hour. While Professor Moreau was waiting for his wife to get ready, he noticed Clara Jane's book and seemed to be impressed.

As soon as the Moreau children were in bed, Clara Jane opened the book. After the first chapter, however, she switched to a copy of *Life* that was lying on the coffee table. The Moreaus subscribed to *The New Yorker* too. There were art books on their shelves, and they let her play records on their phonograph. When people mentioned the wonderful cultural atmosphere of Clara Jane's house, she thought, they didn't know what they were talking about. Her father listened to the Texaco opera broadcasts, and her mother had taken her to hear the Philadelphia Orchestra in Angell Hall, but that—except for her father's fragmentary poetry quotations—was as close as they came to culture; her parents talked mainly about family matters and high prices, and they didn't have a phonograph or a coffee table. She wished she could be one of the Moreaus, speaking French with their parents and listening to *La Traviata*.

When Professor Moreau walked her home that night, he asked

how far she'd gotten with her book, and she only exaggerated her answer a little. But every time she stayed with his children after that, he asked the same question, and she felt obliged to make progress. Near the beginning was an excruciating childbirth scene, unlike anything her mother had told her. It almost made her abandon the book, but she got through the chapter by reminding herself that all this had taken place in Russia long ago; things must be different now.

Besides, she was in love with Prince Andre. At night before she went to sleep, she imagined herself appearing before him in the moonlight. The prince, who looked rather like her General Science teacher, would reach out and lay a hand briefly, burningly, on her shoulder, and then he would make a comment about her eyes. Clara Jane always noticed the colors of people's eyes. Freddie's, for instance, were two different shades of greenish gray, and most purportedly blue eyes were combinations of gray and brown or green. Her own were as rare as blue ones—a light yellow-gray which her mother said was hazel and Prince Andre found fascinating. Her conversations with him tended to dwindle away after the first few sentences, but the touch of his hand on her shoulder felt real.

Grace Davenant prided herself on having explained reproduction to her children, but she hadn't seen a need to deal much with birth. She had concentrated on conception, with the baby as the product. Mothers went to hospitals to have babies, as children went to have their tonsils out.

The first of these conversations had taken place when Clara Jane was six and Mellie was about to be born. The child hadn't asked the expected questions, and she always pulled her hand away when Grace laid it conscientiously against her own abdomen to let her feel the baby move. It was Grace who had to bring up the subject.

"It's all right, Mama," Clara Jane assured her, twisting a piece of gold-brown hair around her finger and looking at Grace with unclouded eyes. "I already know." She was actually not clear about what her little brothers had been before they were born. It had something to do with dust, she thought. But Grace's casual tone was a warning—suggesting that the conversation could end up with Clara Jane's saying something that would make her mother laugh or write it down.

Grace went on, in the same unnatural voice: "The daddy gives the mommy a seed, and it joins with the egg and becomes a baby."

This was a surprise. Clara Jane pictured the two main actors turned modestly away from each other while her father extended his hand behind his back and her mother took something and put it somewhere that wasn't specified. She didn't know where her father would get the seed, unless he ordered it from a catalogue. "Do they have to be naked?" she asked daringly. That was one of the words, like "body," that was embarrassing to say.

"Not really," Grace said, "but it's easier if they are."

That settled it. Clara Jane would never have children.

"Do you understand, dear?"

Her mother never called any of them "dear." Only her father. "Oh, sure," Clara Jane said, and picked up *Eight Cousins* and edged toward the doorway. She had discovered recently that she could read.

"It's a wonderful thing," her mother said. "The most wonderful thing in the world."

"Is it fun?" Because there was a note in her mother's voice that made this a possibility.

Grace wasn't sure how honest to be. She herself had never found much besides frustration in love-making. When she was engaged to Robert, she had felt erotic stirrings but kept them strictly in check; once they were legal, she had assumed, they would culminate in a rush of fulfillment. If this didn't happen—as it didn't—it must be because she was a woman. Men obviously did get carried away by passion, and Grace could see the utility of this in the general scheme of things—however outdated the original plan might be by now. When the human race was just starting out, it would have made sense for men to impregnate everything in sight, and so there had to be some fun in it for them. Whereas women could get everything they needed to carry on the race from just a few sexual en-

counters a year. And so nature just hadn't bothered with female pleasure. Unfortunately. That sort of thing occurred mainly in literature,
where it was the result of male projection. (There were the Samo-
ans, of course, but she suspected there was something fishy about
the data.)

Worse than Grace's own feeble response was what sex did to
Robert. She was disturbed to see him moaning and sweating, at the
mercy of sensations that she couldn't imagine, much less share. On
the first such occasion, during their honeymoon in the Adirondacks,
she was afraid he was having an attack of some kind. By now she
was used to Robert's orgasms, and she knew from diligent reading
that not only were they normal, but she was supposed to be having
them too. But if she didn't, she didn't. When he reached for her,
she knew by now that she wouldn't feel whatever she ought to feel
and wouldn't do what she ought to do, and he would go into those
shuddering spasms, leaving her unsatisfied and terribly alone.

Whether Robert was aware of her frustration, she didn't know;
she was too ashamed to tell him. But if the failure was her own rather
than nature's, the cause might be the lack of instruction from her
mother. So Grace was determined that her children shouldn't be
brought up in ignorance. Still, it was difficult to explain something
that she hardly believed in. The trouble was, sex was *supposed* to be
fun.

"Well, is it?" Clara Jane asked, pausing in the doorway.

"Not fun, exactly." Grace didn't want to encourage premature
experimentation. "But it's very beautiful."

Clara Jane eased out of the room. What her mother had told her
seemed incomplete. The seed, for instance. What did it look like?
If Aunt Eleanor were here, Clara Jane could have asked for details
without the risk of being quoted. However, she passed on the information to the younger children, and they acted it out with their dolls,
making sure the mama doll said "Thank you" when the father
handed her the seed.

Later that same day, working on her column, Grace wrote: "Trying to explain the mysteries of procreation to our eldest. She nods

solemnly, her hazel eyes wide, but have I succeeded in conveying the wonder of it all?"

No, it wouldn't do. Her readers didn't expect her to deal with such risque material.

Years later, babysitting for the Moreaus, Clara Jane discovered Havelock Ellis in the bookcase and found out that there was more to sex than either Nadine Applegate or her mother had mentioned. The thought of her parents, with their large flawed bodies, behaving the way the book recommended, was ludicrous. Besides, it might be noisy; everybody would know. For the rest of her life, a vision was to persist of two shy pale people, like an Adam and Eve by Cranach, standing next to each other while the man politely held out something small and slender like a cucumber seed and the woman politely took it.

XI

The Davenant children, inspired by the curtained archway that separated their living room from the large front hall, produced *The Tack*, the first of their plays, in Easter vacation of 1942. One of the dresses they had found in the attic—a brown crepe number, fringed and long-waisted and dripping with cut-steel beads—seemed meant to be a costume.

Clara Jane had seen very few live performances, except for concerts and school pageants and a silly operetta called *Blossom Time* with her Aunt Eleanor in Cleveland. But in November Mrs. Applegate took her and Nadine to *H.M.S. Pinafore* at the University, and Clara Jane was enchanted; what a playwright ought to do, it seemed to her, was to be silly on purpose instead of by mistake. She suggested to Hal that they produce a play. "My dear Watson," he said, "you are displaying more than your usual acumen." One of the leading characters must be a private detective. "I want to be somebody bad," Freddie said, and Cricket echoed him. The scene would be a schoolroom, Clara Jane decided, and there would be a crime: A student would put a tack on the teacher's chair. On Friday at the beginning of vacation, she borrowed her mother's typewriter. Two days later she finished *The Tack*, with three carbon copies.

That night at the supper table, the children broke the news that a play would be performed next Saturday in the living room. Robert was out of town for the week, as he tended to be during school vacations.

Grace threw a glance down the table toward Mildred, who was pursing her lips. "May Auntie Mildred and I come to it? And Cricket, of course?"

"Cricket is in it," Mellie explained. "He's the villain."

"There might be a lot of people," Hal warned. He was in charge of publicity.

"Isn't that nice," Grace said, already mentally composing an account of the production. And how nice that the children would be occupied this week, while she helped Malcolm Wolfe to put together the summer issue of the *Michigan Science Quarterly*.

Monday morning was springlike, with water trickling into the gutters from melting snow. The children took two orange crates from the doll village and set them up on the front walk with a board across the top. This was the box office, and Freddie and Mellie took turns sitting there or walking up and down the sidewalk distributing handbills printed with the squishy rubber type on Hal's Swiftset press. Hal printed tickets too, to sell at a penny for children and two cents for adults. Everyone made posters and tacked them to trees and utility poles.

Nadine's father bought a ticket, and so did Auntie Mildred and Mrs. Parmelee next door, but that was almost all. It was discouraging. But on Tuesday, Hal had an idea. "We should do it for the war effort," he said. So they wrote, "For the Benefit of the Red Cross" on the posters and handbills, and business picked up. Some people gave as much as a dime.

On Wednesday a reporter from the local paper arrived and took a picture, which appeared the next day on page two. The children suspected Grace, who was in fact innocent; someone down the street had phoned the newspaper. Ticket sales grew, and Clara Jane began to worry. She had rounded up costumes and props and makeup, but none of the actors knew their lines except Hal, and she couldn't get the cast into the house to rehearse. "Come on," she yelled from the front door, but they paid no attention.

She felt the onset of one of the tantrums for which she was famous in the family. When these furies possessed her, a dark mist would rise in the back of her throat and make her want to destroy everything good in her life. Two years ago, after her mother had scolded her unjustly for a room that Mellie had messed up, Clara Jane had unmade both beds, thrown her alarm clock from Grandma against the wall, and smashed her favorite picture of Shirley Temple. But she couldn't let herself get angry now. She took a deep breath: "All right, everybody, time to rehearse."

They went on shouting to passersby, about the play that was bound to be a disaster if they didn't come inside. Freddie, with a poster tied to his tricycle, was riding up and down the sidewalk. Even Hal continued to sit at the box office with the air of an impresario. Mellie was sprawled on the porch with Nadine and Norma Applegate, who were using the poster paper to draw outlines of their hands and decorating the fingers with nail polish and rings. "Clara Jane is so bossy," Mellie remarked.

She must not lose her temper. "Nadine," she said. "Do you want to be in this play or not?"

"Sure," said Nadine, drawing rays around an emerald on the third finger of her left hand.

"All right," Clara Jane said, "you're in charge of getting everybody inside. You can pull the curtains if you want." She had promised the job to Freddie, but that was too bad.

Nadine stood up, legs planted apart in her riding pants, and gave her father's treble whistle. "Come on, you kids," she yelled. "Don't you know there's a war on?" Norma was put in charge of the ticket stand, and the play was rehearsed.

About thirty people were sitting in the hall and on the stairs for two performances on Saturday afternoon, and Grace was amazed. The play began with a monologue by Clara Jane, as Miss Marita Malone, who stood in front of the closed curtains wearing the beaded dress and Grace's blue velvet Greta Garbo hat and wept into a red bandanna. "I am a naive and inexperienced schoolteacher," she sobbed. "I instruct the third grade of the Cherubb Elementary School. I thought my pupils loved me, and I cherished them as I would my own." The curtains jerked open. "*This* is my story!" she said, and stepped onto the stage.

The play, forty-five minutes long, included a raucous performance of the school song, as well as a reading lesson from a Dick-and-Jane primer in which Father killed off the whole family with a shotgun, sentence by simple sentence. In the end, the swaggering red-haired perpetrator was arrested by the egocentric detective, who gave the appropriate warning and hauled him off to jail. The audience laughed in the right places and applauded afterwards, and the children raised almost five dollars for the Red Cross.

Most of those who saw *The Tack* were aware that a local school was called Angell, but Grace Davenant thought other allusions were more obscure, and besides, it was only children playing. The parody of the school song came a little close, but she couldn't be certain that Nadine was singing off-key on purpose.

If Grace had seen the actual script, the mocking tone might not have escaped her, but she made a point of not interfering with her children's projects, from the doll village onward. This policy could lead to surprises, as when the children had borrowed her best hat without asking. Grace only hoped the hat didn't look as foolish on her as it did on her daughter above that hideous brown dress. She was impressed, though, by the way the children had managed the whole thing. Much of the play must have been improvised, but the actors were energetic. Except poor little Cricket, who was cast as a hardened ten-year-old bully. The strain of remembering his part showed on his face.

It was Clara Jane, however, who made the biggest impression. Normally, the child was so speechless in company that Grace wanted to shake her. But from the beginning of the play she spoke her lines with simpering assurance, in an imitation of Miss Sarita Pettibone which Grace prayed nobody else would recognize. Miss Pettibone had a habit of groping in the bosom of her dress, presumably to adjust her shoulder straps. She also smoothed her skirt frequently over her ample hips. And here was Clara Jane doing those same things with her own skinny body and sending the spectators into what Grace, when she wrote a discreet column about it, would describe as stitches.

"It seems," she wrote afterwards, "we may have budding creative talent in the family."

Others in the audience that day were uneasy, but not because of Miss Pettibone; they thought that while the Dick-and-Jane books

were not great literature, perhaps these children shouldn't know it
so well, and they certainly shouldn't take murder so lightly. "Then
Father shot Dick. Then Father shot Jane. Then Father shot Baby,"
Mellie had read in a studious monotone, while Clara Jane, as the
teacher, nodded approval. And did the script contain a hint of amuse-
ment at their mother's expense? Grace Davenant, after all, had a
playful style that was easily parodied. Exactly how conscious were
her children of what they did? Less than two years later, those who
recalled the play wondered even more what had been in the
Davenant children's minds.

XII

In April, Grace made another attempt to bring Mildred and Malcolm Wolfe together. "Though he is a little tall for her, I suppose," she admitted to Robert.

"Maybe," he said, not really thinking about Mildred or Malcolm Wolfe. Robert was packing up his fishing rods in the khaki covers Grace had embroidered in red with his name and a little outline of a trout. The season had begun, and he was about to set off for Hunt Creek, where he might find rainbow trout, as well as ladyslippers and trailing arbutus. When Robert hunted or fished, there was nothing bloodthirsty about it; he was simply fitting into the cycle of nature, finding his place. He spent time in the wilderness and brought home food for his family. At the Fisheries Institute, too, he worked to adjust the balance of human beings in a larger scheme of things. He struggled with bureaucrats and politicians and with businessmen who didn't understand conservation and only wanted to get drunk in a tent and kill more animals than anybody else. Robert loved hunting and fishing but not most hunters or fishermen.

Back the next week with a creel full of fish, he yielded to Grace's pleas and brought home a film from his office to provide a social event for his family and Mr. Wolfe. There were several of these movies, used by the Institute for publicity, and the children's favorite was *Timber Harvest*, a documentary film about lumber camps. There were shots of treetops against blue sky; trees being attacked by saws and toppling to the ground; logs floating down river, guided by nimble men in dungarees and boots and plaid shirts. There was a sound track with soaring music. The best scene showed the preparation of the lumberjacks' breakfast—dozens of eggs being broken into an enormous bowl and poured onto a griddle, pancakes being turned, bacon fried. When a film reached its end, Robert always ran it backwards to rewind it. With some of the other films this was disappointing The children had to remind themselves to laugh at the sight of streams running uphill or bluegills swimming tail-first. But *Timber Harvest* teemed with comic possibilities—trees tilting up from the ground and onto their stumps without a crack showing, eggs slipping out of the pan.

When the movie was shown backwards that evening in April, even Robert and Grace laughed. Even Auntie Mildred. As well as Nadine Applegate, whom Clara Jane had invited in the hope of proving that Robert's job was neither as menial nor as sinister as Nadine assumed. ("Your father's a *fish*erman?" she had asked, and then—with implications of Frankenstein or Dr. Jekyll—"He's a scientist?") Who else had a father who brought movies home from the office? Not Nadine, certainly.

The family, with their two guests, sat in the living room and watched trees leap obediently into place, eggs return to their shells. Clara Jane, noticing her friend's enthralled face, was triumphant.

Grace, too, was pleased. She had managed, not too conspicuously, to seat Mildred and Malcolm Wolfe next to each other, where they could exchange glances during the reactions of Cricket, who sat on the floor at their feet. Surely not even the sourest or most dignified adult could resist his delighted cries.

Not that Malcolm Wolfe could be called sour or overly dignified, but he was definitely shy. James Stewart, she had decided by now, a little more than Gary Cooper. She hadn't been able to keep from pointing this out to Robert, though she had exactly anticipated his wince. He was too much of an empiricist to appreciate an instinctive approach to life; nothing could make him admit the usefulness of instant categories. And yet, she could have said, he was the one who liked poetry, which seemed to her full of unjustified assumptions.

As Grace caught herself thinking this, sitting there in the dim light with the giggling children, she was surprised; she never criticized Robert. Now she glanced at his furrowed face, thrown into relief by the light from the projector. Robert frowned even when he was smiling. If a genie were to present him with an hour of pure happiness, he would spend three-quarters of it looking for drawbacks and the other fifteen minutes trying to find out what he had done to deserve it.

Grace was happy in her work on the science journal, which by now took up all her weekday mornings. Mildred had no early classes on Tuesday and Thursday and volunteered to watch Cricket, who brought back memories of her brothers when they were small. Sometimes she took him around the block to visit Mrs. DeGroff, with whom, to the family's surprise, she had become friendly. Grace increased Mrs. Kepler's hours to three mornings a week, and her own modest salary covered the added expense.

Grace was not only glad to be released from family responsibilities; she loved the work itself—correcting errors, rearranging other people's paragraphs, even ordering paper and dealing with printers. She could be quite firm when she was speaking for someone else, and Malcolm Wolfe, whom she now called by his first name, was a pleasure to work with. He was almost totally uncritical, though when she mentioned this, he said there was nothing to criticize. She was surprised. She had grown so used to Robert's carping, that as soon as she finished a piece of editing, she wondered which things she had done wrong. When she realized that Malcolm approved of nearly everything she did, she grew bolder and worked better than ever.

They were equals, he seemed to think, colleagues working toward a standard they both understood. He had placed a desk for her in a small office adjoining his. During the first weeks, when she had a question, she would enter his office cautiously and wait to be sure she wasn't disturbing him. Later, after they had grown to know each other, they would call companionably back and forth. Grace was contented, in a different way from any she could remember.

However, while she hadn't quite dropped her matchmaking plan, the better Grace got to know Malcolm Wolfe, the more she suspected that he was wrong for Mildred. Her sister-in-law's nervous, obsessive personality, even tempered by marital bliss, might only accentuate Malcolm's natural melancholy. Besides, as Grace had already remarked, he was over six feet tall, and Mildred, next to him, was absurdly short. They would look silly together if they ever went dancing, for instance—not that this was something she could really imagine taking place.

For another thing, Mildred had lately been bringing the name of Professor Baird, her married faculty advisor, into dinner-table conversation, and Grace did just wonder. Professor Baird might be only a new version of the funeral director, but Mildred always did seem to need somebody like that. Malcolm Wolfe was too eligible, Grace suspected, as well as too nice.

XIII

The war kept on. When Clara Jane babysat for the Moreaus, she saw pictures in *Life*: British children hiding from the Blitz; pin-up girls peeking over their shoulders at the camera; dead bodies strewn across the steps of a Chungking air-raid shelter; a puppy attached to a howitzer by its leash; WACs giggling in gas masks; Gypsy Rose Lee, with hardly anything on, entertaining soldiers.

"If we really want to help the war effort," Nadine said in a tough, practical voice as she chewed on a grass stem, "we ought to give ourselves to the boys who're going overseas." She and Clara Jane were lying in the Applegates' back yard on a warm June day, inhaling the fragrance of Mrs. Applegate's roses.

"*What?*" Clara Jane protested. The day had started out so well, with her father making waffles and reciting "What is so rare as a day in June." He did this every year, and Clara Jane never felt summer had begun until he said it. She was stretched out on the grass now, looking into clear blue sky, and she couldn't believe what she had just heard. "*Give* ourselves?" she asked, propping herself on her elbows to see Nadine's face.

"Listen, kid," Nadine said, chewing away on her piece of grass, "they're going to die for us. It's the least we can do."

Clara Jane almost laughed out loud. "Do you really think they'd want us?" She knew more about sex by now, from the books on the Moreaus' bedside shelf. Certain words and certain scenes in fiction or poetry intrigued her too—the word "ravish," for instance, or the love passages that cropped up in even quite reputable poems: What was really going on in "The Eve of Saint Agnes?" Or in *Romeo and Juliet*? Realistically, what actual man would be attracted to either her or Nadine? In the past year Nadine had gotten fatter and developed droopy breasts (which she called tits) and a worse complexion than ever. She had nagged her father into letting her get a permanent, and her hair was out of its braids and drawn back into a turquoise-blue snood or worn in a frizzy blond mass around her face with a pompadour on top. She looked older, but not necessarily better. She still wore her riding pants all the time, with a tight T-shirt, though she apparently never went riding.

As for Clara Jane, she knew her own limitations. From an early age she had understood, from the way her mother brought up the subject, that being pretty was important. The point was that her mother had not been pretty. "Scrawny" was the word she used most often in describing herself as a child. She didn't say "ugly," but it was implied. She praised her sister Eleanor's looks, which had enabled her to get away with anything; whereas all Grace's obedience and striving to please had gone for nothing. Everyone had predicted that she would be an old maid.

"But, Mama," Clara Jane always protested. "You weren't. You married Daddy. You had all of us."

Her mother would sigh then, as if she had achieved such good fortune by a mere fluke. It was only much later that Clara Jane wondered if the sighs could have meant something different.

When Grace disparaged her own appearance, she sometimes ended by referring to Clara Jane's. "And you look just like me," she would say with another sigh. Mellie, on the other hand, was her little beauty. Grace liked to tell how, holding baby Mellie for the first time, she had let out a scream, so sharp that her roommate had rung for the nurse. "My baby!" Grace had cried. "My baby has dimples!"

In childhood photographs, neither Grace nor Eleanor stood out. In fact, they looked rather alike. Still, the message was passed on: There was something wrong with Clara Jane's looks. No soldier or sailor, however love-starved, could want to look at her or hold her hand or kiss her once, chastely, (this was as far as her fantasy went) before being shipped off to his doom. Besides, what could they talk about? She saw soldiers every day on the campus, marching to bagpipes and singing "I've Got Sixpence," but they were real live men—not like Prince Andre, whom she could dismiss whenever she couldn't think of anything for him to say. When Clara Jane tried to imagine a dialogue with an actual person, she couldn't forget how shy she was with strangers. "Cat got your tongue?" she heard the uniformed hero saying before he fled.

But, "Sure they'd want us," Nadine said now, with a knowing look. "Why don't we go down to the Greyhound station? That's where to meet them."

"Let's collect newspapers or tin cans instead," Clara Jane suggested. "Or help my aunt fold bandages over at the school."

"How boring can you get?" Nadine did a brisk handstand and sprang to her feet, brushing grass cuttings from her pants. "All right, then let's put on another play."

Some of Clara Jane's best daydreams were about producing a show for a U.S.O. tour. Soldiers would cheer the Davenant family the way they did Bob Hope and the Andrews Sisters. Even if such a tour was unlikely, a play would be easier than picking up servicemen. "Okay," she said. She could see herself, in her mother's black-and-orange kimono sent by Aunt Eleanor in her Greenwich Village days, as a Japanese spy. Hal would enjoy being a brutal Nazi agent, with a monocle and a square black mustache. Maybe she could work in a death scene.

She borrowed the typewriter again, making sure this time to allow a week for rehearsal before the tickets went on sale.

Grace gave absent-minded permission for the use of the typewriter, the kimono, and the house. She was floating through that summer, paying less attention than usual to her family and thinking more about her job.

And about Malcolm Wolfe. He was such a kind man, so gentle and witty. Days in the office when she helped him with the journal, when they challenged each other over the meanings of words and looked them up in the unabridged dictionary on the stand in his office, held more satisfaction than she had known in a long time. Often she took a sandwich to work, and they ate their lunch together, looking out over the green campus.

During these times they talked usually about the *Quarterly* but sometimes about more personal things. Gradually, Grace learned about Connie's death and about Annabel, whom Malcolm had sent to his sister-in-law because he didn't trust himself to raise her alone. "It was when I took her to the shoe store for the first time," Malcolm said. "I saw I couldn't do it by myself." Annabel, ten years old, had talked him into buying patent-leather tap shoes instead of oxfords. "I was putty in her hands," he said ruefully.

Grace clucked her tongue over the tap shoes. Just like a man. But Malcolm must be a better father than he realized. He was so patient, for one thing. She couldn't imagine him hitting a child.

"It's funny," he said, looking at her almost admiringly, "the way I don't have to explain things to you. The tap shoes. It wouldn't make sense to anybody else."

"It makes perfect sense," she said firmly, gathering up her orange peels and waxed paper.

Malcolm Wolfe did admire Grace, more every day. He scarcely understood how he had done without her before. He had an awareness of her now that let him know, without having to think, exactly where in the building she was, and what she was doing—proofreading at her desk or chatting with a secretary in the hall or searching an obscure corner of the stacks. It was as if she gave off a signal of some kind. She would rush in to work each morning, with an air of having barely escaped from her house and family. A ribbon on her blouse might be untied or a wisp of hair standing up on the wrong side of her part. She would fret cheerfully about the children's refusal to finish their oatmeal or about her sister-in-law's unreasonable crush on Professor Baird, and Malcolm would feel that he was part of a tumultuous, ever-changing household. And then she would straighten her blouse or her hair, and they would set to work.

Grace had given up trying to bring Malcolm and Mildred together. A pity, she thought, but the better she knew Malcolm, the more she saw that he didn't deserve to be stuck with somebody like Mildred.

Malcolm, for his part, was increasingly impressed by the sharpness and flexibility of Grace's mind. She could glance through an article and see right away that a paragraph near the middle ought to be moved to the beginning, or that seemingly essential parts could be eliminated. This ability, she explained, came from experience with her newspaper column, which she often had to shorten or rearrange. Her quick, decisive editing was so different from her often hesitant speech that Malcolm was amazed: Grace Davenant was at least two different people.

He himself was more all of a piece, he thought. He was quiet and melancholy, though no longer profoundly unhappy. He liked his work and loved his daughter. If there was a gap in his life, it wasn't one that he expected to fill. He and Grace might have remained contented fellow-workers for twenty years if she hadn't come to the office one July morning in a more disordered state than usual, with dripping eyes and a quaver in her voice, and if he hadn't inquired whether something was wrong.

She didn't want to tell him. She didn't want to pollute the atmosphere of her working place with family troubles. However, once he had closed the office door, made her a cup of tea, and persuaded her to sit on the leather couch, she couldn't get out of telling.

"It isn't anything," she said, and fumbled fruitlessly for a handkerchief. And it wasn't anything, really. Robert was in one of his rages, that was all, and her interfering father had caused it, and she was caught in the middle. Grace's father, ever since he had found out that Mildred Davenant had come to Michigan, had been writing indignant letters. "He doesn't think it's right," she said to Malcolm, "for Mildred to be living with us." Mildred was a demanding, unstable woman, her father declared, who would do nothing but harm to his grandchildren and to Robert and Grace's marriage. If Mildred must take courses at the University, let her rent a room in somebody else's house.

He had commanded Grace to suggest this to Mildred, but Grace was unable to bring up the subject. "How can I?" she asked Malcolm, and gratefully took the handkerchief he held out. She had explained to her parents more than once about Robert's feeling of responsibility toward Mildred. "It's a question of family ties," he had said. "Family blood." The children were there when he used the expression, and Mellie looked so fascinated that Grace hastened to explain that it wasn't real blood he was talking about. (What a pity she couldn't describe this scene in her column, but of course she couldn't.) It meant, she told the children, that people in the family had to take care of each other.

Grace's mother understood Robert's feeling, but her father didn't. Balderdash! he answered. Fiddlesticks! And now, alas, he had written directly to Robert, who had reacted by blaming Grace. Last night Robert had crumpled her father's letter into a ball and thrown it across the study, and then he had said he was thinking of leaving her. She had known there were times when he wanted to leave, but never before had he come out and said so.

Grace had scarcely slept, and in the morning when she waited for Robert to take back his threat, he had only repeated it in a condensed version. Let Grace's father the banker support the family, he said, if he wanted to run their lives. Let him see how expensive they were.

Robert was right about Mildred, Grace told Malcolm, but her father was right too. Mildred had been doing her best to undermine Grace's authority, not only with Robert but with Mrs. Kepler and the children. Just last night she had criticized the green beans because Grace had served them without the white sauce that her own mother, and Robert's, had always made.

Grace looked up at Malcolm with red eyes above the handkerchief. "But you don't want to hear this," she said.

It wasn't so much that he didn't want to hear it, as that he didn't want it to be true. Sensitive, appealing Grace Davenant shouldn't have to face persecution from petty tyrants. Robert was an admirable person in many ways, but he clearly didn't know how to manage his own life, and he didn't appreciate Grace.

It was then that Malcolm realized how he felt about her.

Not that he could do anything about it. He would keep Grace

near him if he could, and he would enjoy her presence and never let her know. What he wanted to do at that moment was sit beside her on the couch and put his arm around her shoulder, but of course he wouldn't do it.

"Excuse me," she said, sitting up straighter. She wiped her nose, adjusted her glasses, and smiled up at him. "Thank you for listening. I feel better now."

Better, maybe, but nothing had changed. "What will you do?" he asked.

"Oh, Robert didn't mean it. He loses his temper. His leg hurts him, and the children… He has a lot to put up with." She sounded pitying. "I'll write to my father. Maybe Robert will too. Maybe Mildred will move out. Maybe the war will end. Who knows?"

It might all be true, and the Davenant family would continue as usual, but Malcolm's feelings about Grace had changed.

That evening Robert and Grace had another conversation in the study. Robert realized that he had forfeited any moral advantage he might have had over Grace as soon as he hurled her father's letter across the room and threatened to abandon the whole family. But he couldn't apologize because he still felt bound by his duty to Mildred. If Grace would either take better charge of the household or leave the organization to his sister, the problem would disappear.

He explained this in as mild a tone as he could manage, calling Grace "dear" and trying not to hurt her. He did see that it wasn't fair to blame her for her father's meddling. "Take advantage of Mildred," Robert advised. "Let her do all the cleaning she wants."

But Robert didn't have to watch his sister scrubbing away and shaking with exhaustion afterwards. He didn't have to hear her muttered commentary. She had a new way, Grace had noticed, of trembling sometimes. Mildred's head shook on her neck, and her voice quavered. It seemed almost like a symptom of some nervous disease, but Robert couldn't see it. "Mildred's always been nervous," he said. "Who wouldn't be, in her place?"

Grace guided the conversation away from the subject, hoping that no permanent damage had been done.

XIV

One warm day in July, Clara Jane, accompanied by Nadine Applegate, was shadowing her mother. Ostensibly the girls were taking a bicycle trip to the Arboretum. Grace encouraged such expeditions; if the girls were on their bicycles, they couldn't be cooped up in the clubhouse above Nadine's garage, playing cards or reading comic books or heaven only knew what else.

Clara Jane had described her new play to Nadine, who unfortunately coveted the role of the German spy. She would tie her hair back and look as male as possible. "Ve vill crush ze Allies," she said, to demonstrate her German accent. "Ve vill bring zem to zeir knees." She wanted to get into her part by following Grace and finding out her secrets.

"What secrets?" Clara Jane asked as they set off on their bicycles. The whole thing seemed stupid to her, and she certainly wasn't going to let Nadine play the German spy.

"Everybody has dirty secrets," Nadine said.

"Not my mother." Clara Jane, riding along behind, felt apologetic.

"Oh, no?" Nadine called over her shoulder. "You ought to hear what my brother said."

Clara Jane stopped her bicycle and got off. It was too hot to ride uphill anyway. "What did he say?" Wayne Junior had come home for spring vacation and turned out to be even nastier than Clara Jane had feared, with insinuating eyebrows and acne that looked contagious. He had no right to say things about her mother.

"Oh, nothing." Nadine, who had stopped too, looked smug. "He just said she's the sexiest thing he's ever seen."

"My *mother?*"

"In fact, he said he wished he could... You know." She pushed her bicycle ahead. "Come on, we'll lose her."

"But..." Nadine's implication was as ridiculous as her suggestion about the servicemen. Her brother was only sixteen years old, for one thing, and Grace was practically forty. "Oh, really!" Clara Jane said.

They had spotted Grace setting out for the University, hurrying along in her sensible shoes and a flowered voile dress and carrying a worn-out briefcase of Robert's. It was more of a challenge to follow her than a stranger, because they had to stay out of sight. They were at the corner of East University now, and Grace was somewhere ahead. Clara Jane didn't like seeming to agree with Wayne Junior. "Maybe we shouldn't follow her," she said.

"Why not, if she's so innocent?" Nadine squinted. "I'll go down Forest, and you take Packard, so we can keep her between us if she tries to sneak down a side street."

"She's just going to the Science Library." But even if it was only her mother they were shadowing, it was starting to be interesting.

"When you cross a street, ring your bell twice," Nadine ordered.

By July, Grace Davenant found herself in a dilemma. The family had always gone north in August, and it was assumed that—except for Mildred, who was in summer school—they would go this year. They hadn't rented a cottage yet, but they could camp in state parks near the streams and lakes that Robert was studying. Nobody was in diapers this year, and Grace, thank goodness, wasn't pregnant. But she didn't want to go. She had never whole-heartedly wanted to, but in the past she hadn't said so; Robert needed to get away from ragweed, and it was good for the children; if she didn't enjoy camping, that was just too bad.

This year, however, there was her job. The daily contact with Malcolm and other colleagues, the stimulation of exacting work that she did well, had become her own necessity. Without her job, her brain would turn to Cream of Wheat and she would never be able to use it again. Besides, there was gas rationing. If Robert went alone, he could take a state car instead of the big family Buick.

Grace suspected that the children, too, might prefer to stay at home. Though she boasted to outsiders and to the readers of her column about how much the family loved roughing it, she couldn't disregard every single one of their complaints. They liked swimming and rowing boats and being in the woods if there were enough books within reach, but they didn't care for setting up camp every few days and being limited to half a suitcase apiece; they hated evaporated milk, and the smell of outhouses made them gag. Also, this summer they wanted to put on a play.

She mentioned these thoughts one morning to Robert as he was leaning into the mirror to put on his tie, and he reacted as she had feared he would. "No," he said. "The children need to get away." They were picking up too many bad habits and bad language from other children; Clara Jane had actually come to the breakfast table last week wearing lipstick.

Grace admired Clara Jane's daring. The only makeup she herself attempted was a little powder from the Avon lady, rubbed in until it was invisible. (Robert's admiration for Hazel DeGroff was a little unfair, she had often thought. Could he really think her high color was natural?) But this was beside the point. "Would you like to take the children yourself, then?" she asked hopefully. That scheme would be even better.

"It's out of the question." He picked up his briefcase and headed for the stairs.

Grace sighed and scooped up Robert's pajamas from the floor. She loved her children, of course she did, but the mere thought of a vacation from them had momentarily lifted her spirits. "I am a part of all that I have met," Robert sometimes recited in a rolling voice. Tennyson hadn't known the half of it, in her opinion; what if he had been required to split into five new parts, each carrying a bit of himself out into the world? Men surely didn't have to endure this fractured feeling—or not to the same awful extent as women. Grace felt whole only when she knew where all of her children were and what they were doing; and even when this was so, the situation could change in a second. They were growing, forming new cells all the time, for which she was responsible without being able to affect them very much at all.

If children couldn't stay inside their mothers' bodies for their whole lives, they ought not to be there in the first place. Like fish. Did a mother trout feel this anxiety about her offspring—if fish could even feel anxiety? Did a male trout have any notion of which eggs he had fertilized? Clearly not. And human fathers, whatever Robert might claim, weren't much more sensitive. They might fuss at their children and try to make them perfect, but men hadn't had a part of themselves torn out in the process of becoming parents, and most of them didn't even stir when their babies cried at night. No, Grace couldn't send the children away. She went to the closet to look for something cool to wear. The day was already starting out hot and damp.

But, oddly enough, her suggestion had results. In August, seizing the chance of a guiltless escape from ragweed and treble voices, Robert packed up his Complete Shakespeare and *Palgrave's Golden Treasury* with his rods and nets and sleeping bag and set out for the Upper Peninsula alone. Mildred, he was confident, would take care of things at home and see that the children did the chores she had assigned them in a system that involved charts and little metallic stars. And Grace could concentrate on her job.

Clara Jane and Nadine stalked Clara Jane's mother every weekday morning that summer until early in August, when Nadine went to stay with her rich grandmother at Put-In Bay. Even after the spy play, *Axis Evil*, was over, they continued. Though all they ever saw was Grace tripping gaily toward the Science Library, they had come to think of the shadowing as patriotic. "We're practicing to spy on the Japs," Nadine said.

In *Axis Evil*, Clara Jane, wearing the black-and-orange kimono, false fingernails from Kresge's, and Auntie Mildred's satin mules, had turned in another striking characterization, as Madame Cherry-Blossoms-in-Springtime Yatsuma. The hara-kiri scene with a wooden sword was especially fine. Mellie, as Chlorine the lovelorn welder, cried real tears. Hal was a diabolical Baron Boric von Krautheimer, and Nadine pulled the curtain. Some of the audience complained about the fumes from the dime-store incense that smoldered exotically in front of the curtain, and Grace wasn't happy about the gravel the children had sprinkled on the green rug for the outdoor scene, but at least there were no schoolteacher imitations.

Malcolm Wolfe came to the play and brought his daughter Annabel, who was pale and red-haired. The Moreau family was there too, chattering in French. A photograph of the spies being arrested by Cricket in a policeman's hat appeared in the local paper, and the children collected eight dollars and fifty-three cents for the Red Cross. "Once more," Grace typed, "genius raises its head in the family. Might there be a future for our young Thespians?"

Grace, actually, was far too preoccupied in the summer of 1942 to pay much attention to her children. She went to the Science Library in the mornings, and on the days when she wasn't doing volunteer work for the Red Cross, she tended to linger in town through early afternoon, strolling on the campus or through the Arcade on State Street, or passing the music school to hear the splendid cacophony from the practice rooms. Sometimes, to postpone her return home, she rested on a bench near the fountain across from the Michigan League, listening to the bells in the carillon tower.

She was sitting there one day when she saw a plane in the sky and thought of Amelia Earhart. "When I go, I'd like best to go in my own plane, quickly," AE had written. Robert wouldn't allow Grace to ride in an airplane. Not with all her responsibilities, he said, and of course he was right. But it was different for AE, Grace thought now; she had achieved at least some of what she wanted to do.

Grace believed that envy—not the kind she had felt in a half-serious way toward literary characters like Proust's mother, but true, biting envy—was wrong. She had no reason to feel it now: Besides a flourishing family and a husband she'd adored since the day they met, she had a satisfying job, in pleasant surroundings. Yet she was more discontented today than she'd been a year ago. Maybe it was even *because* of her work, which defined her life and set a limit to her ambitions. She used to assume that when she had finally shed family duties, she would go on to her true career. That career, in spite of her day-to-day contentment, now seemed unlikely. She would never be Margaret Mead or Hortense Powdermaker; she didn't even wish to be.

How ungrateful of her, she thought as she sat on the bench under a shower of notes from "Loch Lomond," while statues of Neptune and his sons cavorted greenly in the fountain. Unaware though she was of many of her feelings, she had noticed the inappropriate pangs she'd been suffering lately whenever she came across the name of an accomplished woman from the past. The worst of it was that what she envied George Eliot, Florence Nightingale, or even Amelia Earhart for—as much as their achievement—was their death; her first fleeting thought each time, before she reined in her mind, was of how lucky they were to have earned a chance to rest. Robert was in the habit of saying, quoting Sophocles or somebody, "Call no man fortunate who is not dead," and in spite of his explaining that it wasn't meant the way it sounded but was only something like knocking on wood, she had felt that it was just like gloomy Robert to want everything to be over with. But now she herself was thinking something not too different. Sitting on the bench by the fountain, Grace was surprised at herself.

One day as she was leaving the office, when she jokingly mentioned her reluctance to go home, Malcolm offered her the use of his apartment. Annabel had been staying with him, but she was back in Chicago now, and Grace obviously needed a place where she would be undisturbed. The notion had come to him that she might write a book, a collection of essays on motherhood.

"You mean," she said, "like my newspaper column?"

"No, not like that, nothing like that," he said, so quickly that it struck her that Malcolm might not approve of the column any more than Robert did. If so, it was the first thing about her that he hadn't approved of. "Notes on a Modern Family," Robert had once said, could be seen as fake anthropology of the most amateurish kind.

She was treating her own children as a tribe of savages—with condescension and no objectivity at all. If she wrote that way about Eskimos or Indians, she would be ashamed of herself.

Was that what Malcolm thought too? "Then I don't see—" she said to him, trying to keep the hurt out of her voice. "The column is just a hobby. I don't take it seriously."

"Exactly," he said.

"And it makes the children feel special." Though she wasn't certain of this. Clara Jane and Hal had accused her of exaggeration and even of mendacity. This was natural at their age, of course; if they hadn't objected to her writing, it would have been something else.

"Why *not* take it seriously, though?" Malcolm said. "You could write something really useful. A book of essays, maybe—about what it is to be a mother. Please don't misunderstand me, Grace." His kind, close-set eyes were surrounded with pleading wrinkles. "I don't like to see you wasting your mind—your experience. You could help people."

"But I do help them. You should see the letters I get." She set her chin firmly and picked up a pile of proofs.

"Of course." And they dropped the discussion, but he brought it up again later. If she wrote a book, it needn't be deadly serious; that wasn't what he'd meant.

"No?" Grace laughed to cover her ruffled feelings.

"Though you wouldn't want to resort to humor as a way of evading problems."

She was indignant. "I—" Her indignation faded; he might be right.

"Your graduate degree would give you credentials, and with children of your own... You're such a wonderful example."

"You really think so?" She was already imagining the book jacket, with a picture of herself surrounded by small, pure faces.

"Certainly. Why not?"

"Because..." Because she was a fraud, she thought. This wasn't something she told people, ever; but she had to be honest. "The children were accidental," she confessed. "I didn't mean to have them." And waited for Malcolm's horrified reaction.

An expression of surprise did cross his long, kind face. "Any of them?" he asked, quite reasonably.

Involuntarily, she began to giggle. "Yes. I mean no," she said, nearly breathless. "Not really. I can't..." She shouldn't be talking about such things with her boss—she, a respectable married woman—and on top of that, acting as if the whole situation were hilarious. What must he think? He had stepped back several paces, and no wonder. "I'm sorry," she said, gasping. "Please forgive me." At least she hadn't let him know about Margaret Sanger and the failed diaphragm.

But then he was more admiring than ever; for someone who hadn't planned for a large family, he said, she certainly did an excellent job.

His praise embarrassed Grace. "I'm totally unqualified to be a mother," she told him.

"That's nonsense," Malcolm said. "Absolute nonsense." Her motherhood was her most outstanding quality. He knew she could write about it.

Grace didn't like seeing her children as accessories, though; she preferred to be valued for herself. As for writing a book, she said, the idea dismayed her.

"Don't, then," he said. "Don't write anything at all." She could simply use his apartment while he was at the library. She could read his books and play his records and be free from her family. He would like to picture her there.

So that summer, Grace began to spend a few hours after lunch wandering around Malcolm's empty apartment, singing along with Ezio Pinza or Lily Pons and feeling carefree and expectant, as if the rest of her life might not be predictable after all. The apartment, on the first floor of a Victorian house at the edge of the campus, had high ceilings and comfortable furniture, a piano, and plenty of bookcases. Malcolm's guitar leaned in its case near the fireplace. Sometimes Grace built a fire. She took Malcolm's books from the shelves and examined his signature on the flyleaf and his occasional lightly pencilled marginal comments. She looked through photograph albums—at wedding pictures that showed him young and solemn, next to a bride whose fate was stamped already, Grace fancied, in her white, uncertain face. Connie must have been red-haired like Annabel; her hair in the black-and-white pictures was a medium gray with highlights, and her down-slanting eyebrows were faint.

Annabel's room had a white enameled bed with brass trim, and a quilt made from scraps of Connie's dresses, feather-stitched by Connie's own frail hands (short and stubby, Malcolm maintained, but Grace imagined them long-fingered like her own—her only beauty). A reproduction of Sir Joshua Reynolds's "Simplicity," with the little girl in white ruffles and blue ribbons, hung against the flowered wallpaper above the bed, and dolls and stuffed bears lined the windowsill.

One day Grace put a stack of paper next to Malcolm's typewriter and began to make random notes about her life with Robert and the children and her surprise at finding out how different that life was from what she had imagined it would be. She wrote with concentration, trying to check herself at the first hint of facetiousness. She didn't know whether anything would come of what she was writing, but it was a relief to tell the truth.

Near the middle of the afternoon, reluctantly, she would put her notes away in a folder, cover the typewriter, and start for home.

Grace never mentioned to her family where she spent her afternoons, though she didn't see any real reason why they shouldn't know. Once, coming down Malcolm's porch steps, she saw Hazel DeGroff, tottering along the sidewalk toward the Institute in her tight sandals and unpatriotic silk stockings. They exchanged greetings, and Grace thought Hazel looked at her critically, but then Hazel always looked that way. Still, Grace wished they hadn't met. Her refuge in Malcolm's apartment was the first secret she'd had since her marriage.

Actually, only luck prevented Clara Jane and Nadine, on their bicycle trips, from finding out her secret. They followed Grace unnoticed each morning throughout July, but as soon as she disappeared through the revolving door of the Science Library, they left. Sometimes the girls rode on to the public library, or to Kresge's to order limeade and stretch it out by adding sugar and ice-water. Or they might go to the Fisheries Institute to see the live pink-and-black gila monsters in the lobby and the languid brown bears in the cage outside. Clara Jane associated the Institute's powerful odor of form-aldehyde with her father, who was in charge of the whole building.

By August, Nadine was at Put-In Bay and Clara Jane was spend-ing her spare time in the porch swing with *King Lear*, in which she saw herself as the silent misunderstood Cordelia. Soon afterwards the girls were back in school and tired of the shadowing game any-way. Besides, Clara Jane didn't find Grace as interesting as Nadine did. She was glad her mother liked her job, but the dinner-table conversation was as banal as ever, and the obnoxious newspaper col-umn continued.

It was in early September, when Robert had returned from the north and the children were in school again, that Grace began to wonder whether her feelings for Malcolm Wolfe were stronger than they ought to be. It was all very well to enjoy working with him and to use his apartment when he wasn't there, but now she noticed herself starting at the sound of his voice and choosing her clothes to please him. He liked her in blue, she had learned.

The trouble was, he was so kind. Grace wasn't used to kindness, and it practically made her melt. If that was hard to overlook, it was even harder not to notice the way he gazed at her. And the ques-tions he asked—mainly about the children. Malcolm's respect for her motherhood bewildered her after the reactions of people like Hazel DeGroff, who seemed to consider her fecundity indecent. Even her own parents, who certainly loved their grandchildren, thought that there need not have been so many.

Malcolm did think Grace's children were remarkable. They were the jewels of Cornelia, the angels surrounding the Madonna in a Lippo Lippi painting. They were the children he would never have. And Grace had produced them. He was determined to keep his feel-ings to himself, but one day in September when they were bending over proof sheets of an article about the geology of western Michigan, his hand touched her shoulder and she jumped back as if he had burned her through the thin blue material of her dress. "Sorry," he said, but then something similar happened later that day and she seemed even more alarmed. Could she have sensed his agitation? It was awkward. He couldn't keep apologizing for such trivial accidents.

And then she looked him full in the face, and he understood.

Grace had spent so much of her life trying to feel the way she ought to feel that it was hard for her to recognize a true emotion when it came along. She loved her husband, of course, and even if his love wasn't quite as strong, he must need her, or they wouldn't be together. But that was different from the reciprocal attraction she was beginning to feel now.

Neither Malcolm nor Grace expected to acknowledge their emotions to each other, but they were grateful. Each one was the other's miracle. They continued to work together that summer and to drink their tea in the chairs in front of the window and to take note of each other's good qualities. In the morning when she came into the office, they would look at one another and smile. "How are you?" they would ask, really wanting to know.

XV

November, 1942. Denmark, Norway, the Low Countries, and finally France had been overrun by Germany. The Allies were falling behind.

Robert Davenant was in his basement, stoking the furnace. He pulled open the creaking iron door and shook the ashes down, then shoveled three buckets of coal from the bin and poured them into the hot red heart of the fire. The coal was heavy, and his leg ached, but he didn't mind; he was caring for his family. Tomorrow he would get the two older boys to help him clear out the clinkers. He wished he could afford an automatic stoker. It was all right for him to shovel coal, but he didn't like to think of Grace having to do it when he was away. He dragged himself up the basement stairs, holding onto the banister.

Clara Jane, on the window seat with the curtains drawn, heard ominous sounds from below: First the shovel scraping the rough cement floor of the coal bin, then the banging of metal against the open furnace door. Her father was doing something, she always feared when she heard these noises, that would destroy the whole family and the house too. He was going to blow them all to smithereens—one of these nights if not now. In her search for current events for Social Studies, she had read enough newspaper stories (Dad Slays Family, Self) to know the kind of thing that could happen. She wondered if her mother suspected. Probably not. Her mother was too busy making up whimsical little anecdotes to notice anything real.

It didn't occur to Clara Jane that her own fears might be just as unfounded. All she knew was that she was frightened. She heard her father sigh as he opened the door from the stairs to the kitchen, limped in, and slid the bolt into place.

As well as Nazis and gangsters and her father, Clara Jane still feared school, teachers, talking with strangers, growing up, getting married, and being an old maid. Ninth grade wasn't as bad as eighth—she didn't have a class with Miss Pettibone—but her English teacher, Miss McClure, had pounced on her after returning her first assignment and forecast a future for her as an essayist. Miss McClure seemed to think this was good news, but Clara Jane was disheartened. Just because she liked to read big books, did it mean she had to write them? It was bad enough that her mother took it for granted that she would go to graduate school.

She wished she could be like Nadine, who feared nothing at all, was content to get C in every subject but gym, and dreamed of becoming a horse trainer. (If she couldn't do that, Nadine had announced, she'd be a singer like Helen Traubel or Jeanette MacDonald. When she sang "The Lost Chord," her grandmother had been moved to tears and given her five dollars.) What Clara Jane wanted to do when she was grown up was start a repertory theatre and hire somebody else to write the plays. So she resented Miss McClure's prediction but saw, too, that English wouldn't be hard this year. Algebra and Latin weren't either, but there was still Social Studies—the same old jumble of newspaper clippings and war maps and oral reports. She was supposed to write a term paper on war production, and whenever she thought about it, she hoped she would die before it was due. As she might; if the Germans didn't bomb the school, there was always the chance that her father would do away with the whole family. She thought about this possibility not only when Robert stoked the furnace but when he limped in from work, carrying his loaded briefcase and frowning. He seemed totally miserable, and she knew it was because of her and the other children.

The truth was, in spite of Robert's frowns, that he was more content than he had been in years. The war worried him, and he was losing some of his most promising students to the army, but his children were too young for the draft, and he didn't believe America would be bombed. Above all, Grace had finally stopped showering him with attention that he didn't know what to do with. He couldn't forget how she had spoiled their honeymoon sixteen years before at Cranberry Lake. Robert had always loved the forest—the subtle pattern of sounds, the white swaying of birches, the webs of spiders stretched between the trunks of trees—and he had believed that on that trip, Grace would become part of what he loved. But she didn't respond to the love-making that he had postponed for so long, and she filled the tent with chatter. He had wondered—for the first time but not the last—whether his marriage was a terrible mistake. This fall, her work on the *Science Quarterly* absorbed so much of her energy that she no longer seemed to need more from him than he could offer.

Mildred saw Grace's job as an evil, but that was just Mildred. "I'm working myself to the bone," she said to Robert, her tone almost complacent. "With my classes and the children and all."

"Nobody asked you to," he replied. Robert could be sharp with Mildred when Grace wasn't there.

"To the bone," she said, hefting a tall stack of blue-black textbooks. "Professor Baird is quite concerned."

He didn't ask whether she would rather live somewhere else. Grace's father hadn't written any more autocratic letters, and Robert was glad to have Mildred in charge of things. The household was running more smoothly than he had thought possible.

XVI

B ut Robert, by the spring of 1943, had no reason for complacency. Both Grace and Malcolm had intended to keep their love affair (for that was what it was, they knew by now) on a high plane, with souls and minds—and occasionally hands—briefly touching. They certainly didn't expect to become lovers in a technical sense, but one afternoon in April, when Grace was curled up in Malcolm's blue velvet wing chair with a fire going and *La Boheme* on the phonograph and her notebook on her lap, he came home to get a book, thinking she would already have left. He was so surprised to see her there by the fireplace, with the light flickering on her messy hair, that somehow he came closer to her than he meant to, and then she stood up, and all their careful rules collapsed like the kindling in the fire. It was Puccini's fault, they said afterwards. Mimi was dying, and the music was soaring. Rodolfo cried out, and Malcolm and Grace fell into each other's arms.

After that day, Malcolm returned to his apartment several afternoons a week. As chief librarian, he was free to roam the halls or lose himself in the stacks or visit other University offices. No one could be sure where he was, and he took care not to be gone for long.

He and Grace avoided each other at work. There had been no need, after all, for them to consult as much as they had during the summer. They began to be cautious. While both of them wished they could merge their lives and be together for all the world to see, they knew that it wasn't possible: Grace must preserve her family, and she mustn't betray Robert's trust. She felt more compassion toward him than before. If she couldn't be the faithful wife he thought he had, she was all the more obligated to please him when she could.

Malcolm Wolfe, to Grace's amazement, seemed to feel about her the way she had wanted Robert to feel. And she could respond; she was learning from Malcolm that there was such a thing as mutual attraction—that desire, and even lust, were accessible to unglamorous, overeducated women. She, Grace Davenant, on the jingling brass bed in his apartment, was having sensations that she hadn't even believed in before. There was no mistake; she was having actual orgasms. She felt apologetic toward the romantic novelists she had formerly accused of exaggeration. She was proud of herself, too—as proud as when she had earned her Ph.D. She wished she could tell everybody—well, Robert, at least. With him, she had tried much too hard to persuade herself that she enjoyed love-making. Here was another benefit of her liaison; she was no longer deceiving herself so much.

"I feel so selfish when I'm with you," she said to Malcolm one afternoon as they lay under Connie's quilt, watching bright autumn leaves blowing behind the lace curtains. "No," she explained when he frowned. "I don't mean that it's wrong. It's the way I want to feel, but I never knew it before." Grace had been taught that genuine love extends the self toward another person. This might be true, but it didn't say enough. When she and Malcolm made love, she was able to concentrate on her own feelings—which depended on him but belonged only to her. With Robert, she had worried about what he was thinking; whereas with Malcolm Wolfe she was just herself, so full of sensation and surprise that he didn't exist separately from her. It was as if she had new skin, sensitive and attuned to delight. Perhaps this was the way Robert felt about poetry—which only made her impatient because it wouldn't come right out and say what it meant. This new understanding of Robert pleased her; her feelings for her lover were making her into a better wife.

When Grace and Malcolm met in his apartment, after they embraced and sat on his chintz-covered couch, he looked away from her and began to speak. She watched his shy straight profile as he gazed ahead and slightly down, while he told her what had happened to him since their last meeting. A stranger observing them might have thought that Malcolm didn't know her very well or was confessing some misdeed. But then, after describing a leaky radiator in his car or a minor triumph over the ladies in the cataloguing department, he would glance up sideways and meet her eyes. "Hello," he would say, and reach for her hand. Anyone seeing them then would have thought they had known each other all their lives.

Sometimes she would place her right hand against his left, palm to palm, and she would stretch her fingers until they were nearly as long as his. "Such long, delicate hands," he would say obligingly— or something of the sort—and she would feel how impossible it was that he could ever do anything to hurt her. They never fought. Could this mean, she wondered, that their feelings weren't real? Or was it only that she and Robert bickered so much that she had used up her anger by the time she got to Malcolm? She knew she was responsible for much of the dissension with Robert, because of whatever she said that got on his nerves. But the stories that entertained Malcolm were often the very ones that had irritated Robert. She could talk to him without hearing herself.

None of this was Robert's fault—or she didn't think it was. The responsibility was just as much hers, for having married him without knowing him well enough.

Grace knew that her behavior would appear immoral to most people, but that wasn't the way it felt. Her time with Malcolm didn't seem to take place in the same world as her everyday life. There was no cooking in it, or laundry or arguments or children; it was all talk and love-making. She felt, now, that she had a greater understanding of primitive societies: A Melanesian woman could have two husbands and numerous affairs, and the men might object or try to kill each other, but the woman herself needn't feel that she had sinned. Grace found herself rationalizing, so transparently that she was embarrassed: She and Malcolm made each other so happy that it must be right; they weren't harming Robert or the children and in fact might even be helping them, since some of Grace's newfound love was overflowing onto her family—even onto poor Mildred; she, Grace, was a nicer person than before. And so on. If all these things were true, her previous, more virtuous self knew also that they were comforting lies.

Still, Grace was careful. She omitted Malcolm's name from conversations, and she almost stopped mentioning the Science Library. She must make sure there was no chance of exposure.

So the Davenants got through that school year, with Grace and Malcolm continuing their affair, Robert fleeing to the wilderness when he could, Mildred shining in Professor Baird's classes and nagging the children at home, and Clara Jane actually getting an A- on her impossible paper about war production. Cricket learned to sing "Hi Ho, Hi Ho, It's Off to Work We Go" and "Santa Claus Is Coming to Town" without missing a word or a note, as Grace reported in her column. Wayne Applegate, Junior turned up next door after being expelled from the military academy and made more shocking remarks, which Nadine reported: Grace was a real piece, he said—whatever that might mean. The Davenant girls tried to avoid Wayne Junior, and they, as well as Nadine, were relieved when his mother packed him off to an even stricter school.

XVII

Grace didn't escape guilt completely. Somehow it became understood in the family that she went every afternoon to the junior high cafeteria to fold bandages for the Red Cross, and she didn't trouble to deny it. She did spend several days a week there—including Wednesdays, when Mildred went too—and she worked extra fast to make up for the days she missed, although she didn't feel quite right about using the Red Cross as an alibi. She avoided a regular schedule, since she didn't want a pattern to become apparent. Only she and Malcolm knew in advance whether she would be in the cafeteria or at his apartment.

On one unlucky day, Freddie broke his arm during a soccer game on the field next to the school. The Davenant children usually tried to conceal illnesses or injuries, but Freddie knew right away that his arm wouldn't look normal by dinnertime. Besides, it hurt. Thinking that his mother was in the cafeteria, he stood pitifully outside the windows, desperately searching the room. Some of the ladies saw him, and he was driven home, white-faced and ashamed and trying not to cry. Dr. Wernimont was just opening his bag when Grace drifted in and was struck by conscience.

This was Freddie's third injury in two years. He had broken a finger when he tried to balance upside down on the seat of a tricycle, and he had cracked his collarbone when—dressed as Superman in Dr. Dentons and bathing trunks and a flowing towel—he fell from the maple tree in the front yard. (Almost the worst part of this experience was the humiliation of being rushed to the hospital in costume.) Though it might not be logical for Grace to blame herself for Freddie's injury, she couldn't help feeling that it wouldn't have occurred if she had been at home or in the cafeteria—anywhere but in Malcolm's apartment. To make up for her neglect, she devoted the next episode of "Notes on a Modern Family" to her stout-hearted little son.

Malcolm didn't see why Grace should assume all the responsibility for her children. He couldn't bear her humility before her husband, or the way she made excuses for him. Robert did love the children, she insisted, but even to herself her explanations sounded weak.

She and Malcolm promised each other not to have a child of their own. "Look out," she said lightly to him once, pulling away in the big brass bed with the patchwork cover. "I'm terribly fertile."

But he was conscientious about using condoms, although he confessed that he didn't like them. "Robert didn't either," Grace said, breaking her rule about not comparing the two men. "All he liked was the name, because it was classical."

"Trojans?" Malcolm laughed.

"They seemed too unnatural. The very idea made him uncomfortable." She was becoming uncomfortable herself, discussing the subject. Malcolm would like to have a family with her, she knew. "We have to be careful," she warned.

"I know." He was smoothing her hair back from her forehead, running his thumb over her eyelids, and looking wistful. "Don't worry."

The fault hadn't all been Robert's, though. She, too, had been careless, letting herself slide over and over again into motherhood. Now that there was a future with love and work, she would be more cautious.

Something that pleased Malcolm about Grace was the way her top front teeth met at a slant, just enough to keep the arch from being perfect—a flaw that not everyone, maybe not even her husband, would notice. Without her glasses, her face had a smooth Renaissance look around the eyes, reminding him of those preoccupied madonnas in early Italian paintings. He wanted to know everything about her. What had she been like as a child? Could she show him any pictures? They exchanged childhood photographs to carry in their wallets, Malcolm with long fair curls in a sailor suit, Grace in white, solemnly clutching a china doll with a kidskin body. If Robert ever came across the picture of Malcolm, Grace would allow him to think it was her cousin Ned.

What pleased Grace most about Malcolm was his steady, companionable love for her. Love, as far back as she could remember, had been something which overtook her, inappropriately and alone. When she fell for Robert in sixth grade, she had been ashamed of her emotion; she would have died before letting anyone—especially Robert—know. Her feelings—both the love and the shame—had persisted and grown. While they were both in college, she had continued her devotion from a distance (though at the same time she was unrequitedly attracted to several other men). In graduate school she stopped trying to conceal her passion, but even after she and Robert were married, she knew it wasn't returned in full measure. Her feeling for Malcolm was different: Because it was reciprocal from the beginning, she never felt tricked into making a fool of herself.

Spring vacation, 1943. A week off from school, and Nadine, shuffling cards in the clubhouse, asked Clara Jane when there would be another play.

"Not yet." Clara Jane knew by then that a week wasn't enough. Besides, she wanted to do a horror play next, and Hal hadn't finished designing the monster. His ideas involved buzzers and colored light bulbs.

Then Nadine said. "Why don't we follow your mom again?"

"Because it's too boring." And Clara Jane went home to read *Kidnapped* on the window seat.

So Nadine followed Grace by herself, to the Science Library and out of it again at noon. Afterwards she reported that she had seen Clara Jane's mother go into a white house with a tower on the corner and a porch on the front.

"That sounds like our house." Clara Jane suspected Nadine of making the whole thing up.

"Well, it isn't." Nadine pursed her lips. "I wonder what she was up to."

Two days later, in the middle of the afternoon, the girls crouched behind the overgrown spiraea bushes in front of Malcolm Wolfe's house, eating Hostess Sno Balls that Clara Jane had recklessly bought at Mr. Twist's store. After a picnic in the Arboretum and a dramatic reading of the childbirth scene from *War and Peace*, they had proceeded to the campus and from there to the house Nadine had described. Clara Jane's right hand hurt from a blister she had gotten the day before, digging in her father's Victory Garden. He had warned her not to prick the blister in case she died of blood poisoning like President Coolidge's son. It had broken during the bicycle ride, and the palm of her hand was hot and sore.

As Clara Jane was finishing her cupcake and wondering about the symptoms of blood poisoning, Nadine's elbow jabbed her, and she was surprised to see Grace come down the steps of the big white house, swinging her briefcase. "What do you think she's got in there?" Nadine whispered, brushing coconut off her red T-shirt. "Microfilm for the Nazis?"

"A secret formula for a soybean casserole that will wipe out the entire German army," Clara Jane answered, and when Grace was out of sight they rode down the street a block over, ringing their bells and singing "Off we go, into the wild blue yonder." Clara Jane assumed that her mother's errand had something to do with the war effort; Grace was in charge of bacon fat in their whole section of town.

One afternoon that week Clara Jane, whose blister was healing after all, crept down the back stairs to get Ritz crackers and chokecherry jam and found Auntie Mildred and Mrs. Kepler in the kitchen. Auntie Mildred was sitting at the battered enamel table, and Mrs. Kepler was at the ironing board, sprinkling water over a pile of laundered clothes. Clara Jane recognized her own favorite green dress with the print of little yellow ducks, which had once belonged to Patty DeGroff. The two women looked rather alike except for Mrs. Kepler's bright red mouth—little hunched-up women with conspiratorial brown eyes behind rimless glasses. Clara Jane started to back up the stairs, but then she got interested in the conversation and came down again. Her aunt and Mrs. Kepler were talking about their desire, sometime in their lives, to ride in an airplane. Wouldn't she like to fly? Mrs. Kepler asked.

Clara Jane wasn't sure. "My mother wants to, though," she said, adding rashly, "but Daddy won't let her unless she takes all of us with her."

Auntie Mildred laughed, shooting a knowing glance at Mrs. Kepler. "Well, isn't that nice of him," she said smoothly.

Clara Jane hated being talked down to. "I do know what he meant," she said. "He wants to be sure Mother's here to take care of us."

"Of course, dear," Auntie Mildred said with a wink at Mrs. Kepler.

"So in case the airplane crashes, we'll all die at once and he won't have to be bothered." That ought to show them, and besides, it was true. Clara Jane's father had been teasing her mother, and both of them had laughed, but it made sense.

Auntie Mildred pulled in her mouth. "I know what your father would do if he heard you talking like that," she said. "He'd get out the hairbrush."

Clara Jane doubted it, though he had once spanked Mellie with her beloved blue celluloid brush from Grandma—so hard that it broke and made Mellie cry harder than ever. "And anyway," she added, "I know a lot of things. I bet you think my mother goes to the Red Cross after work."

"Of course she does. I go there too." Proudly, Auntie Mildred fingered the metal button on her lapel. When she and Grace folded bandages, they wore official white headdresses like nurses' caps.

"Not all the time. Sometimes she goes other places." And Clara Jane felt an ambiguous expression on her face, disloyal to her mother, as if she and Nadine were still spying.

"Really?" Auntie Mildred looked at her sharply. "Anywhere in particular?"

"Oh, lots of places." For the first time, the two women were paying serious attention to Clara Jane. "Practically every day," she added recklessly.

"Now, you know that isn't true," Auntie Mildred said, but her dark eyes shone as if she had a twenty-pound bass at the end of a fishing line.

Much later in her life, Clara Davenant would try to recall that day and the days just before it. More distinctly than anything else, she would remember her feeling of disloyalty.

XVIII

The annual Conservation Department picnic took place in a park on the banks of the Huron River, where tables were set near a slope above a flat grassy area with a baseball diamond. Each family brought food to share, and the division heads provided other refreshments. In June of 1943, Clara Jane tried to get out of going to the picnic, but her mother said she needed her help. Clara Jane knew that really her mother was only trying to make her be more social. If she went to the picnic, she might have to play baseball, and she had never been able to hit or catch any kind of ball when people were looking. She took *The Seahawk* along, to protect her from games and conversations.

Grace herself didn't look forward to the occasion. The picnic always made Robert anxious, and she didn't have real friends among the departmental wives. However, she saw it as a chance for her children, and perhaps for Mildred, to expand their circle of acquaintances. Besides, Malcolm would be there, with Annabel.

The two women spent the morning fixing deviled eggs and potato salad, and then Grace put on her blue spotted playsuit with the detachable skirt. She was annoyed to see Mildred come proudly out of her bedroom wearing a similar playsuit in red plaid, but she wasn't going to change just because of that. The children looked as disreputable as usual when they piled into the Buick. Their overalls were ragged, and Clara Jane had covered her nice new striped T-shirt with a worn-out shirt of Robert's which hung nearly to her knees. Still, if they were comfortable, that was what mattered. And the weather was fine. "What is so rare as a day in June," Robert chanted. "Then, if ever, come perfect days."

Although Robert Davenant didn't approve of soft drinks, he had agreed to take charge of an ice chest filled with bottles of Vernor's ginger ale, Hire's root beer, and Dr. Pepper. Ben DeGroff, jovial in a tall white hat, presided at a barbecue grill. Charlie Cline was organizing a baseball game, while Malcolm Wolfe supervised races for the younger children. About seventy-five people were there, Robert estimated, including some very young children and several infants.

The Davenants found a table at the edge of the slope, where Grace could keep the children in sight, and she and Mildred spread out a cloth and unpacked the food. The DeGroffs were just behind them, Grace realized too late as she heard Hazel's voice raised in criticism of the planning committee. Hazel really was an unpleasant person.

But where was Cricket? Glancing at the dandelion-starred grass below, she spotted him near the bottom of the slope, turning somersaults. Over and over, she could see his feet hoisted uncertainly into the air, his legs kicking, his hair shining as he tumbled down the hill. With his bright hair, he was hard to miss. Then, looking back over her shoulder, she saw Clara Jane, trapped by Hazel DeGroff and clutching her book against her chest.

"Rags?" Hazel was saying in astonished tones. "You put it up with *rags?*" She must have complimented Clara Jane's hair, which was out of its braids and flowed over her shoulders in syrup-colored waves, held back by two bronze barrettes her grandmother had sent her. The rag curlers had worked very well, and Grace hoped Hazel wouldn't discourage her. "Clara Jane," she called, motioning down the slope, "would you look after Cricket?" Clara Jane dashed down the hill, grasping her book. "She's such a help," Grace said in Hazel's direction.

Clara Jane, grateful for her mother's strategy for once, went to sit under a lilac bush. There was nobody her age at the picnic unless you counted Annabel Wolfe, who was a year younger and just as bashful as she was. Clara Jane would have liked to make friends with Annabel, but on the rare times when they met, they picked up each other's shyness and couldn't think of a thing to say. Clara Jane was impressed by Annabel's status as an only child and a half-orphan, and she wished that she, too, had a gentle father and a pink pinafore dress and red hair. Annabel's hair was the exact shade of Cricket's, she noticed, a dark red like maple leaves or sumac in the fall.

Grace, at the table above, was noticing the same thing. Cricket and Annabel had been together at the children's play last summer, but Cricket's hair had been hidden by his policeman's cap. Today Grace could see the two matching spots of red, moving from place to place and drawing attention to each other, like a recurring theme in music. The color of new pennies, she reflected, surprised at how poetic she could be. So this was why Malcolm had been so interested in Cricket at the dinner party. Wasn't it a coincidence that each of them had a red-haired child. It was too bad, though, that Malcolm didn't know the rule about red-haired people not wearing pink. The child must have insisted. At least she had on a sensible-looking pair of sandals instead of the tap shoes.

Clara Jane, lost in her dream of friendship with Annabel Wolfe, had failed to safeguard herself from hearty Mr. Cline, who advanced on her now, brandishing a baseball mitt. Before she even noticed him, he came up behind her and hauled her to her feet, saying that she not only had to play baseball but must be a shortstop. "A big strong girl like you," he said in his husky voice, exhaling Sen-Sen or some other kind of sickening breath sweetener; she would be a perfect shortstop. And his dreadful fingers crept under her armpits and rested against the breasts that she had been trying to ignore for the past year. She had always thought Mr. Cline was repulsive, with his black brush cut and his nose with the pores in it.

"No!" she said, and broke free, running back up the hill and evading Mrs. Cline's accusing eyes. Mr. Cline shrugged comically and went to recruit other players.

"What's the matter now?" her mother called in exasperation, and said something to Mrs. DeGroff about "a stage she's in."

"I don't know what I'm going to do with you," her mother said as Clara Jane approached. "You have to learn to enjoy games. Other people do."

This was unfair. The whole situation was unfair. Clara Jane would rather die than tell about Mr. Cline's fingers. "What about you?" she said. "I don't see you playing games." Her mother wouldn't even play Fish or Rummy unless a child had a temperature over a hundred degrees. And besides, she was wearing that embarrassing playsuit again, with the spots that made her look like a clown. Clara Jane flung off down the hill.

Grace smiled and looked around, aware of her audience. "Adolescence is a trying time," she wrote in her head. "I try to remember that our eldest is unfolding her wings and uncertain of her step. She is testing me, I tell myself..." Her thoughts broke off as she saw Freddie, his arm still in a cast, reaching for a baseball bat. The arm had been broken in too many places to heal easily, and Dr. Wernimont had had to set it again. "Clara Jane," she called.

"Never mind, I'll get him," Mildred said wearily, and started down the hill, already shaking her finger at Freddie.

Grace glanced toward the table behind. It did seem as if the very sight of Hazel DeGroff was enough to make her children misbehave. At the moment, Hazel was beaming as her own daughter Peggy, in knife-pleated white shorts, walked past with the oldest Cline boy, a tennis racquet under her arm. However, the day wasn't really going badly. Grace looked down at the children Malcolm had lined up for a three-legged race. Annabel was helping him to tie the racers' legs together. Her bright hair and Cricket's made the same counterpoint as before, moving toward and away from each other. Not new pennies after all, Grace decided; more like polished mahogany, a deep, true red.

"Isn't that remarkable," she heard Mrs. DeGroff say to Mrs. Cline, and realized that they were watching the children too. "The same shade of red. Exactly the same." And then Hazel said, spacing the words out and giving them equal emphasis, "Isn't that interesting." It wasn't clear whether she was including Grace in the conversation.

Mildred returned then, dragging Freddie, who sat down sulkily at the table and crammed a deviled egg into his mouth. "I was just saying to your sister-in-law," Mrs. DeGroff called to Mildred, "how remarkable it is that her baby's hair is exactly the same color as Malcolm's daughter's."

Grace laughed. "Don't tell *him* he's a baby." She pushed a paper napkin across the table toward Freddie, who was chewing with his mouth open.

"Malcolm has been a friend of your family for some time, hasn't he?" Mrs. DeGroff said.

"Not really." Grace wasn't sure what was being hinted.

"Is that so? I thought he was. In and out of the house for years, I thought Mildred said. But then, you see him all the time at work, of course, don't you."

Grace noticed Mildred's eyes gleaming behind her glasses. She could feel her own heart beating.

"I said no such thing," Mildred said. She got up from the table and walked briskly toward Robert, who was standing with his daughters under the trees by the soft-drink cooler.

If Annabel were her friend, Clara Jane was thinking, she could see Mr. Wolfe nearly every day. He would talk to her kindly and maybe even pat her hair as she'd seen him do with Annabel. But that was silly. Clara Jane went to help her father give out drinks. She knew that he didn't like crowds any more than she did. She opened a bottle of root beer and shook it, licking the fizz off the top as it rose. Mellie was there too, digging happily through the ice chips with both hands. "It feels cool," she said. "It feels so cool." But then she pulled her hands out. "My fingers are dizzy," she said, and Clara Jane was grateful that her mother wasn't there with her notebook.

Actually, Clara Jane knew what Mellie meant. Her own hands, which often seemed to be colder than other people's, had a fainting feeling just then that wasn't quite numbness. She saw Auntie Mildred walking down the hill with a grim expression, on the way to scold somebody for something. "Come on," she said to Mellie. "Let's go help Mr. Wolfe with the races."

Grace, still at the table and still bewildered, noticed Mildred talking to Robert in an agitated way, with gestures, and at the bottom of the slope she saw the two red-haired children again, running.

In the big black car on the way home, Grace felt as if an invisible wire were stretched between Mildred and Robert, silently continuing the conversation she had just observed. Robert, at the wheel, held himself stiffly and looked straight ahead, while Mildred, behind him, pursed her lips and nodded. Grace attempted a few remarks, but they died away. "Well, I guess we're all tired," she said finally.

XIX

On the day after the picnic, Robert Davenant got up at six as usual and went to the back yard to work in his Victory Garden. The pea pods were filling out, and the tomato plants had little yellow flowers. Robert was proud of his garden, which he had dug out of the back lawn and fertilized and fenced in with chicken wire. Heavenly Blue morning glories climbed the low wire fence, and moss roses lined the borders. The garden was the most peaceful spot he knew of, outside of the wilderness.

He was troubled this morning, in spite of the flourishing plants and the deepening blue of the sky. Something was wrong between Grace and Mildred. Robert knew that Grace wasn't happy about his sister's living with the family, but he thought she had accepted it. Mildred would have her Master's degree within a year. After that, she was bound to find a teaching job—back in the East, with any luck. She had made perfect grades so far except for a minus on one A which had made her weep, and her professors were sure to write enthusiastic references.

Still, he did wish she and Grace could get along. Last night in the bedroom, Grace had been unusually quiet. Several times she had mentioned the picnic and then had fallen silent, as if waiting for him to continue the topic. Once she said uncertainly, "I don't know what Mildred said to you..." And then stopped, scanning his face.

But Mildred had said hardly anything. He had no idea what Grace was talking about, though it appeared to be connected with Hazel DeGroff. He knew Hazel could be abrasive, but Grace had never even tried to be her friend. Hazel dressed attractively and ran an efficient household and was an asset to Ben. There were things Grace could learn from her.

The picnic yesterday had gone better than Robert had feared. He had enjoyed hearing the children call to each other and watching them run on the grass below the slope; but at one point, Mildred had rushed up to him in one of her states. "About Grace," she said in a stage whisper. "I wasn't going to tell you. I thought it was better if you didn't know, but Hazel says she actually saw her..." She looked around and back up the hill toward the tables, and then she noticed Clara Jane and Mellie, who were standing near the ice chest and waving their hands in a peculiar way. One of their games, no doubt. "No," Mildred said meaningly. "This isn't the time." And retreated, leaving him baffled.

He put his hoe and cultivator away in the garage now and opened the screen door to the kitchen. He was going to Pigeon River the next day, and he planned to take Hal and Freddie. Last night after the picnic he had told them about the trip, which would keep them away for a week. "But, Dad," Freddie said, "what about the monster?"

"What did you say?" Robert supposed it was reasonable for his sons to call him Dad, like a father in a comic strip, but he wasn't used to it yet. Until recently he had been Daddy to all his children.

"We have to work on the monster for the play," Hal said, as anxious as Freddie. "You know." A few days before, at supper, Hal had described his plan for a robot which would light up and make buzzing sounds. Robert remembered now.

"I'm sorry," he said. "You'll have to wait till we get back."

They looked at him with rebellious eyes, standing their ground. "No," Hal said, "we have to stay here," and Freddie echoed him.

Robert was disheartened. It wasn't just that he wanted the boys to go with him—there was no question that they would—but he wanted them to *want* to go. He turned toward the corner behind the kitchen door where he kept the walking stick he had cut from a hickory tree, to use for climbing trails.

"Okay," Freddie said quickly, "I guess I'll go," and Hal looked at him, betrayed.

"You too, Hal?" Robert asked.

Robert and Hal stared at each other. Hal's eyes dropped. "Okay," he muttered.

Robert, who had just remembered Freddie's arm, was relieved. It wouldn't have been fair to punish only Hal. But he was sad, too. A knowledge of plants and animals was the most valuable heritage he could leave his children. He was grateful for his own early fishing trips with his minister father. In fact, he thought the trips had helped to save him; books, Mildred's nursing—and, above all, a hope of visiting the woods again—had sustained him through the first fevers of his terrible boyhood illness and the long recovery afterwards. Robert wanted to give his children, especially his sons, a sense of their own place in nature. He ordered them to pack the next day.

Grace, conscious of her own silences, helped Robert and the boys to round up supplies for the expedition. Every word she said had to be inspected beforehand to see what harm it might do. What was Robert thinking? What had Mildred said to him at the picnic? Grace feared that it had to do with Malcolm. Robert seemed preoccupied, but then, he often was.

She didn't know what was on Mildred's mind either. It was a silly coincidence yesterday, with Hazel DeGroff noticing the two red-haired children and making insinuations. It was absolutely ridiculous. Hazel had seemed to think that Grace and Malcolm ... It was ridiculous; they hadn't even met until Cricket was more than two years old. When Grace understood what Hazel was implying, she had been tempted to point this out. But were Hazel's remarks based on something more than her immediate observation of the two children? She had mentioned a talk with Mildred. It did seem that Grace's sister-in-law had been directing more dark looks than ever at her lately, and she had spoken privately with Robert at the picnic, but Grace didn't see how Mildred could know anything to tell.

Although Grace felt no more guilt than before, she did have misgivings: If Robert or the children found out about her life with Malcolm, they might not understand that it had nothing to do with them. Feeling uneasy and almost sick, she rolled up socks from the laundry pile on the study couch, folded pants and undershirts, and filled a crate with Rice Krispies and prunes and cans of tomato juice. The boys' faces, as doleful as if they already sensed her treachery, made her feel worse.

Cricket, too, was unhappy. Watching her over the edge of the kitchen table, he kept asking, "Why can't I go too?"

"Someday," she told him. Someday all the children would grow up and go away.

The boys, in the end, seemed resigned to the trip. Hal was looking forward to wearing his father's waders, and Freddie flourished the landing net on the way to the car. They left at the first peep of dawn the next morning, and Grace felt relieved. Whatever was wrong, if anything was, she wouldn't have to deal with it yet.

Mildred set off on a journey of her own that day, to visit her brother Wesley in New York. Grace was due for a holiday from the *Quarterly*, but she didn't tell the family. Clara Jane could look after Mellie and Cricket while Grace spent her time as she chose.

"I wish I could paint you," Malcolm said that afternoon as she lay naked across the patchwork quilt. From the intensity of his gaze, she had been able to predict exactly what he was going to say; Robert had spoken the same words more than once at the beginning of their marriage. Either this was what many men said to many women, or she had connected herself with two frustrated artists. Neither of them, so far as she knew, did any actual painting. Perhaps her body simply had some touching perishable quality that moved observers to say such things.

"Not now, but I'm serious," he said. "Would you mind?"

Grace was thinking about Robert, and worrying. "I don't mind." Though she did, a little.

"I'm afraid of losing you. I think that's it." His mouth was sad. "I used to sketch, nothing much." Briefly, he opened a drawer in the bedside table to show her a sketchbook he kept there.

She might have known; it went with the guitar and the Trollope and the chess. But she couldn't think about such things now. "What would we do," she asked, "if Robert found out about us?" If such a thing were to happen, it would be better if the news came from her—rather than Mildred, for instance—so that she could explain at the same time. Not that it would happen. There was no possibility.

Malcolm had been running his hand along her hip, admiring the strong sculpted bones, but his hand stopped moving. "He isn't going to find out," he said. He searched her face, her speckled green eyes. "Is he?"

"No, of course he isn't." She laughed.

"We couldn't see each other again," he said, still motionless. "I don't see how we could."

She caught her breath. "I couldn't stand that. I couldn't."

"Then don't let him." He reached out, and they clung together.

XX

During the time Robert was away, Grace's worries seemed foolish. Even if by some chance he did suspect anything—even if he discovered the truth—she wasn't sure he would mind. He had never in their lives expressed more than a tolerant affection for her, and not long before, he had actually threatened to leave. She didn't mention her fears to Malcolm again.

But, as it happened, Robert did mind. Without knowing why, he felt unsettled. The whole time at Pigeon River—as he tried to keep Freddie from dipping his cast in the water and Hal from reeling in his line before a fish was hooked, Robert puzzled over what had happened at the picnic. Or not happened, because nothing really had. It was only that, in the two days before he and the boys set off, Grace had become mysterious.

Always before now, he had assumed that he knew the limits of his wife's thinking. She might chatter for hours about the children or Mrs. Waterhouse's gall bladder or the eccentricities of Professor Freundlich, and he could predict nearly every word she would say. But after the picnic, a curtain had been drawn over her mind. There were silences, and Robert didn't know what was behind them. He didn't look forward to his return.

Nor did Grace. When Robert and the boys arrived home on schedule, with a bag full of dirty clothes and an ice chest full of bluegills and perch, she went to the back porch as soon as she heard the car pull into the driveway. She didn't run to meet them, though, and she noticed that before Robert kissed her as she held the screen door open, he paused. It was only for an instant, but it was unusual. Her fears came crowding back.

At supper other pauses occurred, during which Grace and Robert looked at or away from each other over the meat loaf and scalloped potatoes. The familiar rhythm of the meal was gone. Even the children were subdued, and Freddie jostled Mellie only twice with his elbow to test whether her new vaccination hurt as much as she claimed it did. Afterwards, when the dishes were done and the children were either in bed or supposed to be, Grace went up to the study and found Robert stacking his fishing equipment in its customary corner. He didn't look up when she came in and closed the door.

"So the great expedition was a success," she said brightly. He obviously didn't feel like talking, but she needed to break the silence. It took time for people to feel easy with each other after an absence, she reflected. It was only natural. She sat on the day-bed and fingered the dark green burlap of the cover. "Was it? The expedition, I mean."

"That's right." He still had his back to her.

"I want you to know that Cricket got over his disappointment before the car was out of the driveway," she went on with a little laugh. "We made ginger cookies in the shape of fish, and he said…" But she couldn't ignore the lack of response. "Robert?" If he would only look at her.

"What is it, dear?" His voice was impatient. He was emptying his green metal tackle box now, taking out the little jars of dragonfly nymphs and blue damselflies and placing them on his desk next to the container of sharpened number three pencils. "You know I'm tired."

The silence was like a block of stone. If Grace hadn't felt guilty before, she did now. Her feelings for Malcolm might not be wrong in themselves, but if they could give Robert as much pain as she suddenly feared, she ought not to have them. "I'm sorry," she said helplessly, and stood up and turned toward the door.

"Wait." Robert pulled the desk chair around to face her and sat down. He was frowning. "Please, Grace."

A serious talk might not be a good idea after all. "In the morning," she said, trying to sound offhand. "When we're not so tired."

"Damn it, Grace, what is it?" His bad leg was stretched in front of him, in its brace.

He must know. He wouldn't use language like that if he didn't. Mildred had somehow found out her secret and told it to Robert. Grace sat down on the day-bed again. "Nothing," she said. She wished she were at the bottom of Lake Erie. What had possessed her to imagine she could get away with anything? "I just want to be sure you understand," she said to Robert. "It has nothing to do with you." But he was still looking at her with that anxious frown. "I mean, it just happened," she explained.

"What? *What* happened?"

She had thought of him as almost omniscient, but now he had a helpless, baffled look. "He...he loves me," she said.

This made no sense to Robert. Could she be referring to one of the boys? "Cricket," he said stupidly. "Cricket loves you?" But of course Cricket did. "What are you talking about?" He tried to read her face.

"It's just something that happened. We didn't know it would happen." She was leaning toward him, and her hair had fallen over her cheeks. "I love you, of course, you know that, I always have, but this is different."

"What are you talking about?" This was Grace, who had scarcely surprised him once in all these years.

"Oh." She paused, backtracking, but it was too late.

"Tell me." He concentrated his full attention on her, peering through his glasses. "What is it, Grace?"

She felt like an amoeba under his microscope; he would never let go of the subject now. "I thought Mildred had..." she fumbled. "I thought you knew." And so she told him. Not about her afternoons with Malcolm, not even who her lover was. But she let Robert know that there was somebody.

He wouldn't believe it at first. How could he? "You're not serious, Grace," he kept saying. "Not you." She had given so much love to him that she *couldn't* have enough left for someone else. It was the whole basis of their marriage.

However, unfortunately, one of the things he still knew about Grace was that she couldn't tell lies. Mildred *had* given away her secret, he realized; more than once, before his trip north, his sister had dropped hints, which he hadn't picked up. Did everybody know? Everybody except him? "Hazel DeGroff," he said, falling back into his chair and taking off his glasses. At the picnic there had been unpleasantness. "Was that what the fuss was about?"

"No!" Grace was affronted. "That was a mistake. She's just jealous because of the children."

He leaned forward, his head in his hands. "Then who does know?"

"Nobody. I told you." She hated seeing him reduced to such weakness by something she had said. Was Robert, whose integrity she had always respected, really worrying about what people thought?

But it wasn't other people's knowledge that appalled him, so much as his own ignorance. "I didn't know," he said.

His disconsolate expression reminded her of Freddie, when the older children had let the Easter Bunny out of the bag; they had tried to undo the damage when they saw Freddie's tears, but it was too late. "Oh, Robert," she said. "I wish I could cancel this whole conversation."

It was what he wished too. He hardly knew what he felt, aside from the disbelief that was already evaporating. More than anything, he wanted Grace to take back what she had said.

Neither of them slept much that night. In the morning Robert went out to his vegetable garden, with thoughts and questions circling his head like insects. The Swiss chard was coming along nicely, and some of the lettuce was ready to harvest. But he couldn't find any pleasure in the garden, and he was almost too tired to stand. He went to the kitchen to make coffee for himself and tea for Grace and carried the tray unsteadily up the back stairs, hoping not to rouse the children. But in the upstairs hall he came across Clara Jane sneaking along in her blue pajamas, two oranges and a pile of toast balanced against her chest. The girls must be having one of their feasts, taking advantage of Mildred's absence. "Jane," he said. "Look after the little ones when they wake up."

"All right." She gave him a wary glance and hurried up to the third floor. He didn't even have the confidence of his children.

Robert took his tray into the bedroom, where Grace lay on her side with her eyes closed. He had never understood how she could sleep so late in the mornings, and he wondered especially how she could do it today. "Grace?" he said softly, setting the tray on the dresser and closing the door. He needed to clear some of the questions out of his mind.

She wasn't asleep after all. "Oh, tea," she said, turning over and looking up at him. "How nice of you." As a rule he was scornful of her preference for tea, and he never brought breakfast to the bedroom except on her birthday. Today he had used the Haviland china. She sat up against the pillows in her faded pink nightgown. It would be impossible to explain herself to Robert, but she had to try.

They held their cups carefully, neither of them wanting to approach the precarious subject.

"Where do you meet?" he finally asked. "Here?"

"No, of course not." Even if it were possible, with five curious children and a hostile sister-in-law, she would never have brought Malcolm there. In her own house, she would be Grace Davenant, incompetent wife and accidental mother; she wouldn't be the fecund but carefree mythological figure she became when Malcolm was with her. There would have been no point. Robert was entitled to ask, of course, though she wouldn't be able to avoid hurting him. "It has nothing to do with you," she said. "Please believe me."

"So you never loved me after all," he said in wonder, looking into his cup. He wasn't going to ask the name of Grace's lover. The name didn't matter.

"Robert!" Where had he got hold of such an idea? "I did! Always. Too much. I loved you *too* much." He had no right to act so crushed now, when he was the one who had always been able to demolish her with a few words. She had truly thought, all this time, that nothing she did could make the slightest dent in his feelings.

She could irritate him, of course—forget to replace the pencil in the budget book or serve dinner ten minutes late or tell the same story over again—but she couldn't harm him; in allowing herself to love Malcolm, she had depended on Robert's strength. Her hands were trembling so much that the tea slopped over the rim of her cup. She held it out to him. "Please take this. I can't…"

"Do you want to leave me?" he asked as he set the dishes on the bedside table. "Is that what you want?"

"No!" How could he think such a thing?

They talked until they could no longer ignore the smell of burning toast and the sound of children's feet pounding through the hallway. "Clara Jane!" Robert shouted a few times, with no effect. He finally dressed and started out for the Institute, feeling that the sidewalk in front of him was twice as steep as usual.

Grace put on her clothes and went to her desk in the alcove of the study. She couldn't face Malcolm today, and besides, the deadline for her newspaper column was tomorrow. Uncovering her typewriter, she typed the heading "Notes on a Modern Family" and sat for nearly half an hour, just looking at it. There was a photograph on her desk, of herself and the children, taken two years ago. It hadn't been easy to round everybody up and make the girls wear dresses and get them all to smile at once. In the picture Grace sat in an armchair, with the four older children grouped around her and Cricket on a footstool in front. He was wearing a little two-piece suit with big pearl buttons at the waist and a sailboat on the pocket and leaning toward the camera with his eyes wide open and a hand on his knee. The very sight of his little scuffed shoes brought tears to Grace's eyes. What was she doing to her children?

She came out of her trance and typed, "The mighty fishermen have returned with mosquito bites and a mess of catfish, boasting to the rest of us about the ones that got away. We mere women know better than to believe them, but we smile and offer praise…"

XXI

Clara Jane sensed trouble. Last night at the dinner table there had been an atmosphere of profound unease. Her parents weren't exactly fighting, but she almost wished they would. They scarcely looked at each other, and both of them were so quiet that the children didn't dare to speak. She wondered how she could get through the years of sitting there in the middle of her suffering family, before she had her own theatre to work in and her own apartment to live in, with two collie dogs and thousands of books. She would never get married, and she would certainly never have children.

She had heard serious voices from the study last night, and today she had waked up early and crept down to get breakfast for Mellie and herself, hoping to avoid her father. She was too late, she discovered when she looked out the kitchen window and saw him staring down at the Swiss chard in his garden. So she made toast and seized two oranges and fled the kitchen, sneaking up the front stairs. However, when she reached the window seat on the landing, she couldn't resist stopping to add a few lines to her new play, tentatively called *The Blue Dragon*. It had come to her that she should include two Supermen in the cast, to rescue the other characters from the monster. So she made her notes and put the script back into the window seat and reached the upstairs hall just in time to meet her father as he limped unexpectedly up the back way. Now he would scold her for taking food upstairs, even though he was doing the same thing himself.

Later in the morning her parents were still in their bedroom, and she wondered if the conversation behind their door could be about her. It sometimes was, she knew—about her temper and how shy she was. She had overheard them one night last fall, when she was sitting on the window seat behind the curtains. They were in their bedroom after a party, talking in the teasing way they used when they thought nobody else could hear.

"She looks," her father had been saying, "as if God had tried to design a pretty girl and been interrupted halfway through." Clara Jane was sure he was talking about her.

She heard her mother laugh. "God? God who?" At this, Clara Jane was momentarily distracted. She had always assumed her parents believed in God. They seldom went to church themselves, but they sent the children to Sunday school.

"I was speaking hypothetically," she heard her father say. "You know what I mean. The two halves of her face don't go together."

"Oh, Robert, what a cruel thing to say."

"Why is it cruel? She can't hear me."

Little did he know. Clara Jane felt the warm tears beginning. She knew she wasn't pretty, but she hadn't known her father knew.

"Poor Miss Everell," Grace's voice said. "I hope you don't insult her in the office."

"I never insult my secretaries."

It had taken days for the last part of the conversation to sink into Clara Jane's consciousness. No, they hadn't been talking about her; she understood that. And yet ever since then, she'd felt that her father had reservations about her looks.

But what she wanted most right now was to finish writing the horror play in time to produce it before the family went north in August. The dramatic Davenant children were beginning to be taken seriously by the whole town. The Red Cross had made them honorary members of the Speakers' Bureau, and requests for performances had come in from an old people's home and the Child Study Club. The radio station had interviewed them.

Clara Jane didn't mind being famous, but with the fame went responsibility. She was still the only person in the family who would do any playwriting. So, after sharing the toast and oranges with sleepy Mellie, she went back down to the window seat again and curled up behind the curtains, trying to figure out how to rescue her characters from the monster they had rashly created. The monster would be played by Freddie, hidden under a silver-painted carton, with red light bulbs for eyes and radio tubes for ears. His only line of dialogue would be "Boo," spoken in a timid voice when his creator plugged him into the wall socket and his eyes and ears lit up. The two Supermen—Norma Applegate and Cricket in Dr. Dentons with towels for capes—would swoop from a concealed ladder at the side of the stage, spot the monster, and flee in terror. Then Hal, as the not-very-heroic hero, would head for the exit and trip over the monster's cord, unplugging it and saving the world.

Clara Jane needed to write this down before she forgot it. She would have liked to borrow her mother's typewriter, but the sound of tense voices from the bedroom warned her not to interrupt. So she stayed behind the curtain, calling every once in a while to the boys to calm down. Why didn't they go outside to play, she shouted. Why not go to the park?

Robert, on his way to the Institute two hours later than usual, felt as if an earthquake had opened the ground under his house and swallowed it, family and all. This wasn't a thing that he had ever believed could happen; it was outside the limits of possibility. His father had sometimes mentioned the Abyss in his sermons, and Robert, in his teens and already a scientist, had scoffed. Now he and Grace and all of their children had plunged into it, and they were still falling, down and down. He could clutch at crumbling ledges, but he hadn't a hope of saving his family, not anymore.

Sometime toward four in the morning, in the midst of other tormenting reflections, the French saying had jumped into Robert's mind about the two participants in any amorous relationship—the one who loves and the one who is loved, or something like that. For more than eighteen years he had allowed himself to be loved, without imagining that his position could change. He hadn't thought it was fair, but it had seemed inevitable. He had never realized how much he depended on Grace's steady flow of worship and obedience; he only knew that it was what she needed to give him and he was willing to accept. At times he had even resented her adoration; it was too hard to live up to. But he had never thought she would withdraw it. He remembered a stanza from Christina Rossetti:

You loitered on the road too long,
    You trifled at the gate:
The enchanted dove upon her branch
    Died without a mate;
The enchanted princess in her tower
    Slept, died, behind the grate;
Her heart was starving all this while
    You made it wait.

Why hadn't he, during all those years, let Grace know that he loved her? Why hadn't he known it himself?

Robert arrived at the Institute and walked past the caged rattlers and gila monsters, through the smell of formaldehyde, down the long empty hall to his office. Most of the staff was away on vacation. Miss Everell was at her desk, though, and he saw her slide a copy of *Vogue* under her blotter as he came in. Poor woman, she would be just as well off reading *Field & Stream*. He went to the inner office, sat at his desk under the varnished and mounted smallmouth bass he had caught years ago, and propped his foot on the bottom drawer, thinking about Grace. Was it his handicap that had done them in? Not because she was troubled by it, but because he tried to behave as if it didn't exist?

He had always made light of his weakness, partly for the sake of his job. Who would employ a conservationist, however qualified, who wasn't strong enough to spend time in the field? But this necessity, as well as his pride, had led to dishonesty. Because he thought he should be as strong as anyone else, at home as well as at work, he had pretended that he was. And his whole household had pretended with him, from the beginning.

On that disastrous honeymoon in the Adirondacks, Robert had set himself the task of carrying Grace across the threshold. When he reached under her knees and hoisted her into the tar-smelling, summer-smelling tent, he was acting ironically and seriously at the same time, putting the whole episode into quotation marks; if he was going to do something traditional, he would do it right. It was meant to be a demonstration of good faith, and yet perhaps it had begun the pretense. The amazement in Grace's eyes was no help, but he could ignore that, knowing that in the deepest part of her own ironic soul she was as sentimental as he.

Both of them, he thought now as he gazed down through green leaves at the campus, might have been ready then to throw themselves straight into a lukewarm bath of romance, if only they could have been sure that no one was watching and laughing.

The rest of the day was no easier for the family. It rained, and neither Robert nor Grace could think about anything but their trouble, and after dinner they had one of their fights. Both of them would have been shocked to learn that their children thought of them as people who quarreled, but the children knew it was true— especially Clara Jane, who had taken on the job of herding the younger children away at the first sign of tension.

The argument that night seemed to her as irrational as any of the others, but this time her father was the one who wouldn't see reason. Usually she mentally sided with him against Grace's non sequiturs and wobbling defenses, but tonight he was obviously wrong. After clearing the table and scraping the dishes, the children had started a Bingo game in the living room. Bingo was one of their favorite games, because of the prizes—a collection of outgrown toys and unwanted presents which they kept in a pillowcase. The game was best when the whole family played and when Robert, for instance, won a broken jack-in-the-box or a pair of lace-trimmed pink underpants.

This evening the strained atmosphere of the last few days had continued at the dinner table, and Clara Jane thought a family game might help. The rain kept the children from going outside to play Statues or Hide and Seek, so she distributed the Bingo cards, and Hal announced the first number.

Then, in the kitchen, voices erupted. "Why did you give it to me," Grace wailed, "if you didn't want me to use it?"

Clara Jane sneaked into the dining room to close the kitchen door. They should have taken the game upstairs. "Because you asked for it," she heard her father say. "How could I know you'd use it to avoid drying the dishes?"

The dish drainer again. There had been problems with this before. The children's father had built the drainer for their mother last Christmas and had mounted it on brackets above the sink. Unfortunately, the very idea of leaving dishes to dry all by themselves grated against Robert's moral sense. The sight of a row of plates and cups sitting there dripping, untouched by any towel, offended him. When he was a boy, Mildred and their Dutch grandmother had washed the dishes immediately after every meal and rinsed and dried them and put them away. Nothing had been left in a rack as evidence of anybody's laziness.

Grace's principles, however, were equally strong. She didn't believe in unnecessary work, and she maintained besides that air drying was much more hygienic than going over every dish with a germ-carrying towel. What was the point?

Exactly, Clara Jane thought as she stood at the kitchen door. And why had her father even brought the sinful dish drainer into the house?

She heard him sigh, and then he said, "You asked me for it, Grace. I do try to please you sometimes."

"I know, Robert," her mother said tragically after a pause, as if what they were arguing about weren't something so trivial. Clara Jane wondered why they were calling each other by name, like the characters in the first act of a play.

There was a silence, and then her father asked, softly and just as sadly, "Do you?" After another silence, he went on. "I thought," he said patiently, "you could stack the dishes there temporarily, before drying them."

What a really peculiar idea. Usually, even when Clara Jane was upset by the way her father lectured her mother, she could agree with his logic.

"I see," she heard Grace say. "I'm sorry, dear."

"But do what you want," her father said, angry again. "You always do. Apparently."

This wasn't true at all, Clara Jane knew. She hoped he wouldn't bring her into the argument by asking why Grace, with all those lummoxes of children, didn't make them do the dishwashing. He often complained about her failure to assign tasks to the children; Grace waited for them to volunteer, but when they didn't—which was usually—she did the housework herself.

Auntie Mildred never used the dish drainer, Clara Jane had noticed. She would be back from New York in a few days, and perhaps the atmosphere might clear. She, at least, knew how to put the children to work.

Clara Jane closed the kitchen door and went back to the living room, where Cricket was squealing "Bingo, bingo, bingo" and begging, as his prize, to be lifted up to stroke Muledeer. (Much later, when Clara Davenant is a grown woman with a profession, she will wonder how she can have spent her childhood with a dead animal looking down from above the fireplace and felt no qualms. None of them minded, though they all wept when their mother read *Bambi* as a bedtime story.)

Robert left the kitchen, wondering at himself. He hadn't meant to criticize Grace—not for using the dish drainer. He had built it because she'd asked for it, but secretly he had hoped she wouldn't use it; he was giving her a chance to please him. He respected his wife's intellectual ability, he really did; but part of him, he recognized with a certain shame, must want to see her on her knees, scrubbing the kitchen floor as his grandmother had.

However, there were more urgent things to discuss. He went up to the study, hoping Grace would follow. Robert didn't exempt himself from his rules about work, he thought as he climbed the stairs. Even reading, one of his greatest pleasures, was justifiable only if he was sick in bed or accomplishing something else at the same time, such as fishing, to provide food for his family. He had chosen his profession on the same principle. Since contact with the wilderness was necessary to his soul, he had found work that would take him there. For Robert to have a hobby—besides fly-tying or archery—would have been unthinkable. The ecology of his existence demanded that everything be connected to everything else, if only by the finest, most imperceptible of threads.

He stretched full length on the green burlap cover of the daybed and thought about Grace. Although he had reason to be angry about more than her housekeeping, anger wasn't his main sensation. Primarily, he felt wounded. Even if he'd been able to foresee this situation, he could never have imagined how much pain he would feel. It was as if the whole atmosphere—every thought that came into his mind and every breath he drew—were poisoned. The analogy, he noted wryly, was a hay-fever one, but his most excruciating reaction to ragweed couldn't come close to what he was suffering now. The word 'jealousy' scarcely seemed to apply: What was most unbearable was the revelation of Grace's secret life—the exclusion of himself, the bestowal upon someone else of attention and love that were rightfully his. (Because, she had assured him, there *was* love; this was not a passing affair.) Her claim of a new and heightened feeling for him—rooted in her new passion—was not believable.

He looked up at the two diplomas on the wall, side by side and not quite level. He had felt uncomfortable when she hung them there, but he had been touched. He had thought he could see straight into Grace's heart.

Yes, that was what he had thought; perhaps the most devastating effect of Robert's new information was the destruction of his past. If he couldn't trust the absolute love he had thought he possessed, what could he trust? Lying there on the coarse green coverlet, he tried to bring back the way Grace had looked as an adoring young girl, but her imagined face fell into a thousand pieces, like a jigsaw puzzle picked up from a table. His present feeling, he thought, was a modern equivalent to the loss of faith that had produced Victorian crises: If the self that believed in Grace had been mistaken, it no longer existed; if it had been his only self, where was he?

He felt some pity for her too—for the failings that she surely wouldn't be able to conceal for long. Could her lover, whoever he was, put up with Grace's cliches? Could he keep from wincing when she referred to his pals at the office or boasted that Freddie was all boy? But maybe the lover lacked Robert's sensitivity; maybe that was why he was her lover. Robert's life had become more interesting than ever before, he thought as he lay on the cot with his eyes closed. Unbearable, maybe, but interesting.

When Grace finally came into the study, he didn't ask any of the questions in his mind. He simply reached out and said softly, "I love you, Grace. I love you."

Later that week Nadine invited Clara Jane to a birthday dinner, at which she was the only guest. Nadine often boasted about her own popularity, but only she and Norma and their parents were there when Clara Jane arrived on the Applegates' porch in her yellow Swiss-organdy dress with the puffed sleeves, bearing a carefully wrapped Nancy Drew mystery, *The Secret of the Hidden Staircase*.

"How much do you weigh?" Mrs. Applegate kept asking gruffly as she waved her cigarette over the dinner table. "You can't weigh a hundred pounds." Clara Jane didn't know what to say, but the meal itself was lovely, and Mr. Applegate was too busy cooking to comment on her lack of conversation. Dinner was fried hot dogs and sauerkraut and mashed potatoes with no lumps. At home, hot dogs were always thoroughly boiled because of trichinosis, but these tasted spicy and rich, and there was dark mustard. The sauerkraut, a new experience for Clara Jane, was better than it smelled. The cake was light and fine-textured, piled with airy white frosting. When the rose-colored candles were lighted, Clara Jane looked at the reflection of the flames in the window and then across the driveway and through another window at her own family, in their own dining room. She saw Cricket clapping his hands and the other children laughing. Even her parents were smiling. They looked like a cover on the *Saturday Evening Post*. She knew they were only having creamed chipped beef and carrots and prune whip, but for a minute she wanted to be in the picture too, instead of with this strange family and their exotic food.

XXII

On the morning after her long talk with Robert, Grace spoke to Malcolm in his office with the door closed. "I've done something stupid," she told him as tears started to her eyes. "I don't know how I could have been so stupid." She flung herself onto the leather couch, which squelched unromantically. She hadn't believed Robert would find out her secret, she said, and she hadn't believed he loved her as much as he apparently did. But she loved Malcolm. She couldn't stand it. If she had to give him up, she would die.

Malcolm stood in the middle of the rug, feeling as if all expression had been wiped from his face. Did she mean that Robert *knew*? Yes, clearly, that was what she meant. But it was Malcolm who had been stupid; he and Grace had seemed so blessed that he hadn't doubted that they would get away with it. He should have known, with his luck, that they wouldn't. He turned the key in his office door and went to sit next to her on the couch. "Are you sure he's found out?"

"Of course I'm sure," she said miserably. "I told him."

"What?"

"Not on purpose. It just happened. I thought he already knew, and so naturally I went ahead and..."

"You did." Grace's transparence was one of the first qualities that had attracted him. But "*Why?*" he asked. He still hadn't taken it in.

"What can we do?" Her face was red, and her eyes and nose were streaming.

For the first time in their acquaintance, he was seriously annoyed with Grace. Enraged, in fact, but there was no time for them to talk. Somebody might knock on the door any minute, and a meeting of the editorial board was scheduled for ten. "Can we meet this after-noon at the apartment? Is it safe?"

"Just this once, I suppose. He doesn't know it's you."

This once? "Well, good," he said sharply. "Let's keep it that way."

A new flood of tears came. "Of course." She reached for the hand-kerchief he held out.

Before the office door had been tried often enough for anyone to wonder what was going on, Malcolm sent Grace to the ladies' room to wash her face and then gave her a long article to proofread, about the habits of the Alaskan musk ox.

Malcolm plodded through the rest of the morning, hoping that the turmoil in his mind didn't show on his face and knowing that probably it didn't. People tended to think of him as mournful but composed, like the Mount Rushmore version of Lincoln, even when he was feeling more like Vesuvius. "You're so calm," they often said.

The editorial board of the *Quarterly* met, and spent two hours trying to decide whether to narrow the margins of the magazine to save paper because of the war. If the margins were too small, the magazine might look skimpy, Grace objected, with more emotion than the subject warranted, and Malcolm wished she wouldn't call attention to herself. They didn't speak directly to each other or meet each other's eyes.

Malcolm couldn't care about the *Quarterly* just now. All he could feel was disappointment in himself, and a terrible sense of loss. At Connie's death, he had thought he was rid of hope. He had thought he had resigned himself. Then he met Grace. When their affair be-gan, he had tried to believe that he couldn't depend on his joy to last; but he had come to depend on it, and now it was gone.

"Is Robert the only one who knows?" he asked Grace that after-noon as they sat in straight-backed chairs before his empty fireplace.

"Mildred." She choked on the word. "I think she suspects."

That was unfortunate. "But you don't know for certain?"

"No, but..." Before Mildred left for New York, Grace said, she had been unfriendly, to say the least. However, with Mildred this wasn't unusual.

"I see." There was a weight on his chest, compressing his lungs.

But whether or not Mildred knew, there was Robert. "He doesn't know it's you, though," she said, as if this would help.

"So you said."

"He didn't even ask."

Robert, with the terrible temper. "He didn't...do anything?"

"What would he do?" The very idea of Robert's attacking her last night was ludicrous—poor Robert, who had been so crushed that she could never respect him again.

Malcolm leaned forward and looked directly into her face. Then he stood up. "Come on," he said in a voice she had never heard before. He grasped her wrist and pulled her roughly toward the bedroom.

"No." She tried to pry his fingers away. "We can't." She didn't know how they could ever make love again, and the thought of this loss had been making her stomach hurt since the night before. But when he began to undo the buttons on her dress, she helped him, crying all the time.

"How could you, how could you," he kept saying, still roughly, as he stroked her shoulders and breasts and pushed her down on the bed and moved on top of her. "Grace. How could you ruin everything? Didn't you want us to be happy?"

This was too much. She braced her hands against his chest and pushed until she could roll out from under him. "Yes. I did. But I didn't know how." He was as bad as Robert. Was this all men wanted—to be smiled at and treated gently and not have to see anyone else's pain? "It's as hard for me as it is for you; don't you know that?"

"Are you still trying to get my sympathy?" he said. "Still?"

"Of course not." How could he think such a thing?

"That was what you wanted, wasn't it? From the beginning."

"What do you mean?" She hadn't dreamed Malcolm could be cruel. He was only supposed to adore her, no matter what she did.

"You needed somebody to comfort you, and there I was."

"No." He was distorting everything.

"Why did you tell Robert?" He sat up and yanked out the drawer of the bedside stand.

"What are you doing?"

"You're so beautiful." He took out his sketchbook and a pencil and gave her a measuring look. "You don't mind, do you? It may be my last chance." He started to draw.

"Are you serious?" She leaped up and grabbed her pink underpants.

"Grace, stop." He abandoned the sketchbook and sank back against the pillows.

Her bra and slip and dress were on the floor, and she hurried to put them on, while Malcolm lay on the bed, watching. She couldn't tell whether he was still angry, but she was. He hadn't listened to anything she was trying to say; he only cared about how her body looked, preferably on a piece of paper. She stuffed her stockings and garter belt into her purse and stepped into her shoes and ran to the door.

"Wait," he said, but she didn't even hesitate.

Two blocks later, with her hair uncombed and her feet sticking to the insides of her shoes, Grace stopped and turned back to the apartment. Malcolm, dressed now, was facing the front door as she opened it, as if he were waiting for her to return. "I'm glad you came back," he said.

"My manuscript. I can't leave it here."

"Your manuscript." He nodded sadly. "No."

"And I wanted to return your key." She sat on the edge of a chair and put on her stockings. They didn't touch each other again.

Starting out once more with the folder of notes in her briefcase, Grace realized that Malcolm was right: What she had wanted from him initially was sympathy, though it had grown into something else. Worse than that, she had expected him to save her from all the problems in her marriage and her life. But he couldn't save her; nobody could. She was glad they had made up after their fight—if that was what it was—but her picture of them together was broken now; it was like a painting on glass that had been cracked and painstakingly mended.

A few days later, Mildred returned on the Greyhound bus from upstate New York, and Grace tried to smile when she saw her carrying her monogrammed leatherette suitcases up the front steps. Mildred looked at her sourly, but perhaps no more so than usual; It was hard to tell. Though Grace no longer visited Malcolm's apartment, she continued to go to her job at the *Quarterly*. He needed her there as much as she needed to go, and besides, Robert might become suspicious if she suddenly stopped. So far, although he was downcast and distant and had made a few references in private to Grace's "friend," he hadn't asked her lover's name.

One Saturday the family took a picnic lunch to Whitmore Lake, and Grace, though she had passed the Red Cross Life Saving course when she was sixteen and still wore the badge sewed to her bathing suit, nearly drowned. "What were you doing?" Robert demanded after he'd towed her back to safety in the one-arm carry. "What in hell did you think you were doing?" She had walked far out into the shallow lake and continued to walk after she reached the six-foot drop-off, just as if she didn't know how to swim. Luckily, the children had noticed and called to Robert, who, in the water, was nearly as strong as anyone else. On shore, she shivered in a towel and turned away, while he marveled at himself: For over a week he had felt an intermittent urge to kill her, and now here he was, forced into saving her life. Had she done it to test his love?

Grace didn't know why she had done it, except that she was miserable, and when she came to the drop-off and found herself in water over her head, she simply hadn't felt like swimming. And so she plunged her toes into the muck at the bottom and held on, wondering how long she could stay under. She opened her eyes in the murky water and saw bubbles rising and felt triumphant. But then Robert arrived, and she had to suffer the indignity of being towed back to land as if she were a fish he had caught. She fought him off as soon as they reached shallow water, though she was almost too exhausted to move. Her nose and the whole inside of her face stung, and tears were streaming from her eyes. She felt humiliated too; it had been a silly thing to do. She huddled in a towel on the dock, watching blue dragonflies spin out across the water, until it was time to go home.

She and Robert didn't discuss the incident. They didn't discuss very much at all now, for fear of upsetting the balance that enabled them to go from one day to the next. Neither of them wanted to look very far into the future.

Disruptions occurred, nonetheless. Robert was even more silent than usual at the dinner table, causing Grace to be more talkative. Since the beginning of their marriage, she had considered it her duty to cheer him up. When Robert was in one of his moods, the slightest remark to him, by anyone, would call forth a dead pause and then an answer that admitted no possible response.

"How did things go today, dear?" Grace might hear herself asking. Often, then, Robert would simply look at her. Or, "As usual," he might bring himself to say. After a few seconds that seemed and perhaps were minutes, she would plunge on. "I hope Miss Everell didn't mislay anything crucial." Because Miss Everell did have her failings, and if Robert could be brought to complain about these, he could be wrenched out of the silence that held him as unbendingly as the brace that enclosed his leg.

But nothing could move him now. Though Grace told herself that he couldn't help it, his muteness was such a punishment to her that she almost felt he was using it on purpose. And yet she chattered on.

Sunday dinner at the Davenants' took place at noon, and on the day after the trip to the lake the family was seated at the table, with Mildred back in place, when Freddie made an unfortunate observation. "Gosh," he said to Clara Jane, "your hair looks repulsive. It's the ugliest thing I've ever seen."

She had left it in rags too long last night, and it was a mass of uncontrolled frizz. Mortified, she looked down at her plate.

The remark disturbed others at the table, for other reasons. The three worst words that the children could say were the ones that substituted for swearing—darn, gee, and gosh. Mildred drew a sharp breath and looked expectantly at Grace. "We don't use words like 'gosh,' in this family," Grace felt obliged to say. "You know that, Freddie."

Robert went on eating his vegetable soup. In the larger context, the word didn't seem like much of an offense. It was surely worse for Freddie to call Clara Jane's hair repulsive.

"Wouldn't it be a good idea to say something else instead?" Grace went on. "Something like 'Yippee.' Every time you feel like saying a bad word, you can say 'Yippee' instead." She looked happily around the table.

A euphemism for a euphemism? Robert wondered whether he loved Grace so much after all.

"*Yippee?*" Clara Jane looked as if she would explode.

"Why, yes." Grace was still smiling.

"A singular situation," Hal muttered. "A singular and sinister situation indeed, my dear Watson."

Hal was as bad as the rest of them, Clara Jane thought. Whenever he was uncomfortable, he turned into Sherlock Holmes. She stood up and slammed her chair against the table, sloshing soup onto the tablecloth. "Mother, that's the stupidest thing I've ever heard!" She ran out of the dining room and up the back stairs to the third floor, feeling the tears begin. She was in trouble now. She wished she could be like Hal, who hated their mother's silliness as much as she did but who didn't cry or throw things. "He's going to be my brilliant one," Grace would say when Hal made one of his cutting remarks. Why couldn't Clara Jane be brilliant?

Half an hour later Robert climbed the stairs to the girls' room. He felt responsible for what Clara Jane had said. She had said it for him.

For the first time in years he found himself thinking of Judith, his lost love. They had met as undergraduates on a chilly February morning in the hall outside the chemistry lab, both nearly late for class. They grasped the same door handle and both drew back, shocked by the contact with the metal. But their fingers had touched. "*Que gelida manina*," he almost said.

What if he and Judith had defied their parents and gone ahead with their engagement? They would at least have started out on a basis of mutual love, no matter what happened later. What would Judith have been like by now? What was she in fact like? They hadn't corresponded. When Robert and Grace were married, both of them had supposed that he was doing her a favor. He was being punished now.

Reaching the third floor, he heard his daughter sobbing behind the closed door of her room. Did she even know what she was crying about?

He didn't want to talk to her. He would make a mess of it. And yet she needed comfort, and she wouldn't get it from Grace. Clara Jane hadn't been easy with her mother since she was two years old. She had never been a cuddly child, like Mellie or Cricket. Grace said it was simply her nature, but Robert suspected it might be a defense against Grace's self-conscious motherhood and her inability to resist a good story. From the time the child learned to talk, she had been quoted and, it might seem to her, ridiculed. Grace still liked to describe Clara Jane's first smallpox vaccination and her exclamation of "No, thank you, Dr. Brown" at the sight of the approaching needle. The doctor, after remarking, "That's the politest baby I've ever seen," had gone right ahead.

It was natural for Grace to be amused by such things, but Robert could see why the children objected to her putting them in writing. If she should come to her daughter's room now to seek an apology, how much of the conversation would appear next week in print? He knocked softly at the door and heard a muffled reply. When he went in, Clara Jane, stretched out in the lower bunk, was sobbing as if she couldn't stop. "Jane," he said.

"I can't stand it," she said into the bedspread. "The things she says. Are you going to spank me?"

He was shocked. "No," he said. "No, sweet."

She, in turn, was shocked. Her father hardly ever called her pet names. But then he sat down on the edge of the bed and patted her shoulder and spoke to her as if she weren't a child. He had loved another woman once, he said, but it didn't work out, and so he had married Grace, and over the years he had come to realize what a good person she was. They hadn't intended to have a family, he said. "We were going to be two scientists. We weren't going to have children."

"Then why did you?" She looked up with a smeared face.

145

"We thought...since Grace couldn't get her degree anyway... You've heard about Professor Freundlich."

"Only about a million times." She hid her face again.

But Grace never directly blamed her professor for the loss of her career—perhaps because she didn't consider it lost. Still, her children might be more understanding if they knew how much they had cost her. "She had given up by the time he died," Robert said. "She didn't know there would be another chance." He patted Clara Jane's shoulder again.

Her sobs died down, and Robert hoped he had consoled her. He lifted the mass of fuzzy hair and kissed the back of her neck and went down to the study, not guessing that his words had rocked the earth as profoundly as what he himself had learned from Grace a few weeks before. Clara Jane had never doubted her parents' life-long mutual devotion: No matter how much they quarreled, they must be in love, simply because they were married.

She hadn't understood, either, that her own birth had put a stop to her mother's career. Clara Jane had heard about the villainous Professor Freundlich all her life, but she hadn't seen him as anything but the subject of her mother's stories. She hadn't made the connection. Without children, Grace Davenant might be studying the Trobriand Islanders she sometimes talked about. By the time she got her degree, she was already trapped. Clara Jane had had no idea.

Seeing her daughter's outraged expression as she left the table, so similar to Robert's, Grace had been dismayed. The child would never get anywhere if she couldn't stop criticizing.

Grace started up the stairs to tell her so, after she had heard Robert trudge down to the study. Mildred, probably not liking to cross through the girls' room while Clara Jane was sulking, had cleared the dining table and, with a put-upon air, was scraping the dishes. She had mentioned earlier that she must study for a calculus exam, so if she did badly on the exam, it would be Clara Jane's fault; or Grace's. But Mildred wouldn't do badly, by anyone else's standards. Last month she had scored ninety-nine on the written part of her driver's test and come home feeling like a failure because of the other one percent.

There was no sound from Clara Jane's room; perhaps she was asleep. Grace knocked faintly, hoping this was the case. Then she opened the door and called, "Clara Jane."

"What?" Clara Jane answered, sounding as if she had a cold.

So Grace went in and delivered her lecture. "I'm afraid there's somebody you remind me of," she said near the end. "I won't say who it is, but she's in our family, and she's very unhappy because she doesn't know how to get along with other people."

"I'm *not* like Auntie Mildred," Clara Jane said from under a pillow.

"Now, I didn't say who it was, but you don't want to grow up to be like her." Grace went downstairs, hoping to take over the dishwashing before Mildred finished it.

Clara Jane went on crying. She felt as if there were nothing left in the world except her brothers and her little sister and herself.

XXIII

Deceiving, Robert thought. She was deceiving me. It was a week later, and he was stripping suckers from his tomato plants. The garden blazed in the morning sunlight. The moss roses along the borders shone in half a dozen colors, and there were good-sized green tomatoes on the vines. He wondered who would look after the garden in August, when they were all supposed to go north to Copper Harbor. He hadn't been able to make concrete plans. The idea of a family trip just now was too much. Maybe he should take only Hal and Mellie, who had the worst hay fever. But he didn't care for the thought of leaving Grace behind.

He wished he could stop thinking about her altogether. Deceiving, he thought again. If he were a character in a Restoration comedy, he would be seen—however unfairly—as a figure of fun. And yet, unfortunately, there was no real question of deception. 'Betraying' was closer, or 'destroying.' If she hadn't told him, he would never have guessed.

The whole situation was more immediate than any seventeenth-century drama, though. It was taking place now, and somehow he related it to the war: He was a pilot, downed in Berlin or occupied France, captured and stoically facing interrogation until the enemy found a way to shatter his morale with unbearable news: Grace, his unquestionably faithful wife, wasn't faithful after all. They must be lying, he thought; if this were true, anything could be. He saw a uniformed German officer with a peaked cap and a riding crop that he slapped against his thigh—and maybe a monocle, like the watch crystal that Hal had squinted through in the children's spy play—breaking the news with detached curiosity and watching his face for the first sign of doubt. Grace was Robert's weak point, but he hadn't known it. He had thought so often of leaving her that it hadn't occurred to him that she could be the one to go.

Not that she had, in a literal sense. She was still there, upstairs in her half of the scratched walnut-veneer bed, probably smiling in her sleep at dreams he couldn't bear to imagine. But she wasn't the same Grace. By a process as effective as the most ingenious torture, she had become unknown.

He went into the kitchen, where he found Mildred spooning coffee grounds into the blue enameled pot that he took with him when he went camping and kept on the back of the stove when he was home. Coffee was one of the few luxuries he and Mildred indulged in. They both liked it strong and harsh, and they drank as much of it as their ration coupons would allow.

Mildred studied his face, clenching her near-sighted eyes. Ever since her return from New York, she had been giving him these searching looks. He didn't see how she could know about his problem, but something must show on his face. He had noticed, when he was shaving, that he was paler now; he frowned without intending to, and his mouth seemed never to have smiled.

Robert could smell the sweet rolls he had put into the oven to warm as he did every Sunday, in the hope of enticing the family to get up early. It never worked. Neither Grace nor the children got to the rolls before nine o'clock, when they were dried to a crisp and the frosting had run down the sides and hardened; but Robert stuck to his principles. Today, pulling a blue-painted chair away from the kitchen table and breathing the fragrance of coffee and cinnamon, he wished he could put his troubles out of his mind. Grace apparently didn't see why their lives should change. She didn't plan to leave him or the children, and she had presumably given up her lover, whoever he might be. Everything could go on as it had before.

Except that it couldn't. If only she would drop her unfamiliar mask and become simple, maddening Grace again, they could survive, but he knew this wouldn't happen.

"Poor Robert," Mildred said abruptly. "You poor boy." She had been talking about their relatives in New York, but she must have noticed that he wasn't listening. "What are you going to do about it?"

"What?" Mildred couldn't have seen into his mind. "What do you mean?"

"I don't believe in divorce, not with all those poor little children," she said. "But I must say I wouldn't blame you." Her head was trembling in the way Grace had mentioned, and her voice was tight.

"What are you talking about?" But it was obvious; Grace had said that she thought Mildred suspected.

"It's common knowledge, I'm very much afraid." She took two thick white mugs from the cupboard and poured coffee. "I can't get over it. Working right there with him in his office and then traipsing off to his apartment afterwards, as bold as you please. What in the name of goodness was she thinking of?"

He couldn't speak. Whose office? he wondered, postponing the only answer that would fit.

"Poor Robert," Mildred said. "I don't know how Hazel DeGroff found out, I'm sure I didn't tell her, how could I, but once she knows something, everybody knows it. That day at the picnic, I was so mortified. I cannot understand Grace."

Malcolm Wolfe. Was it possible? Robert got to his feet, leaving his coffee. "Wake the children up and send them to Sunday school," he said to Mildred. "Would you, please?"

Looking down at his sleeping wife, Robert noted how guileless she looked. In the last weeks she had become anxious and careworn, but in sleep her face was as peaceful as any of the children's. He recalled the worshipful way Grace used to gaze at him. In graduate school she had used his name too often, so that the sound of it irritated him and he asked her to stop. After that she barely pronounced his name at all, and several times he saw her check herself. Over the years, he had hurt her quite a lot.

When did her love for him stop? Now that her lover had become a real person, the situation was real too. Robert gazed steadily at her, willing her to wake up. "Grace," he said finally. She opened her eyes, and her face took on its expression of suffering.

He sat down on the edge of the bed. "I'm sorry, Grace. Please believe me." He didn't have to explain what he was sorry about. They had hardly spoken of anything else since his return from Pigeon River: Robert had blamed himself for the past and made promises about the future. Over and over, he had apologized.

"It has nothing to do with you," Grace said wearily, once again. "It isn't your fault."

She might not think so, but he knew it was. If he could only make her understand how much he loved her now, her devotion would have to come back. The legend of this unending devotion of hers was still so strong that he couldn't let it go; and yet at the same time, he wondered whether it had been real. "Did you really love me?" he demanded.

"Of course I did." She sat up against the headboard, bewildered by his new ferocity. "Robert, what's the matter?"

"Admit it. You were playing a part."

"No. I wasn't."

She must have been. Because what was all this about Malcolm Wolfe? "Malcolm...Wolfe," he said.

"Oh." She closed her eyes, then opened them and looked past him.

"Of all people."

Her face took on a closed expression. "Don't say that. You don't know him."

"Your lover." Robert made himself say it. He wanted to take hold of Grace's shoulders and shake her, keeping on until he forced her to feel the way she ought to feel. She was supposed to love *him*, not some sad-faced librarian. She was still here, after all—still in the room and the bed they shared in their own house; he could see the raveled lace along the top of her nightgown and the pink flowers in the material. It couldn't be too late to cancel the last three weeks. During most of his life with Grace, he had been able to make her happy by a look or a tone of voice. He had known how to keep from hurting her, or how to go ahead and do it. "Why *him*?" he asked.

"You don't know anything about him," she said, grouping her-self with Malcolm and leaving Robert out.

He looked at her obstinate face. Grace and he used to be two fish in the same tank, surrounded by the same element. Now they were separated, and he could see her only through two layers of glass, balancing in a different atmosphere. The comparison couldn't be carried too far, but clearly Malcolm was the one who shared Grace's world now. An odd fish anyway, Robert had always thought— Malcolm with his guitar and his plaintive widowerhood.

"Grace, I love you," he said, as roughly as if he were indeed shak-ing her by the shoulders. If he had spoken those same words a month ago, he wouldn't have been sure they were true, but what he felt now was complicated and passionate and deep. Surely, if he could find a way to convey this feeling, she would become herself again. More than anything, he wanted Grace to return to her adoring, timid, cliche-ridden self. He would know how to value her now.

When Robert left the bedroom, Grace was in despair. She re-membered his shocked face on the night she had let out her se-cret—as if someone (not she, never) had unexpectedly slapped him. He hadn't even wanted to know the identity of her lover; it hadn't seemed to matter. But now he knew it was Malcolm—Mildred must have told him, though Grace didn't know how she had found out— and it mattered after all. Grace would lose her job, for one thing. It had been all right for her to promise not to see her lover again (not as a lover, she qualified in her own mind) before Robert knew who they were talking about, but now it was impossible. She would have to leave the *Quarterly*, and people would speculate, and Robert would never forgive her... She couldn't imagine a fraction of the conse-quences.

There was something else she feared, which she hadn't men-tioned to either Robert or Malcolm: For the last week or so her stom-ach had felt crowded, as if she had swallowed a balloon with a small, hard pain like a stone in the exact center. It was a sensation she recognized all too well. Either the condoms hadn't worked, or she and Robert were back in their same old predicament. She imagined him beating her over the head with the budget book. "The last straw," she heard him shouting. "Don't you have *any* sense of responsibility?" And he would be perfectly right.

She couldn't call Malcolm to her rescue. He might not even want to come—not when he'd heard her latest news. His dream of a large family was only a dream, she had suspected for some time. It was all very well for him to picture the Davenant children as a band of angels, but he had never experienced their terrible constant need or the metallic smell of their bodies at the end of a summer day. Even Annabel, his beloved daughter, spent more time in his thoughts than in his apartment.

He was no more deluded than she had been, though, she knew now: Grace had thought that marriage and children had cut short her career; without them, she would be in Great Russell Street or the Museum of Natural History, drafting a brilliant anthropological article. But it wasn't true. Trying to look back honestly at her years in graduate school, she saw that she hadn't really been sure of what she could do afterwards. If she hadn't married, she would have pursued a career—she would have had to—but she had never been driven by ambition or strong, original thoughts. No matter what she told herself or anyone else, she had gone to graduate school mainly because Robert was there.

And now it was Malcolm, and she was making the same choice all over again. She had no profession, really, not as an anthropologist or a writer—or, now, as an editorial assistant. Not even as a mother. When Grace thought of the notes she had made for her book, she was ashamed. What did she know about motherhood? Her own children didn't even need her as much as she had believed they did. If she were to disappear, they would scarcely notice.

Grace curled up on the rumpled bed and put her hands over her ears. The thought of having to go through one more day—of having to roll her hair at the back of her neck and put in the bobby pins, brush her teeth, and cope with Mildred and the children and, somehow, Robert—was too much. If only she could fall asleep and never wake up. Lucky George Eliot, Florence Nightingale, Harriet Beecher Stowe. She should have tried more seriously to drown herself last week.

She dragged herself out of bed and dressed in her spotted blue playsuit and skirt and went downstairs to remove the scorched rolls from the oven and put in the pot roast for Sunday dinner.

XXIV

Clara Davenant, many years later and with a profession that gives her more authority than she usually wants, still dates most of the events in her life from a night when she was fourteen years old. That was when the real splinter of ice was driven into her heart. She imagined it was there before, when she first heard the story of the Snow Queen, but when the catastrophe came, she saw that she had been wrong.

On that night in July of 1943, Clara Jane couldn't sleep. When she was little, she had loved the bunk bed, where she could pretend to be on a ship, sailing across the ocean. It sagged now, though, and the springs sprawled against each other, making bumps and troughs. Tonight she was turning over and over, thinking that she would never get to sleep. Her back hurt, and she feared the future more than ever. The fights between her parents were worse this summer, though her mother still pretended they didn't take place. Remembering her father's revelation on the day of her tantrum, Clara Jane wondered what anyone could rely on. Something was wrong, not just in her family but in the whole world. She felt as if the war had always been there—as if she had grown up with it. She was afraid of Kamikaze pilots, and more realistically afraid of having nightmares about them.

After tossing for more than an hour, she sat up. She wasn't allowed to read after nine o'clock, and if she turned on the lamp, she would have to listen for the step of Auntie Mildred or her father. The batteries in her flashlight had run out. She wished she could work on the horror play, which they had just begun to rehearse. She planned to cut the hard words out of the Supermen's dialogue and add some lines for Nadine, who was unhappy with her part as the mute housekeeper. Clara Jane was feeling a little bit unhappy herself—a little bit violated—because her mother's current newspaper column was filled with false information about the building of the monster.

Realizing that there was a full moon, Clara Jane decided to sneak downstairs to the window seat, where enough light might shine in to let her make notes. She stole down the ladder past Mellie, who was making little snuffling noises in her sleep.

As Clara Jane walked quietly along the second-floor hall, she noticed a light under her parents' door and heard murmuring voices. There was a light downstairs too, coming from the kitchen. She reached the window seat without being caught, and closed the heavy brocade curtains behind her.

When she pulled the blackout curtains apart, she saw lights in the Applegates' windows on the other side of the driveway. A chalk-white moon shone above the roof of their house, giving nearly as much light as the sun on a foggy day: Clara Jane could see the horses' hooves and their open mouths on the upside-down wallpaper next to her, and she could make out the separate feathery branches of the upside-down trees. Quietly, she took the script of *The Blue Dragon* out of the compartment under the bench and pulled up her feet and began to write. She almost wished she'd dared to cast herself as the fair maiden, Chlorine, but she wasn't pretty enough, and besides, all Chlorine did was stand around and whimper. As the Blue Dragon, Clara Jane would be an educated monster with a blue face, who aspired to create the first monster-made monster. Her costume would be her mother's doctoral gown, and Hal, as the hero, could wear their father's wedding tuxedo and the collapsible opera hat they had found at a rummage sale. (At some point, the hat would be left on a chair and somebody would sit on it—a sure laugh.) Her imagination sped on, churning out ideas so fast that she could hardly record them. I am at the height of my powers, she thought, with the same excitement she'd felt last year when she worked out the mathematical formula.

When she had finished her notes for the play, she composed excerpts from reviews, to be quoted on posters: "'Superb!'" she wrote. "'Horrifying!!'" "'I could hardly stand it...' Brooks Itchkinson, *The New York Times*."

This is what she will remember years later, when she tries to recall the early part of that night. She must have fallen asleep then, right there on the bench. She woke from one of her Nazi nightmares: A fighter plane had been outside the window in the moonlight only a few feet away; she had seen a black swastika on each wing, against a circular white ground, as the plane roared into the driveway between the Applegates' house and her own. The grinning Oriental face of the pilot was so close that she could see his yellow teeth as he lifted a rifle. It didn't make sense, she reasoned as she forced herself awake; he wouldn't have a rifle, and if there were swastikas, he wouldn't be Japanese. But she felt terror, and she wasn't sure where she was or whether it was day or night. She heard voices close by and realized, from her cramped position and the draft against her back, that she was in the alcove on the landing behind the curtain, curled against the glass. A light still streamed through the downstairs hall, from the direction of the kitchen.

She sat up and put her bare feet to the floor; she had to get back to bed before someone discovered her. But then the conversation got louder. Her parents, in their bedroom at the top of the stairs, were arguing. She could hear them even through the closed door, and she noticed unaccustomed tones in her mother's voice. Usually when Grace argued with Robert, she sounded timid and flustered. Tonight there was a note of stubbornness, as if she were repeating the same thing over and over without listening to anything outside her own mind. "It won't do any good," she said at least twice, and then "It's too late."

Her father's voice wasn't familiar either; he didn't sound sarcastic or exasperated or critical. "Can't you *try*," Clara Jane heard him say, and then, after a silence, he began to sob. "Please, Grace."

She was stunned. Her father couldn't be crying, not her father. She drew her feet up onto the bench again and pulled the edges of the curtains together. If she tried to go up to her room, they might come out and catch her. There was the sound of a door opening in the hall above, and a sliver of light appeared under the curtains. "I mean it!" her mother's voice came clearly, with a high singing tone as if she were about to cry too. Clara Jane heard her take a deep, unsteady breath. "I know you don't believe me, Robert, but you'll see."

Slow, uneven steps came toward Clara Jane, and then she heard her father breathing on the landing, and the steps went past her, down the stairs. She wrapped her arms around her knees and held her breath. "Mildred!" her father called below her. "Where are you?" There was a click, and more light came under the curtains as the chandelier in the downstairs hall was switched on. He called again, and then she heard rapid voices further away, in the kitchen. A few seconds or minutes went by, and there were voices again from somewhere, and a muffled crash from upstairs. Clara Jane parted the curtains just enough to catch a glimpse of the bedroom, but all she could see up there was the chair that usually stood against the wall at the foot of the bed. The chair was lying on its side, with its legs sticking out from the flowered cretonne ruffle. Quickly, she pulled the curtains together, just before her father came past again—still breathing hard, laboring up the stairs. "Grace?" he called, "Mildred?" so close that Clara Jane could have put out her hand between the curtains and touched him.

Almost immediately, there was a loud cracking sound.

Clara Jane squeezed her eyes shut and covered her ears. No, she thought; no, no. "Mildred!" she heard her father shout.

More seconds or minutes went by, while Clara Jane crouched, trying to cancel out the terrible sound. Holding still, trying not even to breathe, she concentrated on reversing the action as if it were one of the movies her father brought home from the office: *Timber Harvest*, with trees tilting back onto their stumps and eggs slipping neatly up out of the pan, into the bowl, and back to their shells without out a crack showing. If she could think hard enough, it would turn out that there hadn't been anything at all: Nothing had happened.

But she needed to find her parents. She pushed the curtains apart and crept up the stairs, blinking in the light from the hall and feeling her hand tremble against the railing. Her feet were cold.

The door to the bedroom, directly ahead, was still open, and the light was on. Clara Jane went to the doorway and looked in. The chair was back in its place against the wall where it belonged. Beyond it, next to the bureau, her father was standing perfectly still and holding the gun that he kept in the drawer of the bedside table in case of burglars. He was pointing it toward the floor, as he had taught the children to do when he took them for target practice with his .22 rifle. "Grace," he said in a tragic voice. "Grace."

He looked up and saw Clara Jane and frowned. Motionless, gazing steadily at her, he said, "It was an accident." Then he looked past her, toward the hall. "Mildred," he called. "Come here. There's been an accident."

Her mother, in the blue playsuit and skirt, was lying on the bed with her face turned away. "Mother?" Clara Jane started toward her, but stopped when her mother didn't move. She saw then that Grace was in a position nobody would voluntarily stay in, sprawled on the bed with one leg twisted backward toward the floor. "Mother," she said, more loudly than before, but she didn't dare to go closer.

Then Auntie Mildred scurried in from the hall with her head and hands quivering, grasping a can of oven cleaner. "What happened?" she asked. "Robert? What's the matter?"

That was what Clara Jane remembered, and it was pretty much what she told the police when they came that night and again the next day, when she went to the station with her father and Auntie Mildred. Nobody else in the house had heard anything.

Suicide, everyone said, when of unsound mind. Grace had left a piece of paper in her typewriter—meant apparently as an explanation. It described each of her children and asked Robert to take care of them. Clara Jane, "shy and dependable but has inherited her father's quick temper," and Hal, "brilliant and manly," were particularly annoyed at their characterizations. Even now, their mother could embarrass them.

159

XXV

The next day, Clara Jane went to the police station with her father and Auntie Mildred. "Please don't make me go," she
begged him that morning in the kitchen. "I don't know what happened last night. I wasn't even there."

"You weren't?" But he had seen her, standing in the doorway of
his bedroom.

She looked at the floor. "Not when it...I was asleep."

"In your bed?" He raised his left eyebrow until she could count
five crooked parallel lines on his forehead.

"Not exactly." She studied a worn patch in the linoleum by the
sink. "I couldn't sleep."

"Where were you, then?" His voice was sharp. "Not in the hall.
You couldn't have been."

"On the landing." She couldn't keep her voice steady. "I'm sorry,
Daddy. Behind the curtain."

"And you were asleep."

She had disobeyed, and now look what had happened. He would
be perfectly right to hit her as hard as he could. "It...woke me up."
She couldn't bring herself to be more specific. "Do I have to go to
the station?"

"I'm afraid so." Her father's face looked dry and creased like
paper, and there was whitish stubble along his jaw. He seemed to
be thinking of something far away.

In the car, Clara Jane felt as if she were about to take a Latin
test without having studied the vocabulary. "What am I supposed
to say to them?" she asked her father.

"Just tell them what happened. What you remember."

But she didn't know what had happened, or even what she'd said to the police last night. She was bound to contradict herself. "I don't see why," she said. "I've already told them everything." The night before, after the ambulance took her mother away, a policeman had asked Clara Jane some questions and sent her off to bed, where she had thought she couldn't sleep but obviously had. She woke up in the morning with an aching blank space in her mind, but she could manage to hold back recollection for only a few seconds before it came flooding in.

My mother is dead. She looked at the ceiling a few feet above and sounded out the words in her mind. They felt self-important, as if she were making them up to get attention. Was this the terrible thing that she had dreaded all these years, since she was a small child? But she hadn't believed in it; she had only been scaring herself. It was July, but she was shivering, so hard that the bed was shaking. What she wanted was her mother; she wanted them to put their arms around each other, just to hug each other until everything was all right.

It wasn't over yet, though. Clara Jane's father had made this clear when he saw her standing in the doorway of the lighted bedroom. "It was an accident," he had said, as if she were entitled to an explanation, but Clara Jane, with her mother just lying there absolutely still, hadn't known what she was supposed to do or say.

Mellie was snorting hay-feverishly in the bunk below, still asleep. Someone would have to tell her and the others, but Clara Jane didn't want to be the one. She pulled the covers up and put the pillow over her head as she heard her aunt open the door of her own room and enter theirs.

So it was Auntie Mildred who broke the news and made the children's oatmeal. Mrs. Kepler arrived soon afterwards. She gasped when she heard what had happened, and then she went to lie on the couch with her feet up and a cold cloth on her head. It was a good thing she was there to stay with the other children, because Clara Jane had to go to the police station.

Auntie Mildred, in the front seat of the car, didn't speak. She just sat trying to keep her head still and twisting an embroidered handkerchief between her hands.

Clara Jane was expecting a formal interrogation, with bright lights, and armed policemen firing questions. Instead, there was just one man in a small office, with a secretary sitting in a corner. He wasn't even in uniform. He wore a gray plaid suit with a thin red stripe in the material, and he reminded her of the men who worked with her father at the Institute. Concentrating on details to keep herself from crying in front of a stranger, she made a mental note of his costume in case she wanted to use it in a play. His tie was pale yellow, with a design of red spots that looked like ladybugs. "Good morning, Clara Jane," he said, holding out his hand. "That is what you're called, isn't it?"

"No," she said daringly. "Jane." She hadn't realized she would be questioned alone, without her father and Auntie Mildred.

The man looked surprised. "Oh, pardon me," he said. "Jane. I'm Detective Lieutenant Withrow." He told her he was very sorry about what had happened to her mother and he didn't want to upset her, but there were a few things he needed to know. He asked questions for about an hour.

She admitted that she had sneaked down to the window seat late at night. "I wasn't supposed to," she said guiltily, "but I couldn't sleep."

"Sure," he said, as if it were perfectly natural. "And then what?"

"And then I did go to sleep. Not on purpose." It was important to tell the exact truth. This was much harder than giving a class report or writing dialogue for imaginary characters. "But then I woke up, and I heard my mother and father."

"They were arguing, were they?" He seemed only mildly interested.

"Oh, they always do," she said, embarrassed for them. "This was nothing different." Though it was, but surely that wouldn't matter.

"So they argued a lot, did they?" He looked sympathetic, as if he could see how much this must have upset the children.

The detective was a nice man, with his gray suit and his crinkled gray eyes in a rosy face. She was tempted to tell him all about how

162

much her parents had fought and how frightened she and the others had been, but she was too ashamed. "That's what married people do," she said nonchalantly, as if she were Nadine Applegate. "Isn't it?"

He asked whether she remembered any of the words they said last night, and she repeated the few she could recall: It had been just her father asking for something and her mother refusing. Clara Jane didn't mention the humble, pleading tone of her father's voice. "I was asleep," she kept explaining. "I don't remember."

At one point Detective Lieutenant Withrow offered her a cup of coffee, and, though flattered, she declined. The main thing he wanted to know, it seemed, was exactly when she had heard her father come up the stairs. Because she must have heard him. Was it before the shot—and if so, how long before?

Why should that matter so much? What mattered was that her mother was dead. Clara Jane could hardly remember the shot itself. At the time, she hadn't even recognized right away that that was what it was. She had heard guns in the woods before now, and she had shot at tin cans with her father's .22 rifle, but she had never heard a pistol fired indoors, and she certainly wasn't expecting to hear one last night. It was a loud, crisp sound, and what she had felt first was surprise.

"You write plays, I hear, don't you, Jane?" the detective said. "Well, let's just suppose this happened in one of your plays. There's this crippled man climbing the stairs, and—"

She interrupted, indignant for her father's sake. Besides, she didn't care for the patronizing reference to her plays. "My father isn't crippled. He can walk as well as anybody."

"Oh, really?" Detective Lieutenant Withrow lifted his thick gray eyebrows in apparent puzzlement. "Well, sure," he said slowly. "So he could climb the stairs as fast as anybody else. Is that really so, Jane?"

"Of course." Even if it wasn't quite true, her father wanted people to think it was. "Of course he could."

"So maybe he was already upstairs by the time you heard the shot." His voice sounded casual, but he was watching her face.

She hesitated, avoiding his eyes. "I don't know." This was getting complicated. She was trying to obey her father and just tell what had happened, but that wasn't as easy as it sounded.

"And then what did you do, Jane?" the detective asked. "After you heard the shot."

"Nothing, at first. I was too…" She probably should have done something, but she hadn't. She hadn't been able to move. "But then I went upstairs to the bedroom."

"And what did you see there?"

"My mother. But…" She couldn't talk for a few seconds. She took a breath. "And my father." She didn't want to say that he'd been holding the gun.

"Did he say anything?"

"I don't think so." Her father had said her mother's name at least twice, but she couldn't bring herself to mention that; it was too private. Then she remembered. "'It was an accident.' That's what he said."

"I see," the detective said, drawing out the words and still watching her. "You're sure of that."

"Of course." As if anybody wouldn't remember a thing like that.

"'It was an accident,'" he repeated slowly. "Why would he say that, I wonder?"

"Because that's what it was." Surely that was obvious. She wished she could close her eyes and stop listening to his questions and her own answers.

He raised his thick eyebrows again. "You don't think your mother shot herself? Is that what you mean?"

"Not on purpose. She wouldn't do that." Clara Jane didn't know why people talked about keeping a stiff upper lip; it was the lower one she always had trouble with. The whole thing last night had been an accident. Her father would give the police the details. "Maybe my mother thought she heard a burglar," she improvised. After all, that was why her father had the gun. "And maybe she tripped and the gun just went off." In one of her plays, would such a thing have happened? Not unless she wanted the audience to laugh, but that was because they were plays; she had already learned that actions on the stage have to be made more believable than real life. "Or it was really a burglar, and he got away. Person or persons unknown," she mumbled, recalling the expression from her reading.

"What was that?" Detective Lieutenant Withrow leaned toward her.

Feeling foolish, she repeated the phrase.

"Oh?" He stroked his chin and looked as puzzled as ever. "I see."

They let her go finally, and she rode home in the Buick with her mind racing. The detective had brought up ideas she hadn't anticipated, and she was afraid her responses might somehow have harmed both of her parents. But at least it was over.

She found the other children in Hal's room, huddled on the oval braided rug while he read to them from *The Jungle Book*. Mellie and Cricket were crying, and Freddie stared at the floor, his elbows propped on his knees. "Hi," Clara Jane said from the doorway, feeling awkward. "Do you want me to read now?"

"No, thank you." Hal let the book fall. "What happened?"

"Just now? At the police station?" Though she didn't think that was all he meant.

Freddie looked up. "Yeah. Did they give you the third degree?"

"Shut up," Hal said, and Mellie looked shocked; the children weren't allowed to say that. "I mean last night." Hal looked at Clara Jane. "Were you really there?"

She sat down on the edge of the bed. "No. I don't know anything." But she had been there. And she hadn't prevented it.

She told them as much as she could about the night before, and she told them about the police station and the Detective Lieutenant's plaid suit and the little bugs on his tie and how he had offered her a cup of coffee. They looked at her in silence, and then Mellie said, "A bad guy did it. He snuck in and shot my mother."

"Yeah," Freddie put in. "And we're gonna get him."

"Yeah," Cricket chirped. "Yeah!"

Clara Jane looked at them in despair and ran upstairs to her room.

After a miserable supper from which Auntie Mildred was missing with a headache, Clara Jane tried to escape again, but in the upstairs hall Hal intercepted her. "What really happened?" He stood in the doorway of his bedroom with swollen eyelids and a streaked red face.

"I told you. I don't know." But she knew how he felt. She, too, desperately needed to know the truth.

"Auntie Mildred said she shot herself," he muttered.

"No." She still couldn't believe that. "It was an accident. Daddy said it was." They both knew that their father wouldn't lie. She put her arms around Hal's shoulders, and they stood together in the doorway, crying.

All the children cried, off and on, for weeks. Even four-year-old Cricket, who could still retreat cheerfully to his room to build cities out of colored blocks, often ran to Clara Jane and asked to be rocked or to be held up to rub his face against Muledeer's rough, comforting nose. The children blamed Grace, but they blamed themselves as well: If only they hadn't quarreled so much and if they had kept their rooms neater. Clara Jane explained to the others that nothing was their fault; she knew, though she didn't tell them, that any blame was hers. If she didn't exist, her mother would be a famous anthropologist and still alive; after Grace had had one child, any number of others couldn't make a difference.

Clara Jane knew this was unreasonable. After all, she hadn't been born on purpose. Still, she couldn't forget what her father had told her.

They had to abandon *The Blue Dragon*, of course. Auntie Mildred, two days after Grace's death, was shocked to discover Hal and Freddie spreading out their monster materials in the front hall. The big silver box was ready to be wired, and electric cords and radio tubes cluttered the floor. What did they think they were doing? How could they be so callous? Robert told them he saw why they wanted to go on with the play, but it wasn't a good idea. And he limped to the study and closed the door. The boys reluctantly put away their equipment and went upstairs to read. They couldn't play outside because of all the people who came by and stared.

Clara Jane's plays seemed as childish to her now as the doll village. She shut her scripts away in the window seat and began to read *Henry Esmond*, which was in small type, and ponderous enough to require her full attention.

It was Aunt Eleanor who came to the family's rescue. Grace's energetic blue-eyed sister arrived from Ohio, the back seat of her car loaded with peaches and Fig Newtons and licorice and art supplies. There were packages of colored paper and thick rough manila paper, silver-tipped sticks of charcoal, jars of poster paint, and a box of pastels in a hundred and twenty-four colors. Aunt Eleanor hugged the children and gave them drawing assignments and awarded prizes to everybody.

She also organized the funeral—conferring with the minister, the organist, and the undertaker. Because there did have to be a funeral, she insisted, even if neither Robert nor Mildred wanted anything to do with it. Grace hadn't believed in such things, Robert protested, and the minister hadn't even known her by sight. It didn't matter what Grace had believed, Eleanor said. Her parents would arrive soon, to stay with her at the Michigan League, and they needed a ceremony. Robert allowed her to go ahead.

During that week, with the telephone ringing too much and people dawdling past the house or bringing cakes and casseroles, the children felt quarantined. This was the way it had been when they'd had measles or chicken pox or whooping cough, with a sign on the front door; there was the same sense of disgrace. The children didn't know very many people, but it seemed that everyone in town knew them. Strangers came with brownies and toll-house cookies. Mrs. Waterhouse, whom the children hadn't seen since they moved, appeared in her crimson hat, with a tin of runny fudge. "I saved my sugar coupons," she said, weeping. "Your mother was a lovely lady." Even Mrs. DeGroff showed up in a forest-green Department of Conservation car, bearing a Pyrex dish of Spanish rice.

Clara Jane hated the people who came to stare, and she hated to hear her brothers gleefully opening containers to explore each day's loot. Whenever the doorbell rang, she wanted to hide, but Auntie Mildred had assigned her the job of answering it and making a list of the donors for thank-you notes. Still, this was the first time the children had tasted so many delicacies. They used to suspect that other people's mothers were better cooks than their own, and now they had proof.

XXVI

The several hundred people who attended Grace Davenant's funeral could hardly bear the sight of the sober children—the boys in hastily assembled dark suits and the girls in their outgrown navy-blue sailor dresses. The girls wore wide-brimmed straw hats, though they rejected the gloves Auntie Mildred tried to force on them. They all sat with their father and aunts and grandparents in a graduated row in the front pew of the First Methodist Episcopal Church, displaying well-behaved grief. Their awareness of being part of a performance overshadowed their genuine sorrow—but then, they were used to performances.

Robert didn't fare so well. He shouldn't have yielded to Eleanor about the funeral, he thought as he sat, surrounded by colleagues and hunting companions, under the tall red-and-blue windows. He tried to keep his face as impassive as wood while the minister droned on about motherhood. "This gifted woman, who chose to bestow her gifts upon her husband and family..." He seemed not to have known anything about Grace beyond her public persona. Though how could he? She had projected herself as a devoted wife and mother, and that was the way everybody thought of her.

Or almost everybody. Malcolm Wolfe had haunted Robert's mind for what seemed like forever, but Robert had been trying not to think about him directly. Even the sight of an issue of the *Michigan Science Quarterly*, in a bookshelf at the Institute or on a table at home, was a blow. Now, in church, Robert deliberately made himself think of Malcolm and found that he almost felt pity. Malcolm hadn't intended to cause pain, and he had loved Grace.

Robert concentrated on keeping his face still and limping as little as possible when he walked up the aisle of the church with his family after the playing of "Sheep May Safely Graze." The ragweed season was beginning, but he wasn't sure that his hay fever would be held entirely accountable for his brimming eyes, and he didn't want to weep in public. The quality of the service didn't matter, as Eleanor said; there had been a service, and it was over.

The family, avoiding the use of their beloved Buick, drove home in friends' cars solicited through tactful phone calls from Eleanor. She warmed up two of the donated casseroles for supper and persuaded the children to join her in singing around the piano, hoping to bring their mourning to an end. "To fill the air with joy and gladness," they sang without thinking about the words. "Funiculi, funicula."

For Robert, the ceremony wasn't the end of anything. He knew that the police weren't satisfied with his account of Grace's death, nor with the note she had left in the typewriter. She hadn't signed it, for one thing, and it was worded in an odd way, with no mention of a decision to kill herself—just those descriptions of the children and the admonition to Robert to take care of them, almost like notes for one of her columns. Why should she describe them to their own father, and why should she imagine he might not care for them?

Robert could see why the police were confused. They hadn't known Grace, with her habit of summing people up. She had characterized everyone she knew, but especially her children. This habit had grown partly out of her method of composing "Notes on a Modern Family," but even more, it stemmed from her good intentions as a mother. She had wanted to love her children completely, and this constant analysis was a way of proving her love. Robert wasn't sure the police could understand this.

There was also some uncertainty about what exactly had happened before the shot was fired. Robert told Lieutenant Withrow that he and Grace had been talking in the bedroom and that she had expressed unhappiness. Some people might consider it a quarrel, he admitted—but not over anything in particular. Grace had become hysterical. When she mentioned a wish to die, he had gone downstairs to get his sister, who might help to calm her down. No, Grace hadn't actually threatened to kill herself, or he wouldn't have left her alone. On his way back upstairs after speaking to Mildred, he had heard the shot, and when he reached the bedroom he had found Grace lying on the bed, the gun in her hand and a wound behind her right ear. There was very little blood.

And then he had picked up the gun, the detective said. Why had he done that?

To get it away from her, Robert supposed, because it was dangerous. He nearly laughed then, bitterly, but stopped himself; this was no time for irony. After that, he said, he had called to his sister, who was already on her way upstairs from the kitchen. Clara Jane had appeared then, and, immediately afterwards, Mildred.

Mildred, questioned separately, brought up the name of Malcolm Wolfe, and Robert was forced to give more details. Malcolm must have been brought in for questioning after that, but Robert hoped that his role in the tragedy wouldn't be made public. Why should Grace's reputation and the children's future be unnecessarily stained?

His sister's account wasn't substantially different from his own, he gathered. She had been in the kitchen, preparing to clean the oven, when she had heard voices raised upstairs. Then Robert had appeared, obviously distraught, and asked her to come up to the bedroom. He had left the kitchen, and she had heard the shot and then his voice, calling her. She had run upstairs, to find Grace on the bed and Robert standing near her with the gun. Clara Jane was there too, for some reason; she ought to have been asleep hours before. She, Mildred, had gone downstairs then to call the police.

The involvement of his daughter caused Robert almost as much pain as anything else. Why should his poor little girl not only have to witness such a terrible thing, but also to face questions about it? He would never forget her shocked eyes as she stood in the bedroom doorway, any more than he would forget his own shock at seeing her there. One of his first feelings, on realizing what had happened, had been relief at the thought that his children would be spared the sight. They were all asleep, he was just thinking, and then Clara Jane appeared. Robert had been so careful to shield his children from ordinary everyday things like cheap radio programs and popular music, and yet he hadn't been able to protect them from far greater damage.

He tried to make plans. The entire month of August and the ragweed season had to be lived through before the children could be deposited in school and kept busy enough to distract them. When friends asked what they could do to help, he wished he could request them to spirit the children away for a year or two. His company couldn't be good for them. He still spent most of his waking time thinking about Grace, and at night he dreamed about her; she turned away from him toward a shadowy figure who was almost certainly Malcolm Wolfe; or—worse—she put her arms around Robert and promised never to leave him. He woke from these last dreams to disappointment that lasted most of the day.

Family meals were especially hard. Without Grace to keep the conversation going, there was silence, interrupted only by allergic sniffles or by Mildred's criticisms of the children's table manners. She didn't care for the way they slurped noodles from the rims of their soup bowls or stretched their toasted cheese sandwiches apart to make telephone wires, and she hadn't given up on trying to make them chew their milk. Robert suspected that some of her objections, as well as the children's misbehavior, occurred to fill conversational gaps. He himself, between fits of sneezing, could barely bring himself to speak. He worried about Clara Jane, who had almost given up eating. She was more helpful than before, setting the table or clearing it and washing dishes without being asked; she worked in the garden, fiercely hoeing and yanking out weeds as if they were enemies; but she scarcely said a word.

Grace's parents and her sister Eleanor stayed on at the Michigan League for a few days, but nobody could think of a way to help Robert until Eleanor suggested that she take Clara Jane home with her for the rest of the summer. He and Mildred could go with the younger children to the Upper Peninsula, where they would at least breathe more easily.

When Clara Jane was younger, she had had fantasies of running away to live with her Aunt Eleanor, who, with her pointed features and bright blue eyes and bright red lipstick, was the closest thing to a fairy godmother she could imagine. Once, during a quarrel with her mother, Clara Jane had mentioned this dream, and her mother had burst out laughing. Eleanor, she said, might be artistic, but like all artists, she was unreliable. Once when the sisters were small, they had owned identical dresses and Eleanor had put on Grace's dress by mistake and gone off early to school. Grace would never forget the humiliation of appearing in class in Eleanor's dress, which was four inches too short. To Clara Jane's inquiry about why Grace hadn't worn a different dress, her mother had said, "But we always wore those dresses together."

As an oldest child herself, Clara Jane could sympathize, but she did love Aunt Eleanor. She looked forward to a month in the Ohio town where her aunt taught art in the public schools. She and Aunt Eleanor would lead a bohemian life together, and become so attached that she'd never have to go home.

When they got to Ohio, Clara Jane was surprised to find that her aunt didn't live in a studio filled with easels and canvases, with a lofty ceiling and a skylight. She had a second-story apartment in a normal-looking yellow clapboard house on a respectable street with trees and sidewalks. She kept her easels and other painting supplies in the garage, along with a potter's wheel, several half-finished sculptures, and a vat of damp clay. The walls of the garage were hung with marionettes and hundreds of shellacked papier-mache masks. On the first day, Aunt Eleanor put Clara Jane to work sorting supplies to find out what she had to order before the school year began. Her aunt, Clara Jane realized, wasn't so much an artist as an art teacher, like Miss Andrews at her own school. Her mother would have been surprised.

At Aunt Eleanor's, Clara Jane was as sad as before, but at least she was somewhere new, and she didn't have to do anything about other people's sadness. She was allowed to take long baths and to wash her hair as often as she wanted, with real shampoo instead of soap and vinegar. She wouldn't need to curl it, Aunt Eleanor said, if it were shorter and she washed it often enough. One day she took her niece to a beauty parlor and had her hair cut to a level an inch or so below her chin, and Clara Jane was surprised to find that it turned up naturally on the ends.

Aunt Eleanor bought her an embroidered peasant blouse with puffed sleeves, a broomstick skirt with blue and yellow flowers, a baggy red sweater, a pair of gray wool slacks and a matching jacket and skirt, and white socks and saddle shoes. She also insisted on buying two white cotton slips and three brassieres that made Clara Jane feel strangled, though her aunt promised she would get used to them. Aunt Eleanor pulled down piles of art books from her shelves, and got out stacks of phonograph records. Clara Jane was reminded of her babysitting experience at the Moreaus' house, when she had seen unfamiliar books and magazines and been exposed to a foreign language for the first time. She looked through pages of Raphael madonnas and Dutch genre paintings and Impressionist landscapes, and she tried to like the Picassos that she knew her mother would have sneered at. When Aunt Eleanor put records on the phonograph, Clara Jane was shocked to find that they were often jazz. Her aunt had a ukelele and a big silver saxophone, and sometimes she played along with the records.

Her aunt also, to Clara Jane's greater surprise, turned out to have a boyfriend even though she was thirty-seven years old. He was a carpenter, and his name was Rocky, and he had escaped the draft because of a bad knee. He had met Eleanor, he said, in an evening art class she was teaching. He was the only man in the class, but that didn't bother him. He painted tiny, detailed still-lifes of wild flowers, and Clara Jane thought they were pretty good.

Rocky had rough brown hair and ears like handles and a red face, and he smiled a lot. Clara Jane was afraid of him until she realized he was just friendly and not making fun of her. He called her "kid." "Hiya, kid, what's up?" he would say when he came into the house and found her on the floor, surrounded by books and records. Then Aunt Eleanor would make an omelet or spaghetti, and he would make a salad. After supper all three of them would sit on the couch while he smoked his pipe and Clara Jane looked at more pictures, and Aunt Eleanor, wearing a black kimono with red and white zig-zags, put her feet on the coffee table and played mournful tunes on her saxophone.

They weren't really cheerful during these days, but they were comfortable with each other. For the first time Clara Jane could remember, she was the youngest person in a household.

One day Aunt Eleanor offered to take her niece to see *Now, Voyager*, with Bette Davis. Clara Jane, recalling her experience with *The Letter* and strep throat, felt apprehensive, but Aunt Eleanor said the movie was reputed to be a nice one, with a plot rather like *Cinderella*. However, sure enough, before Bette could change from dowdy to glamorous and captivate Paul Henreid, Clara Jane's eyes began to ache and an unmistakable pain filled her throat. She had to stay in bed for two weeks, with sulfa drugs that made it hard to lift her hands two inches off the bedspread.

She didn't entirely mind, though. Aunt Eleanor brought grape juice and ginger ale with a straw and read aloud from *The Hunchback of Notre Dame* in a stilted translation. Being sick made it less humiliating to cry; Clara Jane could always say it was because her throat hurt. Sometimes Aunt Eleanor cried too, though she didn't have the same excuse. Clara Jane was distressed by her aunt's overflowing eyes and the wobbly pink look of her face. Her mother, to her knowledge, had cried only once, when she'd gotten a parking ticket in the lot behind the courthouse and had to face their father afterwards.

But Clara Jane, lying in her aunt's brass bed with a sore throat, didn't want to think about her mother.

One night at the end of August when she was nearly well, there was a long-distance telephone call from her father. She was alarmed when she realized who her aunt was talking to, and she was more alarmed by the expression on Aunt Eleanor's face. "It's nothing to worry about," her aunt said as she came into the living room where Clara Jane was stretched on the floor with a book of Degas dancers, "but your father thinks you ought to come home."

It *was* something to worry about, Clara Jane learned: The police were conducting inquiries into her mother's death, and they wanted to talk to her again.

"But I already told them," she said as her voice broke and tears ran down her cheeks. "I told them all about it."

"I know you did," her aunt said, beginning to cry herself. Rocky wasn't there, so they didn't have to be brave. Aunt Eleanor's eyes looked even bluer with tears in them, and this time Clara Jane was grateful to see how upset she was; Auntie Mildred would only have told her to stop being a baby. But crying didn't do any good, and the next day, with more tears, they packed the car and drove back to Michigan.

XXVII

The house looked smaller when Clara Jane walked into the front hall with her suitcase full of new clothes, and the wallpaper was less amusing. She had never been away from the other children for so long, and she felt awkward when all four of them appeared in the dining-room doorway and stopped in a clump. Their eyes, the deep-set Davenant eyes that made people spot family members at once, seemed to be judging her. "Boy," Freddie said uncertainly, "does your hair look strange."

Hal punched him, but Clara Jane knew her hair was all right. Still, she was uneasily conscious of her embroidered blouse and her new flowered skirt. The others had on their same old faded overalls and shrunken shirts. Probably nothing about them was different from before, but they looked pathetic, like orphans. Mellie came further into the hall and inspected Clara Jane's clothes. "You're spoiled," she announced. "Just the way Auntie Mildred said."

At supper the house and Clara Jane's family gradually stopped being strange, but she still felt anxious, and afterwards her father asked her to come up to the study and sit down.

He looked even more unhealthy than after the funeral. The lines between his nose and mouth were deeper, and there were gray semicircles under his eyes. He sat down in his desk chair and took off his glasses and rubbed the bridge of his nose.

Robert wasn't sure what to say. He had taught his children always to tell as much of the truth as they knew, but he hadn't visualized a situation in which truth could lead to misunderstanding and straight on to disaster. His whole future might depend on his daughter now, but he mustn't tell her so; she was frightened enough already, he could see from the way she was clenching her fists against her knees. "You know Mr. Staebler," he finally said.

She nodded. Mr. Staebler was the family lawyer, chosen by Grace because he was a Methodist and hard of hearing. He had helped Robert and Grace to draw up their wills and to buy the house. Clara Jane didn't like talking to him because she had to repeat nearly everything she said.

"He'd like to see you," her father said.

"What about?" Clara Jane had imagined another conversation with Detective Lieutenant Withrow, in which both of them would say the same things they'd said before. "I thought it was the police," she said. "And besides, I already told them."

"Of course you did; I know that. But I suppose they want to know something more." Robert didn't want to frighten her, and he mustn't try to influence her. "Mr. Staebler just wants to talk to you for a little while first, and then he'll be with you when you see the police. There's nothing to be afraid of." How Robert wished that Clara Jane had been safely asleep in her bunk on the third floor that night. It was where she ought to have been, as Mildred kept pointing out. They would see Dave Staebler on the following day, and go to the police station afterward.

Mr. Staebler's hearing aid wasn't working any better than it ever had. It kept making squealing noises, and he leaned forward and said, "What? What? Speak up," whenever Clara Jane answered one of his questions. She was reminded of the wallpaper in the front hall; why did her parents always hire people for the wrong reasons? Eventually, however, he took his microphone out of his pocket and set it on the desk between them and was able to hear most of what she said.

He asked her to tell him everything she remembered about the night her mother had died, even if it was something that might hurt somebody else.

She didn't see how something she remembered could hurt anybody. The one who had hurt them all—who had gone away and left them in this mess—was her mother. The back of Clara Jane's throat felt cramped. So this was what happened when people killed themselves: They just disappeared without explaining anything, and other people were left to figure out why. She hadn't realized that death was so complicated. She told Mr. Staebler as much as she could remember, but it was no more than she had told the police. "Don't try to protect anybody," he said several times. The whole family ought to have been protected, she thought, but it was too late.

She mustn't say anything to the police that she wasn't sure was true, Mr. Staebler told her. If she didn't know the meaning of a question, she should ask them to explain. She should think for as long as she needed to, and if she didn't know something, she should say so. She mustn't let herself be talked into anything, though he would do his best to prevent that. That was why he would be there.

So that was why. She had been frightened last night when her father mentioned Mr. Staebler. People who needed lawyers for anything but making wills or deals were usually criminals, she had thought. On top of anger at her mother, she felt confusion and a stupefying guilt. Maybe she deserved what was happening.

In the station with Mr. Staebler and Detective Lieutenant Withrow, she went through the same questions as before, giving pretty much the same answers. The detective, in a dark blue pinstripe suit this time, sounded stern when he got to the question about whether her father had really finished climbing the stairs by the time she heard the shot. He seemed to doubt what she had said to him before, and by now she didn't know whether it was true or not. She hadn't been paying attention to how fast her father was going upstairs; she had just concentrated on keeping her feet out of sight on the window seat, trying not to hear the voices, and hoping she could get to her room before she was caught. "Are you sure he was upstairs by then, Jane?" the detective repeated. "Think carefully. When did you hear him pass you?"

Her father was leaning forward in his chair, watching her face. She recalled Mr. Staebler's instructions about not saying anything she wasn't sure of. But her father hated people to think he was a cripple. "I think so," she said, and felt her face getting hot.

"You think he was upstairs?" Detective Withrow asked.

Mr. Staebler took out his microphone. "Are you sure of that, Clara Jane?" he said sharply.

"No," she admitted with an apologetic glance at her father, "I don't remember."

And then the detective asked what her father had said when she came into the bedroom.

"'It was an accident,'" she muttered.

"What?" Mr. Staebler looked at her sharply. "What was that? Speak up."

She said the words again, and he looked surprised. She had forgotten to tell him this before. "And it *was* an accident," she said. "Obviously."

"You couldn't know that, though, could you, Jane?" the detective said, and she was discouraged. No matter what she said, it wouldn't change whatever he was thinking.

"This whole thing is so stupid," she said coolly to her father in the car on the way home. "Why do they need to know so much when it's all over anyway?"

"I don't know," he said.

And that was all, the children thought, though they worried. School was about to start, and they would have to face outsiders. Over the years the family had grown used to being pointed at, but now, finally, there was a reason. If their mother had simply died, they would have been objects only of interest or compassion. But she had killed herself. There had been blood, and a gun. They wished, as Mellie said with her blue eyes streaming, that they could go to sleep for a hundred years and wake up after everyone had forgotten.

Malcolm Wolfe moved away from town that fall. It seemed that for some time he had been considering an offer from the University of Chicago, and he had finally decided to accept it. Everyone was sorry to see him go, though of course they could understand that he would want to be near his daughter. Annabel might live with him again, he said.

Malcolm hadn't been sure he would survive that summer. He was stunned to find that so strong and pure a love could lead to destruction, and it was the shock of this discovery, almost as much as Grace's actual death, that weighed him down. His interview with the police was an ordeal, unlike any he had ever faced. Nobody came out and blamed him for Grace's death, but they didn't need to; he felt entirely responsible. How could he have led her into a position from which there was no escape but this? He would have been tempted to follow her example if he didn't have Annabel to think of. He wished there were a way to atone to Robert for the damage he had done. As it was, he didn't dare even to send a message of sympathy, and he left town in September with a sense of incompletion and despair.

Robert Davenant was relieved at the news of Malcolm's departure. He had wondered if he should move his own family—but concluded that it might be more traumatic for the children to be uprooted than to stay in the house where their mother had died. The town was so crowded with defense workers that he doubted he could find another place there, and good jobs elsewhere were hard to find. He must simply take the best possible care of his children and help them to forget.

Searching for a better understanding of his wife, he went through her papers—letters, college and graduate school notes, her thesis and a few uncompleted articles, and then the clippings of her newspaper column. There was, too, a thick folder of notes, labeled "On Motherhood: A Meditation," which seemed to have been written recently. He thought first that he should destroy most of these things, but that seemed wrong; the children might want to see them someday. He did throw out a few of the most sentimental columns—the ones that didn't show Grace at her best—but he put all the other papers into a collapsible file and placed it at the back of a filing cabinet.

There were no love letters; she and Malcolm had been scrupu-
lous about not putting anything in writing. They hadn't meant to
disrupt her marriage, Robert was sure by now. But they had been
careless. He couldn't forgive them for that.

XXVIII

The Allies invaded Sicily in the summer of 1943, and Mussolini was ousted. It finally seemed possible that the war wouldn't go on forever.

Clara Jane, in tenth grade that fall, was relieved to find that with the transition to senior high, her classmates had grown more civilized. They didn't know what to say about her trouble, so they didn't say anything. However, she couldn't escape all consequences: She barely avoided being clasped to the bosom of Miss Pettibone's flesh-colored dress. Aunt Eleanor's letters, with comic drawings in the margins, were more comforting. Clara Jane was taking first-year French, which, maybe because she had heard the Moreau family speak the language, came as easily as if she were remembering it from a former existence. Geometry was easy too, and English wasn't bad, though there was a lot of poetry.

She tried to put her mother out of her mind, but one scene kept creeping in, however hard she pushed it back: When she was three or four years old, she had been waiting at the bottom of the staircase, next to the newel post, to go upstairs with her mother. Clara Jane was going to hold the railing with her left hand, and her mother would take her other hand, and they would climb the stairs together. She was sitting there waiting, watching bright flecks of dust in the sunlight from the hall window. She was wearing a white butterfly hair ribbon and a green flowered dress with a big white collar, and she could see her ribbed white stockings and high shoes; she must have been very young.

But then she heard her mother calling her from upstairs. Her mother was already up there; somehow she had slipped past. Clara Jane broke into hopeless tears and was too ashamed to explain why.

She hadn't thought about this since it happened, but now it kept coming back.

If the Davenants had supposed their worst troubles were over, they were wrong. The police, it turned out, weren't convinced that Grace had killed herself; Robert hadn't volunteered information about her love affair but had then admitted that he had known about it. Motive might not indicate guilt, but it was certainly cause for suspicion. And his reputation for a quick temper was confirmed by Grace's reference, in her typewritten note, to her daughter's hereditary rages.

The only two witnesses to Grace's death were prejudiced in Robert's favor—and, furthermore, gave contradictory versions of what had happened: His sister, Mildred Davenant, claimed that Robert had barely left the kitchen when the shot was fired; with his handicap, she insisted, he wouldn't have been able to reach the bedroom by that time. His daughter Jane, on the other hand, said that he could climb stairs quickly. And while she might be overstating her father's agility, she wasn't sure when the shot had occurred. Jane also had heard her parents quarreling.

If it was indeed Grace who had fired the shot, was it certain that Robert, when he went downstairs, hadn't been aware of her intention? He admitted that she had told him she wanted to die. And where was the gun at this time? Still in the drawer of the bedside table? Possibly. Still unloaded? Clearly not. If Robert was to be believed, Grace must have taken out the gun, loaded it, and hidden it nearby—maybe under a pillow—before the argument had started. She must also have written that peculiar note. (They had confirmed that she had written it, since only her fingerprints were on the paper or the typewriter keys. What they weren't sure of was that it was a suicide note.) The wound itself, occurring on the right side of the head of a right-handed person, from a weapon held close to the skin, was consistent with suicide; but someone else could have inflicted it.

There was also the fact that Robert had the gun in his hand when Clara Jane entered the bedroom. Had he taken it from Grace? If so, why?

Too many questions still remained. In December of 1943, Robert Davenant was notified that a preliminary examination would be held in the Justice of the Peace Court to determine whether a crime had been committed and, if so, whether there was probable cause to believe that he had committed it. If the answer to both questions was affirmative, Robert would be bound over to the Circuit Court for trial.

Robert was horrified. Were they talking about murder? he asked his lawyer; they couldn't be serious. Yes, Dave Staebler said, they were, but they didn't have enough evidence to support even a preliminary examination. The case would be dismissed on the first day.

After Robert's initial feeling of shock, his first instinct told him that he needed a more experienced lawyer, but he decided to stay with Dave after all. For one thing, Clara Jane might be testifying, and he didn't want her to have to get used to one more person. Wryly, he reflected that it was loyalty to Grace—who had chosen their lawyer—that had made him call Dave in the first place. Maybe it was time he gave up being loyal to someone who had wronged him so much. Robert was feeling more furious with Grace all the time. She had had no right to cause so much pain to so many people, simply because she couldn't control her feelings. He was angry with himself too, for having married her without enough love, but he no longer felt entitled to all of the blame.

Back at home after talking with Dave, Robert grouped the children around the dining table and explained carefully that the police were still trying to discover what had happened on that night last summer. Since no one but Grace had been there, this was difficult. He didn't tell them what the police suspected, though he feared they would find out soon enough. Mildred was in her room with one of her headaches just then, and he doubted that she would provide much comfort to the children in the weeks to come. Perhaps, he suggested, they'd like to visit their grandparents. Grace's parents had offered to take the young Davenants during the proceedings, which were luckily scheduled for the latter part of Christmas vacation. Robert didn't know what his in-laws thought of him at this point, but they did want to help, and Grace's father had offered to pay for counsel.

The children were glad to hear about the plan, though they expressed scorn for the police. "What could one expect from the blockheads at Scotland Yard?" Hal scoffed.

Clara Jane, assuming that she was included in her grandparents' invitation, ventured to ask whether she could visit Aunt Eleanor instead. No, Robert told her, she must stay at home. She would have to testify.

"I can't," she said, and tears came into her eyes, as they were doing so often now. She couldn't go through all that again. She'd thought so much about it and answered so many questions that she hardly remembered what she had said or even what had happened. She would contradict herself, and that would be perjury, and she would be sent to jail. She felt the splinter of ice in her heart, sharp and cold.

When the time came, Clara Jane helped her brothers and sister to pack, and she rode with them in the black Buick to the train station and saw them off in Hal's custody, feeling as if she were holding her breath the whole time.

On the way home from the railroad station, sitting in the front seat beside her father, she was rigid with apprehension. He sighed several times, but he didn't say anything. Finally she said in a small voice, "I don't know anything more to tell them."

"I know, sweet." There were things Robert ought to prepare her for. He was afraid of what she might hear in court—not only about the reason for the examination, but about her mother and Malcolm Wolfe. The prosecuting attorney would call Malcolm as a witness, Dave had guessed. This could actually work to Robert's advantage, if it could be shown that the affair had driven Grace to suicide. Something else that would come out was that she had been two months pregnant. This last fact had been discovered in the autopsy and had shocked Robert; he had had no idea, though he supposed that Grace had known.

This would all be revealed in the hearing, some of it while Clara Jane was there, and he didn't want her to be taken by surprise. "Your mother," he began, glancing over at her in the car, "was a very loving person." He could see only the side of his daughter's face, behind a curtain of sleek golden-brown hair, as she looked out of the side window.

"Oh, really?" she said. She was surprised to hear him talking about Grace, whom he had scarcely mentioned since her death. She was surprised, too, by what he had said. Her mother had been much too busy and too critical to fit into her idea of a loving person. But maybe her father only meant that Grace had loved him. This was probably true, and if it wasn't, Clara Jane shouldn't tell him so. "She loved *you*, anyway," she managed to say, and turned to see him looking at her searchingly.

"Do you think so?" he asked.

"Of course," she said. Because really, it was true.

"But she loved—other people too," he said.

What people? Grace's parents? The children? Clara Jane didn't believe her mother had loved any of them as much as she'd pretended to, but it would be wrong to say so. She was silent.

"Has anyone... Have you heard anything?" he asked her. "In school, or..."

She shook her head and looked down at the seat, rubbing her thumb back and forth over the rough gray upholstery. They were almost home.

Robert couldn't bring himself to mention Malcolm Wolfe by name, but he hoped he'd prepared his daughter for a little of what she might find out. He didn't know how to talk or even think about Grace. She had laughed at his romanticism, but it seemed to him that she hadn't behaved very sensibly herself. All her life, she had seized any opportunity for self-destruction. When he stopped the car in the driveway, he turned and touched Clara Jane's arm. "Jane," he said. "I would never have harmed your mother. Never. You know that, don't you?"

"Yes." But she didn't know why he'd said it.

Clara Jane learned a little more from Auntie Mildred, who was sitting with Mrs. Kepler in the kitchen when she came in the back door. "I never would of guessed in a million years," Mrs. Kepler was saying. "Mrs. Davenant was so wrapped up in those children, I wouldn't of thought she had time for those kind of goings-on." Her mouth had an eerie gleam, from the Mercurochrome. "Oops." She rolled her eyes toward Auntie Mildred. "Little pitchers."

"Never mind," Auntie Mildred said. "She's bound to find out soon enough." She twisted her apron around her hands and turned to Clara Jane. "Your mother did something that hurt your father very much."

"I'll say," Mrs. Kepler said enthusiastically, and Auntie Mildred gave her a quelling look.

Clara Jane wished they'd stop treating her like a baby. Of course her mother had hurt her father; she had argued with him and ended up shooting herself. What could be worse than that? "Oh, sure," she said. "I know what she did."

"You do?" her aunt said. "Why, Clara Jane Davenant, of course you don't."

"Yes, I do. I always did." She felt as if she had known all of it for years—as if the whole awful scene, with the quarreling and the shot and what she had seen in the bedroom, had taken place years ago.

"You couldn't have," Auntie Mildred said. "He didn't find out himself till last summer, and what a shock that was. Don't you try to tell me that Grace—"

"I did too know." She couldn't stand the smug looks on their faces, the way they kept exchanging glances. "I did too." She ran up the back stairs to her room.

But she hadn't imagined anything like what she heard later that day from Nadine Applegate. Clara Jane had been avoiding Nadine along with everyone else outside the family, but now she needed information. She crept down to the hall and dialled the Applegates' number.

"Oh, kid!" Nadine said through green bubblegum when they met in the clubhouse above her garage, bundled in their parkas. "Don't tell me you don't know about it!" And she explained about Malcolm Wolfe, adding creative details of exactly what he and Grace had done together. "They were even going to have a baby," she said in a hushed voice, "but naturally it died."

"Don't be stupid," Clara Jane said. "That isn't true." It wasn't even logical: Her mother had disapproved of sex games; she certainly wouldn't have taken her clothes off in front of somebody who wasn't a doctor, and what's more, she had too many children already. As for Mr. Wolfe, who lately had replaced Prince Andre in Clara Jane's own fantasies, he would never do anything so undignified and grotesque. "No," she said. "It's impossible."

Nadine shrugged. "Listen, kiddo, everybody in town knows about it."

Clara Jane could only stare. It certainly wasn't true about the baby. It couldn't be.

"When I think of your mom—" Nadine said. "Of course," she added virtuously, "it was pretty obvious she did things like that." The last time she'd brought up the disgraceful size of the Davenant family, Clara Jane had pointed out that Nadine wasn't so pure herself. "What about you and Wayne Junior?" she'd asked, but Nadine had said that was different; the Davenants were grown up.

"At her age!" she said now, snapping her green gum. "I don't blame your father for shooting her."

"What did you say?" Clara Jane stood up, knocking over the can of cigarette butts that Nadine collected from her parents' wastebasket and secretly smoked. "*What?*" she shouted. She felt strong enough to pick up the whole stack of *Terry and the Pirates* comics and rip them to pieces. Nadine's own parents fought all the time, and her father drank and used bad grammar. Nobody would have been the least bit surprised if he had killed his wife. "It isn't true," Clara Jane said. "He did not!" She kicked the stack of comic books, and the top one slid to the floor and splayed open to a series of menacing frames of the Dragon Lady, with her glamorous figure and the blue highlights in her hair. She kicked them again and started a landslide, till comic books nearly covered the floor.

Nadine just snapped her gum again and squinted her eyes in a superior way. "As a matter of fact," she said, "Norma and I aren't supposed to play with your family. If my father knew I was talking to you right now, he'd bash my head in."

"I don't care if he does." Clara Jane crashed open the clubhouse door. "I wish he would." She climbed down the ladder, and ran home and upstairs to her room, where she burrowed under a quilt in the top of the double-decker bed.

Her father didn't tell lies; she was certain of that. On the other hand, she had thought the same thing about her mother, who had turned out to have been fooling them all along. The family had thought Grace obvious, and she had been subtle; thought her ingenuous, and she had been devious; conscientious, and she had been selfish and pleasure-loving. Yes, selfish. Her mother had put her own secret, shameful gratification above the safety of her children. If Clara Jane hadn't known her own mother any better than that, how much could she believe about anyone else?

XXIX

Headlines from Michigan newspapers, December, 1943 and January, 1944:

PROFESSOR AT PRELIMINARY EXAM SAYS WIFE'S
DEATH SUICIDE

SISTER OF SUSPECT TESTIFIES

PROFESSOR AGAIN ASSERTS INNOCENCE

GIRL SAYS MOTHER SHOT SELF

The hearing took place in the Justice of the Peace Court, with Justice Neil Poindexter presiding. The testimony lasted two weeks. Washtenaw County Assistant District Attorney James West was prosecuting attorney, and Attorney David Staebler appeared for the defense.

Clara Jane testified on the first two days of the hearing, and again near the end of the second week. She wanted to wear her new red sweater, but neither Mr. Staebler nor her aunt thought that was a good idea, and she ended up in the dark blue sailor dress again, in spite of cold weather and the fact that she had grown nearly an inch since September. Auntie Mildred said she shouldn't be frightened to appear in court because it was no different from being in a play, but Clara Jane disagreed; in a play she would be somebody else, and her lines would be written ahead of time, and nothing would depend on what she said. Besides, it was obvious that her aunt was just as terrified as she was; Auntie Mildred's head was more unsteady than ever, and she couldn't keep her hands still.

The courtroom was cold and fairly small, with a scraggly Christmas wreath hanging in one window. Most of the people kept their coats over their shoulders. Justice Poindexter wasn't as imposing as Clara Jane had imagined him when she heard his name. He didn't wear a robe. He was about five feet tall, with yellowish-white hair and a green plaid jacket, and he kept peering impatiently at the clock and cupping his hand behind his ear when people were speaking. The idea of two deaf people in a courtroom worried Clara Jane as much as it intrigued her. If Mr. Staebler and the judge couldn't hear each other, what would become of her father's case? "Speak up, speak up," she imagined them saying to each other. She had assumed that adults conducted their ceremonies more sensibly than children, but now she wondered.

During those two weeks, even after the vacation was over, Clara Jane didn't go to school. When she wasn't in court, she stayed in her bunk under the quilt, reading the biggest books she could get hold of. She had finished *Henry Esmond* and was on *The Count of Monte Cristo*, with *The Three Musketeers* and *Twenty Years After* in reserve. Robert closed himself into the study, with pheasant feathers and spools of colored silk scattered over his desk, tying flies for trout fishing; and Auntie Mildred cleaned all the wallpaper in the house with a rubbery pink clay that had a sickening fake-wintergreen smell. Nobody felt like cooking, but casseroles and cookies started arriving again, and nobody had to. And so the three of them got through the time.

A condensed version of the testimony at Robert Davenant's hearing:

At the beginning, Attorney West says he hopes to prove that Robert Davenant, disillusioned and angry at learning of his wife's infidelity, shot her to death.

Attorney Staebler, appearing for Robert, will seek to show that Grace Davenant, torn between love for Malcolm Wolfe and duty to her husband and children, shot herself.

As the first witness, Police Lieutenant Leroy Wilkinson testifies about what he found on the night of Grace's death and what Robert, Mildred, and Clara Jane Davenant told him.

Mildred Davenant testifies that on that night she was in the kitchen cleaning the oven, which, along with the linoleum and the defrosting of the refrigerator, had been shamefully neglected. She heard the voices of her brother and his wife upstairs in their bedroom, and then her brother came down to ask her to go up and speak to Grace. Mildred snaps her mouth shut then, as if she doesn't plan to open it again.

Attorney West asks her what happened next.

Her brother left the kitchen, she says reluctantly, and she immediately heard the shot.

"Immediately?" West asks her.

"Yes." She nods emphatically. "Well, very soon afterwards." When she heard it, she ran up to the bedroom; she does know that. And her brother would certainly not have killed his wife.

The impression left by Mildred Davenant's testimony is that she is telling as much as she knows but isn't really sure of what happened. Also, she is clearly prejudiced in her brother's favor.

Clara Jane Davenant repeats the things she has told the detective and Mr. Staebler, though the story feels artificial to her by now, as if she had written it down and memorized it. It has already replaced her actual memory of what happened. Attorney West asks whether she heard her father climb the stairs before the shot was fired, but she still doesn't remember; however, she says, her father is very strong.

The judge stares, and cups his ear in her direction. "So you think your father could have been upstairs by that time?" Attorney West asks, and Mr. Staebler objects.

Clara Jane goes ahead and answers the question. "If he wanted to," she says, looking down at her father's agonized face. "He could do anything." She hopes he'll see that she at least doesn't think of him as handicapped. "But he didn't kill my mother. My mother did it herself." She tries not to let her voice tremble. "By accident."

Dave Staebler has told Robert that he is not required to testify. Indeed, Dave advises strongly against it. But Robert wants to tell his story. Surely his innocence will work in his favor, he says. Dave has reluctantly agreed.

Robert Davenant, in a voice as calm and clear as he can make it, describes the events on the night of Grace's death: He and Grace, he says, did indeed have an argument, though it started out as a discussion. He didn't know then that Grace was pregnant, but he did know that she had had an affair, and he hoped to persuade her that they could work out their problems and continue their marriage. She seemed to feel that this was impossible; indeed, she became more emotional as the discussion continued, until finally she told him that she wanted to die. At this point, he became alarmed and went downstairs to get his sister. As he was returning to the bedroom, he heard the shot.

Attorney West doesn't understand why Mr. Davenant left his wife alone after she said she wanted to die. Surely it was unwise to leave her in such a state?

"In the first place," Robert says a little impatiently, "I didn't know she was serious. I didn't know she had the gun. And I wanted help. I thought my sister might be able to talk to her."

"But why didn't you call to your sister instead of going all the way downstairs to speak to her? Especially if it was so difficult for you?"

"The children were asleep," Robert says. "I didn't want to wake them. But actually, I believe I may have called to Mildred, on my way down. She didn't hear me. I called her again, of course, after I came back to the bedroom and found Grace."

Attorney West wonders why Grace placed the gun under her ear and killed herself so awkwardly. "Surely she would have aimed at her heart or her temple. Wouldn't that have been more usual?"

"She wanted to die," Robert says. "She wasn't used to the gun, and she just lifted it and fired. I don't suppose she stopped to consider what was usual." Dave Staebler looks quickly at Robert, and he realizes that he has sounded sarcastic.

"Was the gun kept loaded?" Attorney Staebler asks him later.

"No, certainly not." Robert reminds himself not to show impatience. "With five children in the house? Normally it was in the drawer of the bedside table, but I kept the ammunition in a locked case in my study. I hoped that the mere sight of the pistol would be enough to deter an intruder—that it would never be necessary to fire it."

"Did your wife know where the ammunition was?"

"Certainly. And she knew where I kept the key to the case."

"And did she know how to load and fire the gun?"

"Yes, she did," Robert says. "When we were first married, I showed her how to use it. I was often away, and she was alone or with small children in a house in the country. I wanted her to be able to defend herself. I may think now that this was unwise, but it was what I did."

Malcolm Wolfe has been summoned from Chicago for the hearing. Trying to be as restrained as Robert but looking as worn-out as James Stewart near the end of the filibuster in *Mr. Smith Goes to Washington*, he testifies before the filled courtroom: Yes, he says, he and Grace were lovers, but they had no intention of destroying her marriage. In fact, they had given up their affair just before she died.

Attorney Staebler asks him, "Do you think that her separation from you could have caused her to kill herself?"

Attorney West objects.

Staebler rephrases the question. "What was her reaction to the prospect of separation?"

"She was distraught," Malcolm Wolfe says. "Yes. I...see now that she was serious. She said she... If I had realized..." He looks directly at Robert. "She loved her husband and children."

"But she loved you too?" Staebler asks.

"Yes, I think so. I know she did. She was in great distress."

"And this distress was more than she could bear?"

West objects.

"She expressed unhappiness at the thought of separating?" Staebler asks.

"Great unhappiness. Desperation. 'I can't stand it,' she said. I wish I could have talked to her that night. There was no solution; I see that, of course, but I might have been able…"

"Mr. Wolfe," Staebler asks, "at the time Grace Davenant died, did you know that she was pregnant?"

Malcolm Wolfe looks at Robert Davenant again and speaks softly. "No. I didn't know that. If I had…it must have made her situation much worse. I wish I'd known." Justice Poindexter stares at him, then at Robert.

Attorney West calls Mrs. Inez Kepler, who comes briskly to the stand in a two-piece black crepe dress passed on to her by Grace, a smart black hat with a spotted veil, and open-toed shoes. He asks whether, in Mrs. Kepler's opinion, Grace and Robert Davenant were on good terms.

"As good as you could expect," Mrs. Kepler says, "seeing they were married."

West smiles, acknowledging this as a possible joke. "Do you know whether he ever struck her?"

"Well, of course he did," she says, "but it served her right, in my opinion." She nods her head emphatically, several times. "You'd do the same."

Attorney Staebler asks Mrs. Kepler whether she ever actually saw Mr. Davenant strike his wife.

"I didn't have to see it. I knew what was going on." She nods again.

"So you didn't see him strike her." He is attentive and courteous, trying to grasp her exact meaning.

"Not with my own eyes, no. But."

"Did you hear them fighting, then, in a physical way?"

"Do you think he'd do anything like that when I was there? They did argue, though, I can tell you that. But that's marriage, isn't it? Believe me, Mrs. Davenant had nothing to complain about, compared to some of us." Holding out her arm for inspection, she starts to roll up one of her sleeves.

Neither attorney questions her further.

In the final arguments, Assistant District Attorney West starts out by saying that it is an established fact that women seldom use guns to commit suicide. There are a hundred less painful and violent ways. Why didn't Grace Davenant take an overdose of sleeping pills? There was a supply in the house, prescribed for her sister-in-law after nervous trouble. Apart from the improbable method, Mrs. Davenant was known for her dedication to her family. Would such a devoted mother voluntarily leave five helpless children to fend for themselves? Reason tells us that she would not have done such a thing.

Robert Davenant, Attorney West says, is a clever, highly educated man who found himself in an unbearable situation and wanted to be rid of the wife who had betrayed him. Mr. Davenant is well known as a perfectionist who doesn't easily forgive. No matter what promises his wife might have made that night, he couldn't have gone on living with her on the same terms. Mr. Davenant claims that he didn't know she was pregnant, but is this true? Although she hadn't yet consulted a physician, the defense has established that she must have known, and surely she would have told her husband.

There are also the words spoken by Mr. Davenant when his daughter came into the bedroom and found him holding the gun as his wife's body lay on the bed behind him: "It was an accident." Isn't this practically an admission of guilt? In a true accident, nobody bothers to say such a thing; it's assumed to be self-evident. Mr. Davenant has testified that he picked up the gun after it was fired because he wanted to get it away from his wife, but isn't it more likely that he never laid it down?

Attorney Staebler points out that all the evidence the prosecution has offered is circumstantial. It is also a fact, not well enough known, that suicide is fifteen times more common than homicide. For a woman in Grace Davenant's position, it isn't at all unlikely.

She must have made her decision and begun her preparations before her husband came up to bed. She had written the note and loaded the gun by then, and she probably returned it to the drawer when she heard him. As she told him, she wanted to die. There was plenty of time for her, when her husband went downstairs to get his sister, to take out the gun, raise it to her head, and fire.

Robert, on the other hand, would have had to be an athlete to climb the stairs, run into the bedroom, and shoot his wife during the minute or so after Mildred Davenant saw him downstairs and before Clara Jane entered the bedroom. "And as we know, he is not an athlete.

"Robert Davenant's sister," Attorney Staebler says, "has told us that it is difficult for him to climb stairs at any time, and surely it wouldn't have been easier that night, when he was exhausted and under extreme stress.

"Not only would he have had to run up the stairs, but, once in the bedroom, he would have had to take the gun from the drawer of the bedside table or from wherever else it might have been hidden, and then to maneuver his wife into a position from which he could shoot her, from a nearly impossible angle, at very close range. Surely, if he had killed her in a fit of rage, as the prosecution contends, he would simply have fired point-blank from several feet away as soon as he reached the bedroom, and the wound might be in her chest or even her face, but almost certainly not just below her ear.

"On another point, it is not at all certain that Mrs. Davenant would have told her husband about her pregnancy—not if she wasn't sure he was the father. Mr. Davenant says that he didn't know, and nothing we have heard disproves his testimony."

Both sides rested, and Justice Poindexter reported his finding two days later. On the evidence presented, he said, he could find no probable cause to believe that a crime (beyond suicide) had been committed and no reason, therefore, for a trial.

COURT FREES DAVENANT IN WIFE'S DEATH

1986

When the voices of children are heard on the green
And whisp'rings are in the dale,
The days of my youth rise fresh in my mind,
My face turns green and pale.

Then come home, my children, the sun is gone down,
And the dews of night arise;
Your spring and your day are wasted in play,
And your winter and night in disguise.

—William Blake, *Songs of Experience*

XXVIII

"Two things about your mother I never could put up with," the Reverend Clara Davenant's father says crossly. He stops moving his head against the pillow and looks up toward Clara, seeing only a blur outlined by a rainbow. Why do they keep taking away his glasses? It's bad enough being threaded with tubes and suffocated by fumes from a chain-smoking roommate. The nurses here remind him of Mildred, that time he had polio. She liked his helplessness, he could tell, and he fought her as hard as he could—even refusing water to avoid asking so often for the urinal.

"Please, Daddy," Clara says. She grips the white-enameled railing at the side of his bed. She mustn't tire him out, but this could be their last chance to talk.

"In the first place," he says, "Grace bought the wrong kind of washcloths."

"What?" She's startled.

"Fluffy. Too damn thick. Besides that, she emptied my wastebasket too soon."

"Come on, Daddy—"

"She didn't allow for afterthoughts." He gazes past Clara. "If you said something once, you had to mean it for the rest of your life."

"Oh. Yes." Maybe he isn't wandering after all.

"I never wanted to hurt her," he says.

"Her feelings, you mean? Or…"

"Never." His mouth turns down, and he falls back against the pillow.

"Do you wear a robe?" her father asks later. "In church, I mean?"

People in her family keep asking this: Imagine Clara Jane actually being a minister. Is it possible? "Yes, there's a robe," she says. "And a stole too, different colors for different occasions."

"Just like your grandfather. But you always did like dressing up." The windows of the hospital room are black now, laced with diagonal spatters of rain. He gives her an urgent look. "The concept of sin. Does your church believe in it?"

The Davenants seldom talk about morality or emotions without humorous quotation marks. They don't bring such things into serious conversations. But his face is grave now, his expression concentrated. Is he about to confirm the conclusion she reluctantly reached so long ago? "Sin," Clara says. "Yes, I think we believe in it. Individually. We don't have much of a dogma."

He turns his face toward their reflections in the dark window: the high white bed, Clara in the chair beside it. "Because I have sinned," he says, almost too softly to hear.

"Most of us have." She isn't sure, after all, that she wants him to go on.

"To sin, I always thought, is to act against your own principles. But it isn't that simple; you have to think those principles through."

"In order to sin, or in order to avoid it?" She has learned from other sickbeds that pretending to understand doesn't work.

He closes his eyes and opens them, tugs at the hem of the sheet. "Trying not to do harm isn't enough. You have to know how harm can be done." The hollows in his face are blue against the yellowish skin. "I thought I understood your mother... From the time we were in school together. Sixth grade."

Clara smiles. "She never got over the honor, did she? Skipping two grades."

"Little. Skinny. Nine years old. Don't ever think you know another person." He moves his head against the pillow. She notes the faint groove at the end of his nose, the appealing cheekbones. No wonder Grace fell in love. "I didn't talk to you much," he says. "Afterwards. Any of you."

"No." She could have made him talk, she sees now—besieged him with questions till he stopped measuring out his words and spoke without fear of misspeaking. But she too is a word-measurer, never wanting to voice a thing until she's sure of it. Perhaps there have been two of them all these years, both unable to speak. "Daddy," she says, "please tell me—" Tell me what happened that night, she wants to say. Stop talking around the subject and tell me.

He's looking at the dark window again. "I thought I could see straight through her..." He moves his arm and winces, with a glance toward the needle taped inside his elbow. "And then, when I found out..." His mouth is set in a grim, lipless line. "I didn't like being wrong, that was all."

"No, it wasn't all. You loved her." It's true, she finally believes.

"I hadn't realized it." His eyes are squeezed shut.

"Shall I read to you? How about Tennyson?" She has brought him a tape player, with cassettes of Robert Frost and John Gielgud, but he prefers live voices.

He opens his eyes. "'Crossing the Bar'?" His tone is sharp, ironic, intended to hurt. "Not quite yet, I think. 'The Hunting of the Snark.' Can you find that?"

She extracts Lewis Carroll from between Rossetti and Robert Browning on the metal stand beside the bed. Those Victorians. How much are they to blame for the whole anachronistic Davenant family? Clara Jane used to see herself as Alice, the clear-eyed child who relied on logic; she wanted a pinafore and shoes with straps.

"My lovely daughter." Her father gazes up at her, all irony gone. "'I engage with the Snark—every night after dark—In a dreamy delirious fight,'" he murmurs.

Later, Clara hurries down the steps of the University Hospital into the gray Michigan drizzle, trying not to think. But before she can prevent it—before she can even raise her umbrella—the scene begins: She is fourteen years old, in her blue pajamas with the white piping, curled up on a window seat halfway up the stairs. She has awakened from a nightmare about a diving Japanese plane painted with swastikas. She sits up and puts her feet to the floor. And then she hears a sound she has never expected to hear in real life.

Whenever Clara relives this scene—when she recalls being

startled awake and hearing the shot—she sees a stream of blood under her parents' half-open bedroom door, flowing across the hall and down the stairs all the way to the landing, while she tries to avoid stepping in it with her bare feet. But it isn't true: She didn't see any blood that night, not even in the bedroom.

She takes hold of a railing outside the hospital entrance and breathes slowly, willing the vision away. Does Clara think her father killed her mother? It's certainly what she thought when she saw him standing there in the bedroom with the gun in his hand. But then he explained: "It was an accident," he said; Grace—or somebody—had been careless.

It may have been true, but Clara knows more now about the different ways that people—even honest people—see the truth. If her father had struggled with someone who was holding a loaded gun—if the gun had accidentally gone off—would he have admitted his own part in what happened? On that night, as soon as her father spoke to her, she believed him. Later, as the years crept on and the young family grew up, she came to know more about truth and tact and human error. Even her father told social lies, she noticed, though not always successfully: And he would do anything to shield his children.

Was he shielding them in court—if only from damaging knowledge? She doesn't know, but she doesn't believe he told the exact, entire truth.

Clara's umbrella is large, with panels of blue and green and white, a premium from the public television station in the city where she lives now. She unsnaps the band around the spokes, pushes the umbrella open, and makes her way over wet leaves toward the rented room where she'll spend the night. Things My Mother Taught Me: Iron the collar and sleeves first; write the thank-you note on the day you open the present; cut ribbon on the bias; don't touch a light switch with wet hands; carry sharp instruments point down; walk facing oncoming traffic.

Yes, she's still searching for her mother, trying to understand. All of them are.

XXXI

In 1944, after the dismissal of charges against Robert, the Davenants carried on their lives as well as they could. Auntie Mildred stayed on. She enforced table manners and bedtimes, assigned chores and carried out punishments, and Clara Jane, though occasionally resentful, was mainly relieved to have someone else in command. Their aunt pounded out selections from *The Mikado* on the piano, drilled the children in Latin vocabulary, and made angelfood cakes for their birthdays. As for Robert, he went on working and fishing, tending his children and his garden. There was a woman at the Institute, a rather quiet herpetologist with a crown of smooth blond braids, whom he sometimes took to concerts at Angell Hall. When he retired, his department gave him an engraved plaque, which he stored in a drawer somewhere.

Clara Jane read even more after her mother's death, finding unexpected comfort in stories of betrayal and murder. *Anna Karenina* seemed to offer clues to her life, and *Macbeth* and *Hamlet*, assigned in English classes, made her cry in a way that wasn't wholly unpleasant. She no longer sat on the window seat, though; nobody did. And of course there were no more theatrical productions.

So the family got through the years before Clara Jane graduated from high school and went off to college—the same years that led to the end of the war and of an era.

Clara Davenant found out too early about loss, she's thinking as she walks down the street in the rain. As a child, she lived in dread of some looming disaster. She couldn't foresee the details, but the disaster came and she stopped growing, like a plant struck by frost.

Her New England congregation thinks of her as cool-headed and good-humored and in charge. If they only knew; there are grudges she still holds, things she can't face. Her brothers and sister are the same.

Most of Clara's trips to Michigan till now have been only pauses on journeys to other places. She isn't staying in the house on Packard Street yet—though it's empty, with her father in the hospital and Auntie Mildred recently departed for a retirement home in Ypsilanti. Hal and his wife, Daphne, invited her to stay with them, and so did Fred and his new wife, but she's taken a room at the Michigan League. She'll move to Packard Street when Cricket and Mellie arrive from their distant homes.

It won't hurt to look at the house from the outside, though. She walks across the campus to East University and down to the corner of Packard, in rain that's falling more heavily. But then she feels conspicuous—as if, even after all these years, people might recognize her—and turns back. She wishes that she and her father could have talked more today, but that was never possible. Robert can explain why the deer population should be cut down and why trout should be caught with flies instead of worms, but when it comes to human beings, he has never claimed to know many answers. Grace was the one who thought she knew people.

Poor Grace. If she were alive now, there might also be the baby— not the imaginary baby, but an unimaginable middle-aged person whose father was either Malcolm or Robert. What if Grace had been able to get an abortion, though? But she wouldn't have known how: People then didn't even say the word; there were only illegal operations, performed by shady doctors who were almost expected to bungle the job.

Clara's vision of her mother is made up of glimpses, without a continuous thread to string them together. In July she rented a cottage with friends on Lake Winnipesaukee, and one day when she was floating on her back, a dragonfly with a deep-blue body and a double set of black lace wings hovered near her face. There used to be dragonflies at Whitmore Lake, she recalled then, and once her mother almost drowned. But how could that be? Grace was proud of her swimming, Clara does know that much; maybe it was Mildred. This whole memory thing is impossible.

The streets where Clara rode her bicycle are still here, though the principal trees are maples now instead of elms. Miller's soda fountain is gone, and the Graystone Pharmacy has become a copy shop, but the Blue Front convenience store is bluer than ever, and the Michigan League is still across from the carillon tower, with the Carl Milles fountain spouting away on the mall between. Clara stops at a news store and sees a rack of Hostess cakes. She and Hal, with nickels earned for washing dishes or mowing the lawn, sometimes bought cupcakes and smuggled them into their rooms. Their favorites were devil's-food Sno Balls. Now, on an impulse, she buys a package and tucks it into her shoulder bag.

In her room at the League, she rips open the cellophane to the sweet familiar smell, and a recollection surfaces, carrying more associations than she can identify. This isn't like the image of the telephone poles that she willed herself to preserve when she was nearly thirteen. She can still bring back that image when she chooses, along with the look of the poles dividing the sky, and the texture of the Buick's rough upholstery against her cheek—even the way it felt for the family, all seven of them, to sit so close together for a whole day. The reaction the cupcakes arouse is involuntary, and closer to a sensation than a memory: It's a feeling of overwhelming shame. Why should the reminder of a bicycle ride with Nadine Applegate give her this guilty sensation? The very thought of it makes her tingle, as if she had pressed against a blister in the palm of her hand.

She did have a blister, she thinks, from spading her father's Victory Garden. It had broken, and she was afraid of infection. But that doesn't account for the shame.

She and Nadine were riding their bicycles to the Arboretum. They took parallel streets and waited for each other, ringing their bells. Why? In Clara's basket was *War and Peace*, in the brown paper cover she'd made to deflect the comments of grown-up people. She was probably carrying a Thermos of milk and one of those embarrassing whole-wheat sandwiches. Nadine, with her Silvercup bread and baloney and her supply of Nancy comics, would have made scathing remarks.

Clara feels the bell against her thumb, the rattle of the sound.

Elm trees arched green overhead, and sunlight filtered down through small high leaves. She had bought cupcakes at Mr. Twist's. At the edge of the campus, near the Gothic stone buildings of the law school, she rang her bell and listened for Nadine's answering ring.

The bicycle trips. She and Nadine followed her mother—shadowing, they called it. Once, in the kitchen, Clara hinted something to Auntie Mildred without knowing it herself.

"My fingernails are too clean," her father complains the next morning. He lifts his hands above the sheet and forces a smile. She remembers him sliding an angleworm onto a hook, scooping the entrails out of a partridge. He drops his hands, and his eyes close.

Maybe because of Clara's profession, her father has become her charge. It's strange, he said earlier; a minister is the last thing anyone would expect a child of his to be. Not so strange, she thinks, if you consider his worship of nature and his emphasis on morality and self-denial—to say nothing of his feeling for language. He never encouraged her, though. Robert wanted both of his daughters to study science. He saw them wearing neat white lab coats and earning degrees that, unlike their mother's, would guarantee security. They both resisted his vocational advice. In college (where she became reconciled to her first name) Clara majored in English. She didn't know what she would do afterwards, except that she hoped never to write another essay in her life. However, Sunday evening chapel was compulsory, and she soon found, to her surprise, that she enjoyed the services. During the sermon she could let her mind wander, and some of her thoughts excited her. Sometimes she admired the speakers, and sometimes she wanted to argue.

In her senior year Guy Quillen, a theology student, introduced her to new possibilities, personal and professional, before abandoning both her and his vocation at the end of the first term. Clara lived too much in her mind, he said: She seemed unable to feel either anger or joy. She was, in other words, cold. This—especially the part about anger—amazed Clara, who still thought of herself as hot-tempered. But on thinking it over, she wondered: When had she recently been infuriated, when had she thrown things or even wished to throw them? She could be irritable, yes, like anybody, but she probably hadn't felt overwhelming rage since that day in Nadine's clubhouse when she had scattered the cigarette butts and comic books. She hadn't dared to feel it.

Guy knew her history, and he could take it into account, but he didn't think he could live with it. She had no talent for relationships, he said.

Even that last observation of his didn't make her as angry as she thought it should. She could see his point. When he dropped her, she was desolated but picked herself up and went on reading Kierkegaard and Paul Tillich. She had been enrolled in divinity school for some months before it came to her that her intended profession would require her to produce a twenty-minute essay nearly every week of her whole career.

By that time, though, it seemed like destiny. She had always enjoyed performing, she said to her family.

(Guy turned up again a few years ago, sitting in a pew halfway back. Twice divorced—so much for his own talent for relationships—he's a geneticist and spends much of his time with rats; they're quite nice, he says. He's one of the friends who shared the lakeside cottage.)

Even now, Clara hasn't let her brothers and sister know how serious she is about her vocation. She hasn't told them about the times in church when she feels like a messenger, a pure vessel for unexpected news. She can make her congregation think and can even stir them to action. And she enjoys composing sermons after all— the planning of opening words to catch her listeners' interest, the placing of laughs, the conclusion left open but not vague, the shaping of the whole thing into something she didn't know before she wrote it or even before she said it. She thinks her mother would have been proud. Though Grace considered church services one more primitive rite, she would surely have been glad that her daughter could support herself. When Clara ran to the bank with her first paycheck, she felt she was flying.

Hal is now a biochemist at the University. Fred studied law and has become a judge. He's gained forty-four pounds since he passed the bar exam, and is on his third wife. Mellie dropped out of music school to marry an insurance salesman and move to Colorado and have four children. And Cricket, still amiable though no longer eager, is an architect in Corvallis. The Davenants have done well, considering.

They don't see each other, though. They have only briefly been together since the day Clara left home. Their mother's death keeps them apart, she suspects. Each one has worked out a version of what happened, and they don't want their stories disturbed.

"How you doing, Bobby?" A young streaky-blond nurse in T-shirt and painter's pants breezes in and picks up Robert's wrist.

Years of professional hospital visits still haven't reconciled Clara to hearing the staff call elderly patients by their first names. "He isn't used to being called that," she says to the nurse. He should at least be Robert.

His head turns toward her on the pillow. "It's all right," he says faintly.

"Sure," the nurse says, still holding his wrist, looking at a pink watch on a striped band. "Bobby and I are old friends." She gives Clara a complicitous glance.

No, Clara thinks. This isn't the way death should be. It's bad enough that they've given her father a chain-smoking roommate who watches television game shows all day. The nurse is well-intentioned, but she has never heard Robert Davenant recite Tennyson or stood with him on a trail to hear the drumming of a grouse. She hasn't been beaten by him when his standards were too high and his temper gave way.

Does he even know he's dying? He won't say so, though the doctor has drawn him a diagram of the digestive system and discussed the subject like a colleague. Robert knows he can't live without a pancreas, and he knows the cancer is spreading, but when Clara approaches the subject, he changes it. "I'm going to rent the sleeping-porch in the spring," he said yesterday. And, "I'd like to put in asparagus beds next year." On the bedside stand are gifts from his birthday last week—vegetable seeds, a honeycomb, large-type books, and (a risky choice) a Sierra Club calendar. No clothes.

Of course he knows. He must need to talk. "Daddy." Clara takes his hand.

"Jane." His forehead creases. "No, it's Clara now."

"Whatever you like." Her throat tightens.

He's staring at her. "Do you wear a robe in church?" He doesn't seem to remember asking this before.

"Yes, though not everybody likes it." Other problems await her: Last Sunday the Chancel Committee, for some reason, covered the altar with an unbecoming layer of aluminum foil. There are bound to be repercussions. "But that's the way it is," she says.

He fixes her with his eyes and takes a breath. "You think I did it." It's a statement, not a question or a reproach.

She can only look at him.

"I might as well have." He closes his eyes, holding back pain.

Fake cheers and laughter come from the television set, and the roommate chuckles through billowing smoke. "Did you hear that?"

Robert coughs and then looks steadily toward Clara. "You understand? You see why I couldn't..." He coughs again, and starts to choke.

She squeezes his hand and stands up. "That man shouldn't be smoking. I'm going to find the nurse."

"No, Clara. He has his rights." He can hardly get the words out.

"Too bad. It can't be good for him either." She runs down the green corridor, along the yellow line that leads to the nurses' station. What was her father saying? That he hadn't caused Grace's death, even by accident? That he had purposely allowed the possibility to stand? When Clara comes back with the nurse, he has fallen asleep.

Robert Davenant dies that night without saying any more, while Clara and Hal sit beside him.

XXXII

"'The slim and wily rainbow trout,'" Clara reads five days later from the pulpit of the Unitarian church, quoting from one of Robert Davenant's articles on trout fishing, "'was one of my earliest adversaries and first companions.'" Looking down, she recognizes some of her father's former colleagues. Ben DeGroff died years ago, and Mrs. DeGroff, she has learned, is safely tucked away in a nursing home. Auntie Mildred hasn't come either. She disapproves of the whole idea of a memorial service.

When Clara finishes, Hal and Cricket read "Crossing the Bar" and "Fear no more the heat of the sun," and Fred calls on Robert's fellow scientists for brief reminiscences. There's only one reference to his handicap and none to the family tragedy. At the end, Mellie plays a flute sonata. The music is all Bach, though Clara suspects that Robert himself would have chosen Ravel or Tchaikovsky.

Afterwards the family buys pizza and wine to take to the Packard Street house. When Clara pushes open the front door, she has a sense of welcome, in spite of the unswept floor and the chill from the turned-down thermostat. Facing her are the stairs and the window seat, with the brocade curtains sagging in threadbare folds. She can see into the living room, where a cot is set up and spent matches litter the Dutch-tiled hearth. In the dining room, a record player with a lucite dust cover sits on a scratched metal cabinet that holds albums of Puccini and *Fred Waring and the Pennsylvanians.*

The Davenants—all five of them, besides the two wives—take their places around the oak dining table. Seated under Aunt Eleanor's still-lifes of green grapes and patty-pan squash, in the setting where some of their most anxious moments took place, they're nearly silent. The two circles of pizza, pepperoni and onion-mushroom, steam fragrantly on the table, next to a container of Greek salad and half a gallon of Almaden Mountain Red, but nobody moves. "Jane," Cricket finally says, "would you like to say grace?"

Clara is disconcerted. Even with strangers this request isn't always easy to fulfill, but Daphne and Mellie and her brothers are looking at her with sober faces, while Fred's young wife bows her pale tangled curls above her plate. "We are grateful," Clara improvises, "to be here again together, all of us who love each other—" Her voice threatens to break. "Who love each other, to remember a man we loved." Yes, they did, even when they were afraid. "We are grateful," she finishes. A tear is making its way down Mellie's cheek, and Fred's wife has her eyes tightly closed. "Hal," Clara says, "will you open the wine?"

He pours it into seven plastic cups and raises his. "To Robert Davenant," he says, and all of them lift their cups. "All right, who wants pepperoni?"

During the meal they talk half-humorously about Hal and Daphne's son who wants to drop out of college to write computer programs and about Cricket's expensive twin daughters who are both freshmen at once. The conversation reminds Clara of their mother's cheery newspaper columns: Nobody mentions the twins' drug problems, though everybody knows. And did one of them really have an abortion last spring? Did Fred's oldest boy smash up his Mercedes? You wouldn't know it from anything anybody is saying. Mellie seems contented enough, though she's had an astonishing number of operations, from a hysterectomy to the removal of a neuroma from the sole of her foot. Nobody speaks of their childhood at this same oaken table, and nobody mentions Robert or Grace.

To an outsider, would the Davenants seem like an ordinary bereaved family, understandably grave but grown up and in charge of their lives? Clara isn't sure. For one thing, all of them look unnaturally young. It's a matter of expression, somehow; they seem startled and wary—not as if they haven't known suffering, but as if they haven't come to terms with it. However, she realizes, these aren't their everyday faces. Here, in this echoing cobwebby house with the gritty floors, they have slipped back into their childhood roles as if into those Disney figurines she gave them one Christmas. Grumpy. Sneezy. Dopey. If Cricket is no longer Happy, what is he? What is she herself? Anxious? Bossy? She doesn't know.

Fred pushes away his plate and glances around the table. "Well," he says. "Are we going to talk about it?"

Freddie the judge. The tune of "Who's Afraid of the Big Bad Wolf" goes through Clara's mind, and then Mellie says, "What do you mean?" Cricket's elbows are on the table, his head sunk in his hands.

"We ought to," Hal says. "It could be our last chance."

Freddie looks straight at Clara with his mismatched eyes—one gray-green, one gray-brown. "What do you think, Clara Jane? Did he do it?"

Mellie draws a quick breath, and Hal says, "Fred, come on."

A reporter asked Clara the same question yesterday on the telephone. She hung up without answering.

"Come on, Fred," Hal says. "She doesn't know any more than anybody else."

"No?" Fred is still looking at her. "I've always thought you knew more than you said in court."

"In other words," Hal says to him, "you think he did it."

"Didn't he?" Fred asks her.

Clara can't answer. She has thought so, in a way.

"He was always criticizing her," Hal says.

"Not for anything important," Clara says. "Only when dinner was late, or when she used a cliche. That night was different. He didn't sound angry. I think he was crying." She never told this to the police or even admitted it to herself, but she heard him sobbing.

"Oh, please, can't we talk about the good things?" Mellie's hair is pulled back into two graying wings above her high pure brow. "How he tied flies? How he used Cricket's hair?"

"Or quoted James Russell Lowell?" Fred asks sharply. "No. Go on, Clara Jane."

"I don't know any more," Clara says. "Though I was there, of course."

"Yes, you were." Fred is a solid presence, in a well-cut suit with a vest.

"But I was in court too, and I don't understand that either. I didn't tell the truth."

"Really?" Mellie's eyebrows reprove her.

"About how fast he could climb the stairs," Freddie breaks in. "Right."

"How do you know so much?" Clara asks. He's talking as if he'd been there and heard her testimony.

"The papers covered it pretty thoroughly," Hal says, and Fred nods.

At the time of the hearing, she didn't understand that reporters were actually sitting in the courtroom and writing down what she said, to be printed in the paper for everyone to read. Her father banned newspapers from the house during those weeks, but she thought it was because of the war news. "You've read the stories?" she asks now. She hasn't seen them herself.

"Only about once a year," Cricket says with a half-smile, looking past her toward the stained-glass panels in the window.

Mellie barely nods, without speaking.

So they've been as haunted as she has. Maybe more; they were younger when it happened, and they were asleep: They woke up to find their mother gone. "It wasn't very bright of me, was it?" she says. "Bragging about how strong he was."

"Oh, I don't know," Fred says. "Maybe it even helped his case. They figured you wouldn't have said it if you knew he was guilty. Not unless you wanted to get him in trouble." He lifts one eyebrow in a question.

"No," Clara says, "Just the opposite." She has been through this herself, over and over, without finding any motive but an ill-conceived wish to support her father. "I think I was showing off," she says.

Fred goes on, interrogating her. "So, did he do it?"

"Not on purpose, I've never thought that."

"An accident, then?"

"That was what he said. I don't know. The police just kept on asking about the stairs—whether I heard the shot before or after he passed me."

"Oh?" Freddie must have behaved like this in court before he became a judge—pacing up and down, pouncing, playing to the jury. "Surely you realized why they asked that."

"But I didn't know the answer. I didn't know anything." The sound of the shot had knocked chronology out of her mind. She had tried to roll time backward like a movie reel. She looks around the table at all those eyes. "All I remembered was the voices and the chair."

She's startled by her own words. What chair? Why did she say that?

Hal looks at her narrowly, his Baker Street look. "A chair?"

"The one in the bedroom." She's confused. She doesn't think there was anything about a chair in the testimony, but she heard it fall and she sees it now, just visible between the curtains—her mother's small upholstered chair, lying askew like the knocked-over furniture in Hogarth engravings she's come across since then.

"What about it?" Hal asks.

"Nothing." It must be a false memory: When she reached the bedroom, nothing was out of place. "I've never thought he killed her on purpose."

"You think there was a struggle?" This seems to be what Hal thinks.

"Maybe. It's hard to believe she would have done it herself." Though there are other things Clara wouldn't have expected her mother to do—take a lover, for instance.

Hal is looking at her with Robert's most attentive expression. "So you don't go for the suicide theory."

She recalls her own rages, when she might well have done irrevocable things if a weapon were at hand. However, Grace didn't get into rages. "Maybe she considered it…"

"A lot of things didn't come out in court," Hal says. "Who took the gun out of the drawer, for instance? And loaded it?"

"Mother did. I suppose." Though Clara has trouble with this.

She can see Grace firing the gun—frantic and scarcely aiming—but not loading it. She has never been able to imagine her mother, in that unbecoming blue playsuit, picking up actual bullets and putting them into the gun. "I don't see how we'll ever know."

"We shouldn't be talking about it," Mellie says. "We have no right."

"No right?" Fred turns to her, ignoring his wife's nervous touch on his sleeve.

Clara recalls what her father said in their last conversation: "I might as well have." Which meant that he hadn't.

XXXIII

After supper, in the living room with a fire crackling and Muledeer looming through his cobwebs, they talk more easily. "We were such a strange family." Mellie is counting stitches in the maroon football sweater she's knitting for her third son. "No wonder nobody liked us."

Clara is surprised. People liked Mellie, always. But she only says, "Everybody's strange." She thinks about the faces she sees on Sundays under the stained-glass windows representing Education and Music. Sometimes she visualizes her parishioners' secrets floating above their heads like balloons in a comic strip: The overflowing woman in the third row resents her children and hides in the bathroom to eat Milky Ways; yet she volunteers for the most tedious jobs on the R.E. Committee. The man who looks like Hairless Joe writes resentful verses about his former wife. The woman with purple eye makeup claims to be a feminist and stalks out of church whenever a hymn mentions mankind or brotherhood, but she's constantly involved with sadistic men she refers to as her lovers; "My lover tried to run me down with his motorcycle," she complained last week.

"Strange?" Clara says. "You should see my congregation."

"Well," Mellie says. "*Your* congregation." Mellie is an Episcopalian now.

"Everybody's strange," Clara says. "Some people are just more public about it."

"We were public, all right," says Freddie the judge, as if he were in pain.

Clara doesn't know whether he's talking about their mother's newspaper column or her death—or about the plays that she herself dragged the children into, parading them before the whole town, as it may have seemed to him. He loved to sell tickets but would never play more than a minor part.

"Face it; we were strange," Mellie says.

"Yes," Cricket says. From this angle, Clara recognizes the same shallow dimple that Robert had at each side of his mouth, and the way he bent his head to listen. Are Cricket's daughters afraid of him? She can't imagine it.

When all of them were young, Clara was afraid they would change, and of course they have. She was a math prodigy for the space of one afternoon. Later she hoped to be an actress or a journalist. There's no telling what, in a child, will endure. The strangeness they complain of—whatever it was that marked the Davenants—was part of what she loved.

Before they separate for the night, they hug each other in turn, without speaking.

After the ones who live in town have left, Clara takes a bath. The bathroom has scarcely changed. A shower has been added, but the square white tiles and cracked grout look the same as when she was a child. She bathed before that dinner party their mother made them attend—in this same tub, with the clawed feet and the faucets she turned with her toes. Was Malcolm Wolfe a family friend by then? Was he her mother's lover?

There's a fantasy that Clara sometimes calls up: Some Sunday after the service, a woman of about her own age will shake her hand and say, "I'm Annabel Wolfe." Clara used to picture the woman with fading red hair like Cricket's, but now she makes it silvery white. Annabel's face is long and kind, the way Clara remembers Malcolm Wolfe's. The two of them will go to the Pewter Pot near the church, and Annabel will explain what happened to Clara's mother. It doesn't matter that the actual Annabel can know even less than she; the Annabel in her imagination understands everything.

219

Later, in the sun-porch that was once Hal's room, Clara doesn't sleep easily. A few years ago Robert, when his eyesight had begun to fail, shot a hen pheasant and reported himself to a game warden who would have preferred to overlook the whole thing. If her father broke a law, however accidentally, he didn't lie about it. Still, if she can't imagine Robert telling lies in court, she can see him holding information back.

"You have all these morbid memories," Mellie says to Clara the next day. "Don't you remember anything good?" They're packing some of Auntie Mildred's clothes—still in their original wrappings, with price tags—in a suitcase for Clara to take to her the next day in the retirement home. "This was Auntie Mildred's trousseau, you know," Mellie says.

"It was?" Clara feels a tug of pity.

Mellie holds up a sea-green slip of heavy satin, with a deep border of ecru lace. "Isn't this pathetic?"

"Oh, my," Clara says. "The wicked undertaker never got to see that." She's chagrined to hear herself laugh.

"Undertaker." Mellie's laughing too; the word has set her off. Both of them sit on the bed, choking and giggling. "It isn't funny," Mellie protests.

"No." They're still laughing. "Of course there were good things," Clara says. "We had a lot of fun. Laughing at Auntie Mildred, for instance."

"More than that. What about going camping? And on trips?"

Clara can't believe this. "You hated camping. You got carsick."

"I did not." Mellie goes back to the underclothes. There must be half a dozen negligees with matching nightgowns. "Never."

"It always rained. Seven people in a wet tent." Clara can't forget the misery and failure and fear. "Somebody always touched the canvas, and the water came pouring in."

Mellie's mouth opens, as if to say that she was never the one.

"Mother's root beer was good, " Clara says. "She used to put it up in Mason jars. And the trees we planted whenever a new baby was born. Yours was a peach tree, I think. But then we moved away."

220

Why does she have to qualify everything? Is she afraid to identify happiness?

"Do you want to hear my theory about Mother and Daddy?" Mellie asks softly. "About why he married her?"

"Oh, that was because…" Clara recalls the day her father came to her room, after she had yelled at her mother and spilled her soup. "There was somebody he couldn't marry, and then…" He seemed to be apologizing for having chosen Grace as his children's mother, but he didn't offer a reason. "Because she was there, I suppose."

"Because she *followed* him there." Mellie's voice is firm now, as if she's thought long and carefully about what she's saying.

"And listened to his troubles. He did tell me that."

"She seduced him."

"Literally, you mean? Oh, come on. Not—" Not my mother, she wants to say, as if she were fourteen-year-old Clara Jane protesting to Nadine.

"I used to wonder," Mellie says. "I never could imagine them in love."

Clara wondered the same thing. "You're not saying she was pregnant, are you?"

"Oh, no." Mellie puts on her shocked face.

"Because I wasn't born till later. After the famous Professor Freundlich episode."

"She wouldn't have to be pregnant. Just one time would make him feel obligated."

"That's true."

"It's only a theory," Mellie says.

Clara lies back on the candlewick spread and looks up through the window, past the Applegates' former house. They moved away years ago, and Clara has heard, variously, that Nadine has become a prison guard, a riveter for Henry Kaiser, and a typing teacher in the Upper Peninsula. Wayne Junior works in a drugstore.

"My seduction theory," Mellie says later, as Clara drives her to the airport in their father's ancient green Nash Rambler with the Trout Unlimited sticker. "I think I got the idea from Mother's book."

"What book?"

"The one she was writing when she died." Mellie looks out the window. "I always forget how flat everything is here. Absolutely flat."

"You mean her columns? Was she collecting them into a book?" The children were spared that, anyway.

"No, haven't you seen her papers? This was a sort of memoir, only about forty pages, more serious than her columns. It's probably in the attic."

At the airport, Clara notices her sister looking at her and away again, starting to speak and breaking off. "Is something the matter?" she asks as Mellie picks at the handle of the flute case she carries.

"Not really." But Mellie frowns. "You manage everything so well. You always did. And here you are, actually making a living out of telling people what to do."

Clara restrains herself. "That isn't what I do."

"Isn't it?" Mellie looks down at her with melancholy blue eyes. She's taller than Clara now, with wide shoulders and long arms. "The truth is, I wish you could tell *me* what to do." Her married life isn't going well, she says, glancing up toward the loudspeaker that will announce her flight. Her husband no longer likes her looks.

"But, Mellie," Clara says. "You're so beautiful. I've been noticing all over again."

"If I am, he doesn't know it." She plays with the catch on her flute case, clasping and unclasping it. "He fights with the boys. He doesn't like their politics. I don't know. He's just disappointed, and worried about his heart."

He should be, Clara thinks; he should worry about his heart. Her lovely little sister, who was so inventive in their plays. "You were the best actor in the family," she says.

"Oh, no, I never had any talent. Not even for music, really."

"You were the best." Clara wishes Mellie could believe it.

XXXIV

As soon as Clara gets back from the airport, she hurries up to the attic. It's a hopeless mess—cartons, trunks, snowshoes, fishing equipment, toys, broken furniture. How could her fastidious aunt bear to live in the same house with this clutter?

She's searching for her mother's papers, in particular for the memoir that Mellie mentioned. The first box she sees, though, is marked with her own name. Inside, she finds school assignments and report cards and scripts of her plays. At the bottom is a scrapbook with a double-winged airplane on the cover. Clara's mother gave it to her on her eighth birthday, along with a batch of clippings about Amelia Earhart. Grace was hoping her daughter would continue the collection. No such luck: The latter part of the book is filled with pictures of Shirley Temple, stuck in with lumpy home-made paste. Here is Shirley—showing her dimples, saluting as the Little Colonel, endlessly tap-dancing—nothing like gallant Amelia with her tousled hair and tomboy grin. The play scripts are fragile and yellowed and marked with stage directions. *The Blue Dragon*, fourteen single-spaced pages, is on top, its margins filled with the notes Clara scrawled behind the curtains on the landing, with only the moon for light. She remembers how inspired she felt, how quickly she wrote. But of course the play was never produced. She puts the papers away in her grandparents' metal-bound trunk, to send to her own home.

In another carton she finds the costume collection—the brown crepe beaded dress and the collapsible opera hat and all the rest—which she supposes will go to Goodwill. She looks through the other boxes without finding anything written by her mother, either on the typewriter or in her unmistakable Palmer Method hand. It's strange that there's nothing at all. Grace was always writing, whenever she wasn't reading or talking; even her letters were longer than most people's. Could Robert have destroyed her manuscripts? All of them?

From a box of books Clara extracts Palgrave, as well as Robert's marked copy of Shakespeare and *Andersen's Fairy Tales*, with the smudgy Dulac watercolor illustrations. Cricket has already taken some books and fishing equipment to Oregon. Mellie took linens and a music rack. The rifles, in their khaki cases embroidered in red, will go to Robert's hunting companions. Hal and Daphne can deal with everything else.

At almost midnight, Clara tries Auntie Mildred's room. There's nothing of her mother's, but she discovers a fat leather album filled with photographs and newspaper clippings that celebrate family achievements or weddings and births. Auntie Mildred has saved the articles about the children's plays, and besides these—placed between two pages but not pasted in—there are accounts of the inquiry into Grace Davenant's death.

Clara can't ignore them any longer. Kneeling on her aunt's white hooked rug with the pink roses, she reads through the news stories. Two of the accounts understate her father's age, she notes, and all of them refer to him, erroneously, as a professor. Apparently he testified for hours and endured rigorous cross-examination. She didn't know that—or know, either, that Malcolm Wolfe had been questioned.

The paper describes Clara as having been on the verge of tears during her own testimony; she remembers how hard she tried to keep her composure. And she sees that she did, indeed, exaggerate her father's strength, but the judge had the sense to question her statement, and Auntie Mildred set him straight. Clara lives through her anxiety all over again: Detective Lieutenant Withrow, in his glen plaid suit with the discreet red stripe, clearly suspected her father, but he wanted to be fair. The Lieutenant was relying on her to come up with the truth.

The next day, as Clara sets off for Ypsilanti to see her aunt for the first time in several years, she's as tense as if she'd drunk five cups of coffee. Why did the investigation concentrate so much on her father and her? Mildred Davenant did testify, but not for long— and nobody questioned her seriously. The more Clara thinks, the harder it is to see her aunt as a mere bystander that night. Auntie Mildred was certainly in the kitchen when the quarrel began, but did she stay there until her appearance in the bedroom doorway with her can of oven cleaner? Didn't the police even notice the back stairs?

Clara temporarily loses her way and pulls into the parking lot of the retirement home ten minutes late for lunch. She has neglected to bring a present, and the small grocery near Happyrest Haven offers only licorice whips or drab, ungiftlike boxes of chocolate nonpareils. She settles for the nonpareils and puts them into the suitcase with the lingerie.

Mildred Davenant, in a corrugated hairdo and a double-knit coral pants suit, stands inside the glass doors of the building, waving energetically. She must be in the active phase of her medication. Parkinson's disease was diagnosed years before, and she has only brief periods of control over her movements, Hal has reported.

"I'm sorry," Clara says. "Have you been waiting long?"

Auntie Mildred's body has closed in on itself, and her shoulders hunch into a high question mark. "Well, Clara Jane, it's a pity you couldn't get here to help me dress, but if you couldn't, you couldn't." She looks Clara up and down. "Is that what you always wear?"

Clara has substituted a dark green suit and silk shirt for the sweater and jeans of the last few days, and she's wearing her amber earrings, but evidently this isn't enough. "Isn't there some kind of a robe?" Auntie Mildred asks in obvious disappointment.

"In church there is. Not here." Clara takes her fragile knobby elbow, which feels like loosely wrapped china, and they progress down the corridor over slick green linoleum. In Auntie Mildred's room, greeting cards and family pictures lean in rows on every flat surface. The bed holds stacks of cushions embroidered by nieces.

On the walls, between more photographs, are acrylic paintings of turquoise lakes which she has done in the recreation room downstairs. She unpacks the suitcase and adds Clara's candy to a hoard in her desk. "In case they run out in the dining room," she says with a wink that may be voluntary.

Recalling her aunt's ban on food in the Packard Street bedrooms, Clara is disconcerted. This woman is nothing like the wicked witch of her childhood. Does she even remember the night that Clara wants to ask her about?

"It might be a good idea to use the bathroom before lunch," Auntie Mildred says with another wink. "We don't want an accident." When Clara declines, her aunt frowns. "Stubborn as ever, I see. Well, don't say I didn't warn you."

They take another slippery corridor to a dining room where two smiling ladies wait. "How refreshing to see a pretty young face," one of them says, and Clara, fifty-eight, feels oddly youthful. When her aunt introduces her as "my minister niece," she sees that Auntie Mildred is proud of her.

Lunch consists of Franco-American spaghetti, canned peas, and frozen biscuits that have passed through a microwave oven. Dessert is an icy green pie. "Key lime," Auntie Mildred guesses, stabbing at it and bouncing her fork to the floor. "He didn't want a funeral, you know," she says with a reproving look at Clara.

"It wasn't a funeral." Their two companions are looking interested.

"Memorial service, whatever. He didn't want it."

Maybe she hasn't changed so much after all. "And it wasn't for him," Clara says. "It was for—"

"It was for you," Auntie Mildred interrupts. "You children always did go right ahead with whatever you wanted." She chips at the green pie with her spoon. "Orange crates all over the bedroom, dirt on the rug. And you were the ringleader."

"Some of his friends were there. People from the Institute."

"He didn't want it."

"I don't think he would have objected." What Clara's father

minded was dying—not the dying itself, but the missteps that had led to it. He had tried to create a perfect family, and look what had happened. Clara herself used to have that same ideal, but even before her mother's death, she had felt that sliver of ice in her heart, stealing along her veins and making her hands so cold that people jumped back from her touch. Raynaud's phenomenon, a doctor explained recently, but Clara still thinks of it as an outward manifestation of something more.

After lunch, Auntie Mildred leads Clara downstairs to the painting studio in a windowless room next to the furnace. The clogged brushes and pots of cracked paint and the small muddy canvases all have an air of disuse. It's pitiful, Clara thinks. But there are questions she needs to ask—about Grace's papers if nothing else. "Auntie Mildred, what happened to my mother's things?"

"Her clothes, you mean? We gave them away. Clothes, books, everything. Packed them all off to a rummage sale." Her aunt thrusts a stray paintbrush into a jar. "I don't know why they can't keep this room picked up. No sense of responsibility."

"What about the things she wrote?"

"Her letters? Or those so-called newspaper columns?"

"And her research materials, everything." There must have been stacks of them.

"Oh, those. I cleared those out long ago," Auntie Mildred says with satisfaction. "We had a nice big bonfire."

"My mother's *papers*?" The condescension and distortions in her mother's newspaper column bothered Clara almost as much as her own inability to keep from reading it. The memoir was probably only more of the same, but now she'll never know. "Her papers?" She feels cheated. Her interfering aunt, right now, is scraping cherry-red paint off a tabletop with her thumbnail—working diligently away as if she'd been assigned to tidy up the universe. Clara feels the beginning of an immense, familiar fury; she hasn't forgotten how to be angry after all. She isn't going to scream or scatter paintbrushes as her childhood self might have done, but she's going to get some answers. "Auntie Mildred," she asks, "what happened that night?"

She doesn't have to say which night she means.

Auntie Mildred's hand stops moving. "Silly little Grace," she says with an attempt at a laugh. "Making a scene like that in the middle of the night. Knocking over the chair and all."

So the chair was real. "You picked it up," Clara says. It isn't a question.

Auntie Mildred peeks sideways at Clara's face as if trying to assess her mood. "Well, somebody had to," she says with a martyred sigh, and goes back to the dried paint.

Of course. And Clara's aunt was upstairs when the gun went off. Before it went off.

"It was an accident," Auntie Mildred explains. "Robert said so himself."

"Yes, I remember." There's no use in asking any more. It isn't that Clara's anger has gone, but there's nothing to do with it: Her aunt isn't even the same person who did these things, and Clara isn't the same either. "Let's go," she says, and escorts Auntie Mildred to the outside door.

Partway down the hall, a heavily made-up woman in alligator pumps and a mink coat sits on a bench, staring out at the parking lot. Auntie Mildred nudges Clara. "Every blessed day," she says, sotto voce, "and not one visitor. Poor Hazel."

Hazel DeGroff. My mother's enemy, Clara thinks instantly, and wonders why. Is it only because Mrs. DeGroff treated the Davenant family with such disdain? Or was there something else? The spark of a sermon appears in her mind, on the futility of revenge: If only she and her siblings, all those years ago, could have foreseen this shrunken woman in the fur coat waiting by the cold glass doors.

She embraces her aunt, though not warmly—not yet—and goes out to the car, where she sits quietly for a few minutes. Before Clara was three years old, when she was placed in charge of her first little brother, she took responsibility for keeping order in her family. She has more in common with Auntie Mildred than she ever knew: Is there such a thing as a Hamlet complex, reserved for the eldest child? O cursed spite, she thinks. No wonder she chose such a highhanded calling.

She drives to a park where trees overhang the river and where her family used to take picnics. She walks along the bank in the cool autumn sunshine, looking down at the clear water running over mottled brown stones. What did happen on that night in 1943?

Clara's scenario has two possible beginnings: In the first one, sometime during Grace's last day she gave up on both of her lives; perhaps she had just discovered her pregnancy. That evening she typed her note and loaded the gun and perhaps slipped it under a pillow. Robert came in then, and pleaded with her to love him again, and she said it was too late. (Clara actually heard some of this.) When she said she wanted to die, Robert went downstairs to get his sister, and Grace took out the gun.

In Clara's second—and less likely—version of events, Robert was the one to find living unbearable—to take the gun and bullets from their separate places. (In that case, the sheet of paper in the type-writer might have been a draft of Grace's next newspaper column, the opening of a reflection on parenthood. After all, whatever might be true biologically, she and Robert were legally due to become, once again, parents.)

No matter who loaded the gun, it was left in the bedroom when Robert went to fetch his sister.

Clara stops and leans against a tree, running her fingertips over the rough bark. For a long time, she has assumed that her mother did try to kill herself and that her father failed to prevent her. The scene Clara imagines now isn't very different, but her aunt has re-placed her father: As soon as Robert spoke to his sister in the kitchen, she is almost sure, Mildred ran up the back stairs and tried to wrest the gun from her sister-in-law. ("No, no, Grace, you mustn't do that," Clara hears her muttering through clenched teeth.) The chair was knocked over as they struggled. The gun went off and Grace fell onto the bed—just as Robert, having climbed up the front stairs past the window seat, entered the bedroom. "Mildred!" he shouted, seeing his sister, and ordered her back to the kitchen.

She went, after replacing the chair, and he took the gun and per-haps wiped off fingerprints. When Clara Jane appeared in the doorway, he must have been thunderstruck. "It was an accident," he said—and called to his sister, who ran back upstairs with her can of oven cleaner. Clara doesn't think the can was a deliberate prop; her aunt probably grabbed it for something to hold onto.

In his testimony Robert managed, without telling many actual lies, to prevent suspicion from falling on Mildred. If he should be charged with murder, she could step forward. The only one who told the truth was Clara Jane, and even she edited and exaggerated.

Clara sinks onto a bench and gazes across the water at the curving branches of trees that have lost most of their leaves. She must let Hal and the others know. She'll call them tonight.

Once she saw a dog burying an orange popsicle under a forsythia in the park. Would he come back to claim it? she wondered. Would he even remember? It seems to her now, as she sits on a bench by the river, that her own buried grudges may at last have disappeared. If she tries to dig them up, she'll find that they've melted away.

William Blake's "Nurse's Song" is running through her head— the second version, from *Songs of Experience*. A side effect of Clara's profession is that she's always exposed to poetry, always looking for readings for the Sunday service. "The days of my youth rise fresh in my mind,/ My face turns green and pale." Well, yes. She can use that next Sunday: When I was a child, she writes in her mind, I was fearful. I didn't always know what I was afraid of—teachers or doctors or bombs or even our minister, who put jokes in his sermons but had no sense of humor—but the fear was always there, in the back of my mind. And then, one night, something terrible happened.

Her congregation is aware of the story, although she hasn't spoken of it. It has built a fence around her, and her silence has built it higher. But they know where she is this week, and a notice has appeared in the bulletin; sympathy cards and African violets must be crowding her desk already. She can tell them, briefly, about her father's death, and then about her mother's. (She won't mention her aunt.) It was a disaster, she'll say, a family misfortune. What she hopes to do is to open up her past and take away some of the fear. There is always (*always*) the risk of giving her own experience too much importance, but if it can help anyone else, it ought to be told.

She reaches into her pocket for the pencil stub and scrap paper she keeps there—and pauses. She's missed the point about the dog and the popsicle: It wasn't a shameful secret he was burying, but a treasure. What if he were to dig for it later and find it still there? Not expecting anything else, he wouldn't even be surprised. He would never know what a miracle it was.

THE END

ACKNOWLEDGMENTS

My thanks to Attorney George Krause for information on the Michigan legal system in 1943, and to Marie E. Kingdon for putting me in touch with him;

to Ann, Elsa, Grant, Jane, Judith, and Katherine, who read the book in an early stage;

and to Vera Gold, the MacDowell Colony, and Yaddo.

A chapter of the book appeared, in slightly different form, as a short story in *96 Inc* in 1996.